Kristy and her friends love babysitting and when her mum can't find a babysitter for Kristy's little brother one day, Kristy has a great idea. Why doesn't she set up a baby-sitting club? That way parents can make a single phone call and reach a team of baby-sitting experts. And if one babysitter is already busy another one can take the job. So together with her friends, Claudia, Mary Anne and Stacey, Kristy starts THE BABYSITTERS CLUB. And although things don't *always* go according to plan, they have a lot of fun on the way!

COLLECTION 6

Book 16
JESSI'S SECRET
LANGUAGE

Book 17
MARY ANNE'S
BAD-LUCK MYSTERY

Book 18
STACEY'S MISTAKE

Ann M. Martin

Scholastic Children's Books,
Commonwealth House, 1 – 19 New Oxford Street,
London, WC1A 1NU, UK
A division of Scholastic Ltd
London ~ New York ~ Toronto ~ Sydney ~ Auckland

Jessi's Secret Language
Mary Anne's Bad-Luck Mystery
First published in the US by Scholastic Inc., 1988
First published in the UK by Scholastic Ltd, 1991
Stacey's Mistake
First published in the US by Scholastic Inc., 1987
First published in the UK by Scholastic Ltd, 1991

First published in this edition by Scholastic Ltd, 1998

ISBN 0 590 19884 X

Typeset by Rowland Phototypesetting Ltd,
Bury St Edmunds, Suffolk
Printed by Cox & Wyman Ltd, Reading, Berks.

1 2 3 4 5 6 7 8 9 10

CONTENTS

JESSI'S SECRET LANGUAGE

1st CHAPTER

I happen to be very good at languages. Once, my family and I went to Mexico on vacation, and during the week we were there, I practically became bilingual. (Which, in case you're not sure, means able to speak two languages really, really well. In this case, English and Spanish.) If I weren't so good at languages, this story might never have happened.

The story also might never have happened if I weren't so good at ballet. If you think about it, ballet is just another kind of language, except that you talk with your body instead of with your mouth. I feel like I'm talking in circles, though, so let me start my story. I'll begin it on the morning of the day I was going to audition for a part in the ballet that my dance school was planning to put on. My family and I had only been living in Stoneybrook, Connecticut, for a few weeks at that time. . .

I woke up before my alarm went off. I've always been able to do that. But for some reason, I always set it anyway. Just in case I should have a mental lapse and *not* wake up on time. The reason I get up early is so that I can practise my ballet.

Every morning, I wake up at 5:29, hit the alarm before it can go off and wake everyone else up, chuck my nightgown and put on my leotard and warm-up stuff. Then I tiptoe down to the basement. No matter how quiet I am, I know Mama always wakes up and listens to me make my way to the basement. That's just the kind of mother she is. I hope she goes back to sleep after she sees that everything is as it should be. But I'll probably never know. Even though she and I are very close (which is how I know she wakes up when I do), I'll probably never ask if she goes back to sleep, and *she* probably doesn't know that I know she wakes up. It's not the kind of thing you need to talk about.

The *barre* in the basement is one of the nice things about moving to Stoneybrook. As I mentioned earlier, we haven't lived here very long. In fact, until we moved, we had lived in a little house on a little street in Oakley, New Jersey. I was born there. Well, not in the *house*—in Oakley General Hospital—but my parents were already living in the house.

4

Maybe I should tell you a little about my family now. (I'll get back to the *barre* in the basement in Stoneybrook. Really, I will.) Here are the people in my family: Mama; Daddy; my eight-year-old sister, Becca (short for Rebecca); my brother, Squirt (whose real name is John Philip Ramsey, Jr); and me—Jessi Ramsey. I'm eleven, and my full name is Jessica Davis Ramsey.

My family is black.

I know it sounds funny to announce it like that. If we were white, I wouldn't have to, because you would probably *assume* we were white. But when you're a minority, things are different.

Of course, if you could see me, there wouldn't be any question that I'm black. I have skin the colour of cocoa—darkish cocoa—soft black hair, and eyes like two pieces of coal. That's how dark brown they are. They're the darkest brown eyes I have ever seen. My sister Becca looks like a miniature version of me, except that her eyes aren't quite as dark. Also, she doesn't have my long, long legs. Maybe that's why she's not a dancer. (Or maybe it's because of her stage fright.) And Squirt looks like, well, a baby. That's really all you can say about him. He's only fourteen months old. (By the way, he got his nickname from the nurses in Oakley General because he was the smallest baby in the hospital. Even now, he's a little on the small side, but he makes up for it by being extremely bright.)

As I said, we used to live in Oakley. I liked Oakley a lot. There were both black and white families in our neighbourhood. (Our street was all black.) And Oakley Elementary was mixed black and white. So was my dancing school. My grandparents and a whole bunch of my cousins and aunts and uncles lived nearby. (My best friend was my cousin Keisha. We have the same birthday.)

Then Daddy's company said they were going to give him a big raise and a big promotion. That was great, of course. The only thing was that they also wanted to move him to the Stamford, Connecticut, branch of the company. That's how we ended up here in Stoneybrook. The company found this house for us in this little town. My parents like small towns (Oakley is pretty small), and Daddy's drive to Stamford each morning isn't long at all.

But—I don't think any of us expected the one bad thing we found in Stoneybrook: There are hardly any black families here. We're the only black family in our neighbourhood, and I am—get this—the only black kid in the whole entire sixth grade at Stoneybrook Middle School. Can you believe it: I can't.

Unfortunately, things have been a little rough for us. I can't tell if some people here really *don't like* black people, or if they just haven't known many, so they're kind of wary of us. But they sure weren't very nice at first. Things are getting better, though. (Slowly.)

Things started getting better for me when I met Mallory Pike. I think she's going to be my new best friend. (Actually, she *is* my new best friend, but I feel funny saying that—like it might hurt Keisha somehow.) Mallory is this really nice girl in my class who's part of an eight-kid family. And she got me into a group called the Babysitters Club, which has been great.

Well, now I'm way, way ahead of myself, so let me get back to the *barre* in the basement. *Barre* is just a fancy French word for "bar." You know, that railing that ballet dancers hold onto when they're practising their *plies* and stuff? Our new house is so much bigger than our house in Oakley, and Daddy's job pays so much more money, that he and Mama set up this practice area in the basement for me. It's got mirrors, and a couple of mats (for warm-ups), and of course, the *barre*.

On the morning I've been telling you about, I practised in the basement until I heard Mama and Daddy making coffee in the kitchen. That was my clue that it was time to shower and get dressed for school. I kissed my parents good morning, and then ran upstairs. As I passed Squirt's room, I heard him babbling away, so I went inside and picked him up.

"Morning, Squirts," I said as I lifted him from his crib.

"Ooh-blah," he replied. He says only four real words so far—Mama, Dada, ba (we're pretty sure that means bird), and ackaminnie (which we *know* means ice cream). Otherwise, he just makes funny sounds.

I carried Squirt into Becca's room. Becca was still in bed. She has a terrible time waking up in the morning, so I dumped Squirt on top of her. I can't think of a nicer way to wake up than to look into Squirt's brown eyes and hear him say, "Go-bloo?"

Becca began to laugh. She tried to scold me at the same time. "Jessi!" she cried, but she was laughing too hard to sound cross. It's easy for me to make people laugh.

Becca and I got ready for school, and I changed Squirt's nappy. Then the three of us went downstairs and joined Mama and Daddy for breakfast.

Breakfast is one of my favourite times of day. Another is dinner. This isn't because I like to eat. It's because I like sitting at a table and looking around at my family, the five of us together, joined by something I could never explain but that I can always feel.

"So," said Mama, as soon as we were served and had begun eating, "auditions today, Jessi?"

"Yup," I replied.

"Are you nervous, honey?"

"The usual, I guess. No—more than the usual. It's not just that I want to be in *Coppelia*. It's also that I don't know how auditions are going to go at the new school." The ballet school that I got into in Stamford is bigger, more competitive and much more professional than the one I'd gone to in Oakley. I know I'm a good dancer, but even though I'd auditioned and got into the advanced class at the new school, I was feeling sort of insecure. The most I could hope for at the auditions that afternoon was not to make a fool of myself. I don't plan on becoming a professional ballerina—I just like ballet, and the way I feel when I dance—but still I wanted to do my best at the auditions.

"What's *Coppelia*?" Becca wanted to know.

"Oh, it's a great ballet," I said with a sigh. "You'll love it. We'll have to go see it, even if I'm not in it. It's a story about a dollmaker named Dr Coppelius, this really lifelike doll he creates—that's Coppelia—and Franz, a handsome young guy who falls in love with the doll. He sees her from far away and thinks she's real." I realized I was getting carried away with the story, but Becca looked interested, so I continued. "That's not the only problem, though. See, Franz is engaged to Swanilda (she's pretty

9

much the star of the show), and when Swanilda thinks Franz has fallen in love with another woman, she feels all jealous and hurt. After that, the story gets sort of complicated. Swanilda even changes places with Coppelia, and poor Dr Coppelius thinks his doll has come to life. In the end, everything is straightened out, and Swanilda and Franz get married, just like they'd planned."

"And live happily ever after," Becca added.

Mama and Daddy laughed. And Daddy said to me in his deep voice, "I know you'll do fine this afternoon, baby."

"Maybe," I replied. "We'll see. Thanks, Daddy. I just hope I don't fall over Madame Noelle or crash into a mirror or something."

That time we all began laughing, since I'd never done anything like that and wasn't likely to. I was still nervous, though.

"Okay, girls. Time to get a move on," Mama said a few minutes later.

Becca and I swallowed the last of our breakfasts, flew upstairs, and had a fight over who would get to use the bathroom first. In the end, we went in together and brushed our teeth in record time. Then we began the mad scurry to get out the door and on our way to school. I always think there's not that much to do in order to get ready, but one of us usually loses something, and then Becca gets into a panic about school. (Lots of things about school upset her.)

That morning it was, "Mama, we're having a *spelling* test today!"

"Becca, you're probably the best speller in your class. Don't worry."

"But I can't get up there in *front* of everyone."

"Think of me," I told her. "Auditions this afternoon. I have to dance in front of my whole school."

Becca didn't look comforted.

I took her hand and led her out the front door. "Don't forget," I called over my shoulder to Mama. "After ballet I have a meeting of the Babysitters Club."

And then Becca and I were off. Our day had begun.

2nd CHAPTER

"Hi! Sorry I'm late!"

I start most meetings of the Babysitters Club that way because I'm usually rushing to the meetings from either a ballet class or a sitting job. This time I was rushing in from auditions. They had gone reasonably well, but I wouldn't *really* know how I'd done until my next class.

"That's okay," Kristy Thomas replied. She spoke briskly, but then she smiled at me, so I knew it really was okay.

I sat down next to Mallory Pike, feeling relieved. Mallory and I are the two newest members of the club, so we don't want to upset anybody. Especially Kristy.

Kristy is the chairman of the club.

Kristy started the club in order to help out parents in the neighbourhood who need sitters, and to earn money, of course. But for me, the club has done something

12

else. It has helped to pave my way here in Stoneybrook. I'm meeting lots of people, especially people in my neighbourhood, and those people are finding out that I (a black girl) am not scary or awful or anything except just another eleven-year-old kid, who happens to have dark skin. (And who also happens to be a good dancer, a good joke-teller, a good reader, good at languages and most important, good with children. But a *terrible* letter-writer.)

I think I'm getting ahead of myself again, though. Let me go back and tell you about Kristy, her club and the rest of its members. For starters, Kristy and all the other girls except Mallory are eighth-graders. Mal and I are not only newcomers to the club, we're lowly sixth-graders. Anyway, as I said, Kristy was the one who began the club. She started it about a year ago when she saw how hard it was for her mum to find a sitter for Kristy's little brother David Michael. Mrs Thomas was making phone call after phone call and not getting anywhere.

Kristy thought, wouldn't it be great if her mother could make one call and reach a whole lot of sitters at once? So she teamed up with three other girls—Mary Anne Spier, Claudia Kishi, and Stacey McGill—and they formed the Babysitters Club. (Stacey's no longer living in Stoneybrook, and Mal and I and another girl, Dawn

Schafer, have joined the club, but I'll tell you about all that later.)

Anyway, the club meets on Monday, Wednesday, and Friday afternoons from five-thirty until six. People who need a sitter call us at those times (the club advertises a lot, so our clients know how to reach us), and when they call, they reach *six* sitters! Kristy, Claudia, Mary Anne, Dawn, Mal and me. They're bound to get a sitter for their kids with just that one phone call.

As chairman, Kristy keeps the club running very professionally. Long ago, she got a record book in which we write down all sorts of things—our job appointments, of course, plus information about our clients, as well as all the money we earn.

Kristy also makes us keep a club notebook. We're supposed to write about every job we go on. The notebook is a sort of diary telling about which kids we sat for, what went on, how the kids behaved and any problems we ran into. Once a week, each of us is supposed to read the last week's entries so we can stay on top of things. We all agree that this was a good idea of Kristy's, and that reading the notebook is helpful. But writing about the jobs can be a pain. Oh, well.

I know why Kristy is the Chairman of the Babysitters Club. It's because she's a take-charge kind of person who is brimming with ideas. Kristy's one of those people who's always beginning sentences with, "*I* know, let's. . ." or "Hey, how about. . ." She has a big mouth and loves to be bossy. Some kids don't like her, but I do. I like lively people who surprise you now and then.

Kristy has a mum, two older brothers named Sam and Charlie (they're in high school), and her younger brother David Michael, who's seven. Also, since her mum (who was divorced) got remarried, Kristy now has a stepfather, Watson Brewer, and a little stepsister and stepbrother. Karen is six and Andrew is four. (Kristy's father left the Thomases a long time ago, and Kristy hardly ever hears from him.)

Kristy used to live right across the street from Claudia Kishi (we hold our club meetings in Claudia's bedroom) and next door to Mary Anne Spier, but when her mother and Watson got married, the Thomases moved across town to Mr Brewer's mansion. (He's a millionaire or something.) Kristy's having sort of a hard time adjusting to her new rich neighbourhood (boy, can I relate to that), but she still sees her old friends, the club members. We use part of our club subs to pay Kristy's brother Charlie to drive her to and from Claudia's house so that she never has to miss a meeting. Plus, she still goes to Stoneybrook Middle School, and she and Mary Anne are still best friends. (They had lived next door to each other since they were babies.)

Kristy has brown hair, brown eyes, and is on the small side. She *always* dresses in jeans, sweaters, and sneakers, and she has no interest at all in boys. She thinks they are gigantic pains. (So do I.)

The vice-chairman of the club is Claudia Kishi. This is mostly because Claudia has a private phone and private phone number, so it's very convenient to hold our meetings in her room. When job calls come in, they don't tie up anyone else's line. (Once Mal and I tried to start a babysitting club of our own at her house, but her brothers and sisters always wanted to use the phone, so that never worked out. Also, our club needed some older members, not just us two sixth-graders.) But when Claudia's phone rings during a meeting, we can be pretty sure it's a job call.

Claudia is absolutely the most exotic, sophisticated thirteen-year-old I have ever seen. She's Japanese-American, and has long, silky, black hair which I don't think I've ever seen her wear the same way twice. She braids it, puts it in ponytails, winds it around her head, and decorates it with clips or ribbons or scarves or whatever she feels like. Her eyes are almost as dark as mine and she has a complexion I once heard Kristy say she would kill for (not that there's anything wrong with Kristy's skin). And her clothes! You should see Claudia's clothes. Mallory and I have talked about her outfits. Claudia wears things our mothers won't let us wear until we're forty-five, if then. Don't get me wrong. Her clothes aren't, like, revealing or anything. It's just that they're so *wild*. Mallory and I are absolutely in awe of her. I think Mary Anne is, too, a little. Claudia wears the newest, most up-to-date fashions (whatever they happen to be), and adds her own personal, slightly crazy touches. She loves art and sometimes makes herself jewellery, especially big earrings. (Claudia, of course, has pierced ears, which Mal and I want desperately but are not allowed to have yet. All we're going to get is braces on our teeth.)

Anyway, Claudia doesn't just love art, she's a really good artist. Unfortunately, she's a terrible student. Being a poor student is bad enough, but when you have an older sister who is a genius, like Claudia's sister, Janine, it's really tough. Claudia manages, though. She does as well as she can in school, and otherwise concentrates on her art and babysitting. She lives with her parents, her sister and her grandmother, Mimi.

Mary Anne Spier is the club secretary. She's in charge of keeping the record book in order, except for the money stuff. (That's Dawn Schafer's job, since she's the treasurer.) It's hard to believe that Mary

17

Anne and Kristy are best friends. This is because in a lot of ways they're opposites. Oh, they look alike, all right. They're the two shortest kids in their grade and they both have brown hair and brown eyes, but that's where the similarities end. Kristy is loud and outgoing, Mary Anne is shy and introspective. (*Introspective* is one of my favourite words. It means thoughtful, looking inside yourself.) And Mary Anne is sensitive and caring. I notice that the other girls usually go to her if they have a problem. She's a good listener and takes people seriously.

Mary Anne, believe it or not, is the only club member with a steady boyfriend. She used to dress very babyishly, but now her clothes look pretty cool. She's changing. Claudia says she's becoming more mature. And I think that's hard on Kristy. Mary Anne lives with her dad and her kitten, Tigger. Her mother died when she was a baby. I think Mr Spier used to be really strict with her, but he's lightened up lately.

Okay. Remember that I said there used to be a club member named Stacey McGill? She was the original treasurer of the Babysitters Club, but her family moved back to New York City, where they used to live. Guess what. *Our* family moved into her old house! Anyway, when Stacey moved away, Dawn Schafer took her place as the treasurer. Dawn had moved to

Stoneybrook from California several months after Kristy started the club. She got to be good friends with Mary Anne, and soon she had joined the club. I like Dawn a lot. She lives near Mallory, so I see her more often than the other older girls in the club.

Dawn would be the first one to describe herself as a true California girl. She has long (and I mean *long*) hair that's so blonde it's almost white. She loves health food (won't touch the junk food that Claudia's addicted to) and always longs for warm weather.

She's going through a rough time right now. The reason she moved east was because her parents got divorced. She came here with her mum and her younger brother, Jeff. But Jeff was so unhappy that he finally moved *back* to California to try living with Mr Schafer. As Dawn pointed out, her family is now ripped in half. I think Dawn is a survivor, though.

The other club members are Mal and me. You already know about me. And you know that Mal has seven brothers and sisters. She loves to read, write stories and illustrate her stories. She thinks her parents treat her like a baby, and she can't wait for the day when her braces will be off, her ears will be pierced and her glasses will be gone. She's dying for contacts and wishes she could straighten out her head of curly hair.

As Mal once said, being eleven is a real trial. Mal and I are junior club members since we are only really allowed to sit after school and on weekends; hardly ever at night (unless we're at our own houses taking care of our brothers and sisters).

So those are our six club members. We do have two associate members, who don't come to meetings. They're people we can call on if we really get in a fix—if someone needs a sitter and none of us can take the job. One of those members is Logan Bruno, who just happens to be Mary Anne's boyfriend! The other is a girl named Shannon Kilbourne, who lives across the street from Kristy in her rich new neighbourhood.

And that's about it. At our club meetings, we mostly take phone calls and line up jobs. In between, we talk. We talk about us and what's going on in school or in our lives or with the kids we sit for. Sometimes we get silly. For instance, during the meeting that was held after my ballet auditions, Dawn announced that she'd heard that if you were able to touch your nose with your tongue, it meant that eventually (like when you were eighteen) you would need a very big bra. Well, this was pretty intriguing for all of us, especially Mal and me, who don't need bras at all yet, and even though I didn't see the vaguest connection between tongue-touching and bra size.

"I can do it! I can do it!" Kristy shrieked, but she had to calm down in the middle of her shrieking because the phone rang. Kristy, who always sits in Claudia's director's chair, wearing a visor and looking official, dived for the phone. So did Mary Anne, Dawn and Claudia. Mal and I didn't dive for it. We're too new for that. We're still in the middle of the fitting-in process.

Kristy picked up the phone and said, "Hello, Babysitters Club." She paused. "Yes? . . . Oh, I see. . . Well, we've never sat for a deaf child before, but that doesn't make a difference to any of us. I mean, if it doesn't make a difference to you. We like all children." (Long pause.) "Training? Well, that makes sense. Listen, let me talk to the other babysitters and I'll call you back in a few minutes. Just give me your number. . . Okay. Thanks. 'Bye."

Kristy hung up the phone and turned to us. "That was a new client. Her name is Mrs Braddock. She's got two kids. Haley is nine and Matthew is seven. The Braddocks have just moved to the neighbourhood. There are two hitches here. One, she needs a regular babysitter, two afternoons each week. And two, Matthew is deaf. He uses Ameslan, whatever that is. So she needs a sitter who can come every Monday and Wednesday afternoon, and she needs someone who'll be willing to learn this Ameslan thing. Mrs Braddock says she'll train the sitter. She sounds really nice."

The six of us got into a big discussion. Dawn and Mary Anne didn't want regular afternoon jobs. They wanted their schedules to be more free. Claudia couldn't take the job because she has an art class on Wednesday. Kristy lives too far away to be convenient to the job. That left Mal and me. Mal was interested, but she often has to watch her brothers and sisters on Mondays when her mum volunteers at Meals on Wheels.

So Kristy called Mrs Braddock back and I got the job! I was so excited. Working with a handicapped child sounded really interesting.

The meeting was over then and we were all rushing out the door to our homes and our dinners when Mal cried, "Hey, Jessi, how did the auditions go?"

"Oh, fine!" I replied lightly. "But I won't know anything until my next class."

"Well, good luck!" said the others.

"Thanks." I replied. But I was a whole lot more nervous than I let on.

3rd
CHAPTER

"And *one* and *two* and *three* and *four* and *plie* . . . *PLIE*, Mademoiselle Jones. Bend those knees!"

Sometimes Mme Noelle gets a little carried away in ballet class. She has this big stick (Becca saw it once and called it a club, but it really isn't) that she bangs on the floor in time to her counting. This is only when we're exercising at the *barre* at the beginning of class.

"And *one*" (bang) "and *two*" (bang), "and *three*" (bang) "and *four*" (bang). "On your toes. Up, up, *up!*"

I wished it were the end of class instead of the beginning. At the end, Mme Noelle was going to announce the parts in *Coppelia*. Not everyone from our class would wind up in the ballet. Kids in all the other classes at the school had tried out, too, and there were simply not enough parts to go round.

23

I looked at the students in the room. We are an advanced *en pointe* class, which means that we dance in toe shoes. I will never forget how thrilled I was when I got my first pair of toe shoes. That is absolutely the most exciting thing in the life of a young ballerina. But you know what? We work out so hard that we need new shoes constantly. We just wear out one pair after another. Mama and Daddy admit that this is expensive, but they know I'm serious about my dancing even if I don't want to become a professional, so they go along with it very nicely. I put quite a bit of my babysitting money toward shoes so that my parents don't have to pay for all of them.

In my class are eleven other girls. I'm the youngest and the newest. The next oldest are two twelve-year-olds and the others are thirteen and fourteen. Mme Noelle said I'm the first eleven-year-old to be in this class in a long time. In fact, she sort of made an announcement about it. Right away I could tell that Hilary and Katie Beth were upset. Hilary and Katie Beth are the twelve-year-olds. Until I came along, *they* were the youngest in the class.

They do not like me.

Well, I'm sorry I took their special positions away, but I couldn't help it. I mean, I didn't do it on purpose.

"And *one* and *two* and *three* and—Pay

attention, Mademoiselle Romsey!"

Mademoiselle Romsey. I mean, Ramsey. That's me! It always takes me a second to remember that.

In Mme Noelle's class, you don't apologize when she scolds you. You just shape up and work extra hard. Which I did.

But not until after I noticed Hilary and Katie Beth gloating at each other. They were happy to see me in trouble.

We finished our *barre* work and started in on some floor exercises. *Tour jetes* and stuff like that. We practised head work, too. When you turn, you have to spin your head around faster than your body. It's sort of hard to explain. Anyway, then Madame began to teach us a complicated routine that involved groups of four girls dancing with their hands crossed and joined.

Nobody wanted to hold my hands.

Oh, okay. That's not true. It's just that Hilary and Katie Beth were in my group and neither of *them* wanted to hold my hands. The only solution was for me to dance at the end of the line, holding the hand of the fourteen-year-old in our group who was mature enough not to care about petty little things.

Mme Noelle finally ended class five minutes early.

"Okay, *mes petites*," she said, which is French for "my little girls." Considering the fourteen-year-olds in the class, *mes petites* seemed sort of odd, but she calls us that all the time.

She banged her club on the floor and said, "Gother 'round, please. I am going to announce those of you who have earned parts in *Coppelia*."

My heart began tap dancing in my chest. On the day of auditions, all I had cared about was not doing something stupid. Since I hadn't done anything stupid, I was hoping that maybe, just *maybe*, I would be given a teeny little part, like one of the townspeople.

Mme Noelle cleared her throat as my classmates and I stood before her nervously. Most of us were nervous, anyway. But Hilary and Katie Beth looked smug. They thought of themselves as Madame's favourites, so I guess they weren't worried about getting good parts.

Madame began by announcing the smaller roles.

"In this closs," she said, "Mary Bramstedt and Lisa Jones will be two of the townspeople. Carrie Steinfeld will participate in the Donce of the Hours. Hilary, although the Chinese Doll is usually played by a male dancer, you have been given that part. I think you can do it. Katie Beth, you will play Coppelia herself."

Madame paused.

I nearly died. I wasn't even one of the *towns*people. How humiliating. And Hilary and Katie Beth were gloating up a storm. The Chinese Doll. What a role. And Coppelia herself. Oh, well. There probably weren't any black people in little European towns hundreds of years ago anyway. How could I have thought I'd get a role in *Coppelia*?

I was so busy feeling sorry for myself that I almost missed the next thing Madame said: "One role more. I am very pleased to announce that the part of Swanilda" (she's the star, remember?) "has been awarded to one of the students in this closs."

Just about everyone in the room gasped. I'm surprised there was any oxygen left to breathe.

"Swanilda," Mme Noelle said, "will be played by Mademoiselle Jessica Romsey."

Jessica Romsey? Oh, Jessica Ramsey. That was *me*. ME! I was going to be Swanilda, the star?

"I admit," Mme Noelle went on, "that Jessica is a bit young for the role, but I think she can hondle it. Jessica, your audition was wonderful. That is all. Soturday rehearsals will begin this weekend for those in the performance. Closs is dismissed."

I walked into the changing room in a fog. I wasn't sure how to feel. I was delighted, thrilled, scared to death. It was encouraging that Madame didn't seem to mind a black Swanilda, but could I really learn the part? I began to imagine myself on

27

stage in Swanilda's lovely costume.

First I saw myself *pirouetting* and *tour jeteing* to beat the band.

Then I saw myself leaping through the air toward the open arms of Franz, missing, and sailing into the scenery, which comes crashing down, knocking three dancers unconscious and ruining the performance.

With a little shudder I slipped off my shoes and leg warmers and searched around for my jeans.

"Congratulations, Jessi," said Mary Bramstedt and Lisa Jones.

I shook myself out of my fog.

"Thanks," I said, looking up gratefully. I smiled.

They crossed to the other side of the room and began sorting through their clothes.

"Congratulations, Jessi," said two more voices, only this time my smile faded. The voices were not friendly. They were nasally, mimicking what Mary and Lisa had just said. Imagine somebody noticing that you've totally botched something up, and saying, "Oh, that's *nice*. Real nice." That was exactly how those voices sounded.

I didn't have to glance up to see who the voices belonged to.

Hilary and Katie Beth.

What was I supposed to say?

I decided to ignore their tone. "Congratulations to you, too," I replied. "The

28

Chinese Doll. That's a great part. And Coppelia, Katie Beth. That's terrific."

"Oh, come off it," replied Katie Beth nastily. She had unpinned her long hair and flipped it over her shoulder. "Coppelia barely does anything. She just sits there. She's a doll, for heaven's sake. They could put a dummy on stage, and it would be the same thing."

"No, it wouldn't," I told her.

Katie Beth just tossed her head. Then she took Hilary by the arm, and they sat down not far from me.

It was while I was pulling my shirt on over my leotard that I heard it.

"Teacher's pet," Hilary whispered to Katie.

They were talking about me.

"She just got the part because she's Madame's favourite. And she's the favourite because she's the newest and youngest," agreed Katie Beth.

"Yeah, just wait until another girl joins the class," Hilary added. "Then she'll see."

Were they right? Had I got the part of Swanilda because Madame favoured new girls, not because I was a good dancer? If that were true, I couldn't stand it. That would be worse than not being in the production at all.

When I was dressed, I slunk out of school like a dog with its tail between its legs.

4th CHAPTER

I didn't worry about my role in *Coppelia* for long. In our house, it's hard to keep worries inside. Everyone notices when you're brooding. Even Squirt, who tries to make you laugh by blowing raspberries.

I hadn't been home from class for more than ten minutes before Mama dragged the whole story out. Then she began talking some sense into me. "Didn't we agree that the Stamford school was the best ballet academy in the area?" she asked me.

"Yes," I replied.

"And didn't we look into its reputation, and even the reputation of Madame Noelle?"

"Yes."

"And did we find anything that wasn't professional?"

"No."

"So," said Mama, who was really being

a lot gentler than this sounds, since she was sitting close to me on the couch and smoothing back my hair as she talked, "do you believe what those girls were saying? Do you think Madame Noelle would risk the whole show, would cast the starring role with a dancer who wasn't the best for the part, in order to play favourites?"

"Nope," I replied.

"I don't think so either," said Mama, and she pulled me close for a hug.

"Thanks, Mama," I whispered.

And that was the end of that. Hilary and Katie Beth were jealous, and I'd just have to live with that. It was their problem, not mine. The only way for me to feel bad about it was to *let* them make me feel bad. And I wasn't going to do that. Why should I?

I concentrated on Matthew Braddock, my new babysitting charge. I was supposed to go to his house for my first training session. I decided that before I did, I should at least know what Ameslan was. So the night before I met Matthew I went into our study and looked up some things in our encyclopaedia. It turns out Ameslan is sign language and that signing is a way of talking with your hands—so that deaf people can *see* you talk, since they can't hear you. The book says signing is a lot easier than reading lips, because so many spoken words "look" the same. Stand in front of a mirror. Say "pad" and "bad." Do they look any different? Or try "dime" and "time." Do *they* look any different? Not a bit.

But signing is a language especially designed for the deaf, in which words or concepts are represented by different signs made with the hands. Actually, there are different kinds of sign languages, just like there are different spoken languages. American Sign Language (or Ameslan) was the language Matt had learned.

When I thought about it, even people who can hear use signs pretty often. We have always accused Daddy of "talking with his hands." He absolutely cannot hold them still when he talks. If he's talking about something big, he holds his hands wide apart. If he's trying to make a point, he pounds one hand on the table. If he wants to show that something is unimportant, he sort of waves one hand away. If he says your name, he points to you at the same time.

Well, I couldn't imagine a different sign for every word in the world, and I couldn't imagine the sign for a word like "shoe." Or how, for instance, would the sign for apple be different from the sign for orange?

I would find out soon enough.

I rang the Braddocks' bell at 3:15 on a Monday afternoon. I realized that from then on, my schedule was going to be very busy. Mondays—Braddocks, then a meeting of the Babysitters Club. Tuesdays—dance class. Wednesdays—same as Mondays. Thursdays—only free afternoon. Fridays—dance class, then club meeting.

Whew!

The door was answered by a pixie of a girl who must have been Haley, but who looked small for nine. Her blonde hair was cut short with a little tail in the back (*very* in), and her brown eyes were framed by luscious dark lashes. Her face was heart-shaped, and she gave me this wide, charming grin that showed a dimple at the right corner of her mouth.

"Hi," she said. "Are you Jessica?"

"Yup," I replied, "but call me Jessi. You must be Haley."

"Yup." (That grin again.) "Come on in."

Haley opened the door and I walked into a house that looked pretty much like Mallory's, only without all the kids. A lot of the houses in this neighbourhood look the same. They were all built by this one guy, Mr Geiger. I guess he didn't have much imagination.

As soon as I stepped inside, I was greeted by Mrs Braddock. She looked like a nice, comfortable kind of mum to have. She was wearing blue jeans and Reeboks and a big, baggy sweater, and she rested one hand reassuringly on Haley's shoulder while shaking my hand with the other.

"Hi, Jessica—" she began.

"Jessi, Mummy," Haley interrupted. "Call her Jessi."

Mrs Braddock and I laughed, and I was ushered into the living room. Then Mrs Braddock told me to sit on the couch. "Matt hasn't come home from school yet, but he'll be here any minute. As you know, I'm not going out this afternoon. I mean, you're not here for official babysitting. I just want you to meet Matt and Haley, and I want to introduce you to sign language. If you're interested in learning it, we'll go on from there."

"Okay," I said. "Let's start. I love languages."

Mrs Braddock smiled. "Terrific."

"Can I be the teacher, Mummy?" asked Haley.

"Does Haley know sign language, too?" I asked.

"We all do," replied Mrs Braddock. "It's the only way to communicate with Matt, and we don't want him left out of anything." She turned to Haley. "You better be the assistant teacher, honey," she told her. "Why don't you start by finding the *American Sign Language Dictionary*? We'll lend it to Jessi for a while."

Haley ran off and Mrs Braddock con-

34

tinued. "Before I begin showing you actual signs, I should tell you a little about teaching the deaf, I guess. One thing you ought to know is that not everyone agrees that the deaf should communicate with sign language. Some people think they should be taught to speak and to read lips. However, in lots of cases, speaking is out of the question. Matt, for instance, is what we call profoundly deaf. That means he has almost total hearing loss. And he was born that way. We're not sure he's ever heard a sound in his life. He doesn't even wear hearing aids. They wouldn't do him any good. And since Matt can't hear any sounds, he can't hear spoken words, of course, and he can't imitate them either. So there's almost no hope for speech from Matt. Nothing that most people could understand anyway."

"And lip-reading is hard," I said. "I experimented in front of the mirror last night."

"You've been doing your homework," said Mrs Braddock approvingly.

"How come everyone wants deaf people to speak and read lips?" I asked.

"Because if they could, they'd be able to communicate with so many more *hearing* people. Matt, for instance, can only communicate with us and with the teachers and students at his school. None of our friends knows sign language and only a few of our relatives do. When Matt grows older, he'll meet other deaf people who use sign language, and maybe even a few hearing people who can sign, but he'll be pretty limited. Imagine going to a movie theatre and signing that you want two tickets. No one would know what you meant."

I could see her point and was about to ask why the Braddocks had chosen signing for Matt, when Mrs Braddock continued. "We're not sure we've made the right choice, but that's the choice we made. At least we've been able to communicate with Matt for a long time now. Most kids take years to learn lip-reading and feel frustrated constantly, even at home." Mrs Braddock sighed. "Some families," she added, "don't bother to learn to sign. The deaf children in those families must feel so lost."

Haley returned with a big book then and dropped it in my lap. "Here's the dictionary," she said cheerfully.

I opened it to the middle and looked at the pages in front of me. I was in the K section. The book reminded me of a picture dictionary that Becca used to have.

"Key" was the sixth word under K. I saw a picture of two hands—one held up, the other imitating turning a key in an imaginary lock on the upright hand.

"Oh, I get it!" I said. "This looks like fun."

"It is sort of fun," agreed Mrs Braddock. "But there are several thousand signs in there."

"Several *thousand*!" I cried. I knew there were a lot of words in the world, but I hadn't thought there were *that* many.

"Don't worry," said Mrs Braddock. She took the dictionary from me and closed it. "Right now, I'm just going to teach you a few of the signs that Matt uses the most. When you're at home you can use the dictionary to look up other things or things you forget, okay?"

"Okay," I replied, feeling relieved.

We were just about to start when the front door opened and a little boy came into the living room. I caught sight of a van backing down the Braddocks' driveway.

"Well, there you are!" cried Mrs Braddock, speaking with her voice and her hands at the same time. "Home from school."

The boy was Matt, of course, and his face broke into a grin just like Haley's, with a dimple on the right side of his mouth. He waved to his mother and then ran to her for a hug.

"Believe it or not," Mrs Braddock said to me, "that wave was the sign for 'hello.' It's also the sign for 'goodbye.'"

"That's easy to remember," I said.

Mrs Braddock turned Matt so that he could look at me. Then she turned him

37

back to her and once again began signing and talking at the same time. She was introducing us.

"Is there a sign for my *name*?" I asked, amazed.

"That's a good question," Mrs Braddock replied. "And the answer is 'Not exactly,' or perhaps, 'Not yet.' What I did just now was *spell* your name. I used finger spelling, which I'll explain later. However, since it takes too long to spell out names we use a lot, such as our own names, or the names of Matt's teacher and his friends at school, we make up signs for those people." Mrs Braddock signed something to Matt, saying at the same time, "Matt, show Jessi the sign for your name."

Matt grinned. Then he held up one hand and sort of flew it through the air.

"That," said Mrs Braddock, "is the letter M for Matt being tossed like a baseball. Matt loves sports."

"Oh!" I exclaimed. "Neat."

"Show Jessi the sign for Haley," Mrs Braddock instructed Matt.

Another hand flew through the air.

"That was the letter H soaring like Halley's Comet. When you know finger spelling, you'll be able to tell the signs apart more easily. Also, we'll have to give you a sign soon."

Mrs Braddock asked Haley to take Matt into the kitchen then and fix him a snack.

38

When we were alone again, she began showing me signs.

"The word 'you' is easy," she told me. "Just point to the person you're talking to."

(What do you know? I thought. My father knows sign language!)

"To sign 'want,'" Mrs Braddock went on, "hold your hands out like this—palms up, fingers relaxed—and pull them toward you, curling your fingers in slightly."

Mrs Braddock went on and on. She showed me signs for foods, for parts of the body, and for the words "bathroom," "play," and "come." Finally she said, "I think that's enough for one day. I'm going to start dinner. Why don't you take Matt and Haley downstairs to the playroom so you can get to know them better?"

The Braddocks' playroom looked like any other playroom—a TV, a couple of sofas, a shelf full of books and plenty of toys.

"Ask Matt what he wants to play," I said to Haley.

Haley obediently signed to her brother, a questioning look on her face. Matt signed back.

"He wants to read," Haley told me.

"Read!" I cried. "He can read?"

"Well, he *is* seven," Haley pointed out, "and he's been in school since he was two. It's really important for him to be able to read and write."

Of course, I thought. Reading and writing are other ways to communicate.

Matt found a picture book and curled up with it.

"How can I get to know him if he reads?" I wondered out loud.

"How about getting to know *me*?" asked Haley impatiently, and she shot a brief look of annoyance at her brother. Luckily he didn't notice.

That one annoyed look said a lot. Something was going on between Matt and Haley, I thought, but I wasn't sure what.

That night I finished my homework and settled into bed with the *American Sign Language Dictionary*. Tons of questions came to me, and I wrote them down so that I'd remember to ask Mrs Braddock. How do you sign a question? Do you make a question mark with your fingers? How do you make a word plural? I mean, if there's a sign for "apple," what's the sign for "apples"? What's finger spelling? (Mrs Braddock had forgotten to explain.) And can you string signs into sentences, just like when you're speaking? (I wasn't sure, because I couldn't find signs for "the," or "an," or "a.")

Even though I knew I had a lot to learn, I decided I liked sign language. It's very expressive—almost like dancing.

5th CHAPTER

Wednesday

Brat, brat, brat.

Okay. We all agree that Jenny is spoiled and a little bratty, but I've never minded her too much. At least, not until today. Today she was at her worst. Mostly, she just didn't want to do anything. She wasn't dressed for anything fun and she wouldn't change into play clothes. Finally I took her outside and we ran into Jessi and the Braddocks! Then Jenny's brattiness just came pouring out. That kid needs a few lessons in manners. Really. Maybe we should start a class.

I have to admit that running into Mary Anne Spier and Jenny Prezzioso that afternoon was not the best experience of my life, but I guess it could have been worse. And it was not Mary Anne's fault. I bet Jenny was born a brat.

Oh, well. I'm ahead of myself (again). Mary Anne's afternoon at the Prezziosos' house began right after school ended. Mrs P. let Mary Anne inside, where she found Jenny sitting at the dining table having a snack. Now, come on. How many kids do *you* know who get afternoon snacks in the dining room? At our house, it's strictly kitchen. Usually we don't even sit down. Becca and I just open the fridge, stand in front of it until we see something we want, take it out and eat it on the way to our rooms or (in my case) on the way to a babysitting job or to Stamford for dance class.

But Jenny was sitting at the dining room table eating pudding from a goblet with a silver spoon. She was wearing one of her famous lacy dresses. (Mary Anne once told me that she thinks the Prezziosos support the U.S. lace industry all by themselves.) On her feet were white patent leather shoes and in her hair were silky blue ribbons.

Now don't get me wrong. Jenny wasn't off to a birthday party or anything. Her mother dresses her like that every day. (I hope the time will come when Jenny will rebel and refuse to wear lace anymore. Or ruffles. Or ribbons. Or bows.) Another thing. The Prezziosos are not rich. They're just average. But Jenny is their princess, their only child. (They call her their angel.)

Anyway, Mrs Prezzioso finally left, and Mary Anne and Jenny were on their own.

"Finish up your pudding, Jen, and then we can play some games," said Mary Anne brightly.

"I eat slowly," Jenny informed her. "And don't call me Jen."

(Keep in mind that Jenny is only four.)

"Sorry," Mary Anne apologized. But already her hackles were up, because she added tightly, "I didn't mean to insult you."

Jenny slurped away at her pudding. "All finished," she announced a minute later, holding out the spoon and goblet.

"Great," replied Mary Anne. "Go and put them in the sink." She wasn't going to do Jenny's work for her.

Jenny did so, scowling all the way.

Mary Anne knew they were off to a bad start and began to feel guilty. "Okay!" she said. "Let's play a game. How about Candy Land? Or Snakes and Ladders?"

Jenny put her hands on her hips. "I don't wanna."

"Then let's read. Where's *Squirrel Nutkin*? That's your favourite."

"No, it isn't, and I don't *wanna* read."

Jenny and Mary Anne were arguing in the kitchen, Jenny's hands on her hips.

"I know!" cried Mary Anne. "Finger painting!"

"Finger painting?" Jenny sounded awed. "Really?"

"Yes. . . If you'll change into play clothes."

"No. No no no. This is my new dress and I'm wearing it."

"Okay, fine," replied Mary Anne. "If there's nothing you want to do then you can just stand here all afternoon. I'm going to read a book." (As you can probably imagine, quiet Mary Anne doesn't say things like that very often.)

Jenny looked at Mary Anne with wide eyes. "You mean you're not going to play with me?"

Mary Anne sighed. "What do you want to play?" she asked.

"I don't know."

"Dolls?"

"Nope."

"House?"

"Nope."

"You want to draw a nice picture for your mummy?"

"Nope."

Mary Anne had reached the end of her rope. "That does it," she muttered. She opened a cupboard door, pulled out Jenny's light coat (of course Jenny didn't own a sweat shirt or anything), and put it on her. She buttoned it up, Jenny protesting the whole time, put on her own jacket, and marched Jenny outdoors.

"Now," said Mary Anne grimly, "We're going to have fun if it kills us."

But Jenny, if you remember, was wearing white patent leather shoes. They're kind of hard to have fun in. The only activity Mary Anne could think of for them was a nice quiet walk.

That was how they ran into Matt and Haley and me. I was at the Braddocks' again and had just had another signing lesson. I had memorized over twenty signs by then. (The Braddocks knew about a million, but I was new at this. They'd been at it for years.) Anyway, after the lesson, Mrs Braddock had asked me to take Matt and Haley outside to play.

Mary Anne and I were surprised to see each other.

"Hi!" we exclaimed.

Then we had to do a lot of introducing, since Jenny didn't know me or the Braddocks, Mary Anne didn't know the Braddocks, I didn't know Jenny and the Braddocks didn't know Jenny or Mary Anne.

Haley translated for Matt, and I jumped in whenever I knew a sign. I noticed that Jenny was watching us with her mouth open.

"What are you doing?" she finally asked Haley and me.

"Matt's deaf," I explained. "He can't hear us, but we can tell him things with our hands. Then he can see what we're saying."

Jenny approached Matt and yelled right into his ear at the top of her lungs, "CAN'T YOU HEAR ME?"

Matt just blinked and backed up a few paces.

Haley signed to him to say hi to Jenny.

Matt obediently waved.

"He just said hi to you," I told Jenny.

"You mean he can't talk, either?" asked Jenny, aghast.

"He can make *sounds*," Haley told her defensively.

And just then, Matt caught sight of a bug wriggling along the sidewalk. He laughed. His laugh was a cross between fingernails on a blackboard and a goose honking. I had to admit, it was one weird sound.

Jenny cringed against Mary Anne. "Let's go," she whispered—loudly enough for Haley and me to hear her. "He's weird. I don't want to play with him."

"Well, you're not the first one to say so!" Haley shouted.

"We better leave," Mary Anne said quickly. "I'm sorry, Jessi. I'll call you tonight so we can talk, okay?"

I nodded.

46

As they left, Haley shot a murderous glance at her brother, who was now on his hands and knees, watching the bug.

"You know what?" she said to me, and her great grin was gone. "Having a brother like Matt really stinks." Then she stood behind him, tears glistening in her eyes, and shouted, "You stink, Matt! You STINK!" Of course, Matt didn't hear her.

"It is so horrible!" Haley went on. "People think Matt's weird, but he isn't. Deaf is not weird. Everybody's unfair." Then she stormed into the Braddocks' house and slammed the door behind her.

Ah-ha, I thought. I was beginning to understand Haley and Matt. The Braddocks had just moved to a new neighbourhood and Haley wanted to fit in, but Matt was making that a little difficult.

Well, I could sympathize. In Stoneybrook, being black wasn't any easier.

6th CHAPTER

My first real babysitting job for Haley and
Matt! I have to tell you that I was a little
nervous. I was even more nervous than I'd
felt at the most recent rehearsal of *Coppelia*.
The rehearsal had been hard work and I'd
felt sore afterward, but not nervous. I was
fairly self-confident. So if I could dance the
lead in a ballet, you'd think that a job
babysitting for a nine-year-old and a
seven-year-old one afternoon wouldn't be
hard at all. And ordinarily it wouldn't be.
But Matt is not your ordinary seven-
year-old.

I still knew only a handful of signs, so I
started imagining all sorts of problems.
What if Haley wasn't around and Matt
didn't feel well? I couldn't ask him what
was wrong, and if he tried to tell me, I probably wouldn't understand.

But there was no point in worrying about

things like that. Of course Haley would be there to help me, and Matt would be fine. Besides, he could write, and anyway, Mrs Braddock was only going to the grocery store. She'd be gone for an hour and a half, at the most.

When I got to the Braddocks' house I could tell that Mrs Braddock was a little nervous, too. She kept reminding me about things.

"Be extra careful outdoors," she said. "Remember that Matt can't hear car horns."

"Right," I replied.

"And he can't hear a shouted warning."

"Right."

"And inside he can't hear the doorbell or telephone."

"I'll take care of those things."

"Do you remember the sign for 'bathroom'?"

"Yup."

"For 'eat'?"

"Yup. . . And I can do finger spelling. I memorized the alphabet last night." (Mrs Braddock had explained to me that there was a sign for every letter in the alphabet, just like there were signs for words. So, for instance, if I wanted to spell my name, I would sign the letters J-E-S-S-I. Finger spelling takes longer than regular signing, but at least you can communicate names and unusual words that way.)

49

"The whole alphabet?" Mrs Braddock repeated. She sounded impressed.

I nodded. "The whole thing. Oh, and I thought of a name for myself. Look."

I shaped my right hand into the sign for the letter J (for my name), pointed it downward and whisked it back and forth across the palm of my left hand. That's the sign for the word "dance" except that you usually make a V with your right index and middle fingers, to look like a pair of legs flying across the floor.

"See?" I said. "A dancing J! Anyway, don't worry, Mrs Braddock. You know how many signs I've memorized. I'm not too good at sentences, but Matt and I will get along. No problem." I sounded a lot more confident than I felt.

"Besides," added Haley, who had appeared in the kitchen. "You've got *me*, right?" She sounded a little uncertain—as if I might say I didn't need her after all.

I put my arm around Haley. "I'll say!" I exclaimed. "You're the best help I've got."

Haley turned on that smile of hers.

"Well. . ." said Mrs Braddock. She glanced down the hallway and out the front door, looking (I think) for Matt's special school bus. "Matt should be here in about ten minutes. I told him this morning that you would be here when he got home from school and that I'd be back soon. Haley can help you remind him if he seems anxious, but I think he'll be all right. He really likes you, Jessi."

"Thanks," I replied.

Mrs Braddock left then, and Haley and I sat on the front steps to wait for Matt. The school bus was prompt. It pulled into the driveway exactly ten minutes after Mrs Braddock left.

Matt jumped down the steps of the van. He waved eagerly to the driver, who waved back, and then signed something to a giggling face that was pressed against a window of the van. The little boy signed back. A second boy joined in. Matt and his friends were talking about football. (I think.)

It was odd, I thought, to see so much energy and so much communication—without any sound at all. Watching the boys was like watching TV with the volume turned off.

The bus drove away and Matt ran across the lawn to Haley and me, smiling. (Mrs Braddock hadn't needed to worry about anxiety.)

"Hi!" I signed to Matt. (A wave and a smile.)

He returned the wave and smile.

I showed him the sign for my name (which he liked), and then I asked him about school. (The sign for school is clapping hands—like a teacher trying to get the attention of her pupils. When I found that out, I wondered what the sign for "applause" or "clap" is, since it seemed to have been used up. This is the sign: You touch your hand to your mouth, which is part of the sign for "good," and *then* clap your hands. It's like applauding for good words. See why I like languages? They make so much sense.)

Matt signed back, "Great!" (He pointed to his chest with his thumb and wiggled his fingers back and forth—with a broad grin.)

After Matt had put his schoolbooks in his room, he ate a quick snack. I'll give you the sign for the snack. See if you can guess what the snack was. You form your hand into the sign for the letter A, then you pretend to eat your thumb. That's the sign for . . . apple! Eating the letter A. Isn't that great?

Anyway, as soon as Matt was finished eating, I took him and Haley outdoors. I had a plan. I hadn't been able to stop thinking about what happened when the Braddocks and I ran into Mary Anne and Jenny Prezzioso. And I was determined that Matt and Haley were going to make friends in their new neighbourhood. I remembered how horrible Becca had felt when nobody in Stoneybrook would play with her. Then one day Charlotte Johanssen, who's just her age, had come over, and Becca was so happy she barely knew what to do.

I began marching Matt and Haley over to the Pikes' house.

"Where are we going?" Haley asked me.

"We," I replied, "are going to a house nearby where you will find eight kids."

"Is one of them my age?" Haley sounded both interested and sceptical.

"Yup," I replied and suddenly realized that we were leaving Matt out of the conversation by not signing. I told Haley to sign.

"I hope the nine-year-old isn't a boy," Haley said, hands flying.

(Matt made a face at that.)

"Nope," I said. "The nine-year-old is a girl. Her name is Vanessa. She likes to make up rhymes." There was no way I could sign all that, so Haley did it for me, to keep Matt informed. Then she told him where we were going.

"Is there a seven-year-old Pike?" Matt signed.

Haley looked at me.

I nodded. Then I signed "girl," and Matt made a horrible face. It wasn't a sign, but it could only mean one thing—YUCK!

"Tell him there's an eight-year-old boy," I said to Haley.

Matt brightened, and I finger spelled N-I-C-K-Y.

We had reached the Pikes' front door by then. Matt boldly rang the bell. It was answered by Mallory, and I was relieved.

I'd told her we might come over, and I wanted her to help me with the introductions.

"The Barretts are here, too," she whispered, as we stepped inside. "They're friends from down the street. Buddy is eight and Suzi is five." She turned to Haley and Matt, said hello, and waved at the same time. She knew that much about signing from me. I loved her for remembering to do it. That's one of the reasons she's my new best friend.

"Well," said Mallory, "everyone's playing in the back garden.

We walked through the Pikes' house, waving to Mrs Pike on the way, and stepped into the yard. It looked like a school playground.

The Pikes and the Barrets all stopped what they were doing and ran to us.

The introductions began.

The signing began.

The explaining began.

The staring began.

And Haley began to look angry again.

I glanced at Mallory. "Ick-en-spick," she whispered. And with that, a wonderful idea came to me. Mallory and I love to read, and not long ago we'd both read a really terrific book (even if it was a little old-fashioned) called *The Secret Language*, by Ursula Nordstrom. These two friends make up a secret language, and "ick-en-spick" is a word they use when something is silly or unnecessary.

"You know," I said to the kids, "maybe Matt can't hear or talk, but he knows a *secret language*. He can talk with his *hands*. He can say anything he wants and never make a sound."

"Really?" asked Margo (who's seven) in a hushed voice.

Mallory smiled at me knowingly. "Think how useful that would be," she said to her brothers and sisters, "if, like, Mum and Dad punished you and said, 'No talking for half an hour.' You could talk and they'd never know it."

"Yeah," said Nicky slowly. "Awesome."

"How do you do it? asked Vanessa. "What's the secret language?"

This time, Haley jumped in with the answer. "It's this," she replied. She began demonstrating signs. The kids were fascinated.

"Say something," Claire, the youngest Pike, commanded Matt.

"He can't hear you," I reminded Claire.

"*I'll* tell him what you said," Haley told Claire importantly. She signed to Matt.

Matt began waving his hands around so fast that all I could understand was that he was signing about football again.

Haley translated. "Matt says he thinks the Patriots are going to win the Super Bowl this year. He says—"

"No way!" spoke up Buddy Barrett. Haley didn't have to translate that. Matt could tell what Buddy meant by the way he was shaking his head.

Matt began signing furiously again.

"What's he saying? What's he saying?" the kids wanted to know.

Mallory and I grinned at each other. We sat down on the low wall by the Pikes' patio, relieved, and watched the kids.

"Your brothers and sisters are great," I said.

"When you grow up in a family as big as mine," Mallory replied, "you end up being pretty accepting."

"Thank goodness."

After a while I looked at my watch and realized that Mrs Braddock would probably be back from the grocery shop soon.

"I better take Haley and Matt home," I said and began to round them up. But in the end, I only brought Matt home. Haley was having too much fun at the Pikes' to leave, and swore up and down that she knew the way back to her house. I left her teaching the kids how to sign the word "stupid." I had a feeling there was going to be a lot of silent name-calling in the neighbourhood for a while.

7th CHAPTER

Friday

Oh, no! Jessi what have you started? Mallory and I were sitting at her house last night and guess what happened. You won't believe it.

Well, she might believe it. Don't jump to any conclusions. After all, most kids like languages, and this one reminds my brothers of football signals.

Okay, so she'll believe it but anyway, Jessi, get this. It started when the Pike kids went totally wild last ni

Not me! I wasn't wild!

No, of course not, Mal. You were one of the sitters. I meant that your brothers and sisters were wild.

Oh, okay.

I have to stop Dawn and Mal's notebook entry here. It goes on forever. Let me just tell you what happened while they were sitting. (And by the way, Dawn was right. I did sort of start something.)

Mr and Mrs Pike were going to a dinner party that evening, so Mallory and Dawn were in charge of the Pikes from six o'clock until eleven o'clock. They had to give the kids dinner and everything. I know you met some of the Pikes in the last chapter, but just to refresh your memory, I'll include all their names and ages here:

Mallory—the oldest, of course. She's eleven, like me.

Byron, Adam and Jordan—ten-year-old triplets.

Vanessa—nine

Nicky—eight

Margo—seven

Claire—five

Those kids are a handful, even for two experienced sitters.

When Dawn arrived, which was just as Mr and Mrs Pike were leaving, the kids were angry and clamouring for dinner. Sometimes Mrs Pike let the kids eat up leftovers when babysitters are in charge, sometimes it's up to the sitters to make sandwiches or something. But this time Mrs Pike had fixed a huge pot of spaghetti (a food that every single Pike will eat) and left the sauce bubbling away on the stove.

"Well, if everyone's hungry," said Mallory as her parents' car backed down the driveway, "then let's eat."

Dawn had sat at the Pikes' often enough that she was prepared for what happened next: The kids swarmed through the kitchen and had the big table set and the food served in about thirty seconds. (Well, maybe I'm exaggerating, but it was fast.)

Then they sat down to their dinner. Since there are so many Pikes, their kitchen table looks like a table in the school dining room—very long with a bench on either side and a chair at each end. Four kids sit on one side, four on the other and Mr and Mrs Pike sit in the chairs.

That night, the boys were lined up on one side, facing Vanessa, Claire and Margo. Mallory was sitting where her mum usually sits and Dawn had taken Mr Pike's chair. Something about boys *versus* girls seemed a little dangerous to Dawn, but there are almost no rules in the Pike house, so she didn't ask them to change places. She just hoped for the best.

That was before the worm song began.

Things started off innocently. Adam, one of the triplets, formed his spaghetti into a mound and placed a meatball at the very top. Then he began to sing, "*On top of spaghetti, all covered with cheese, I lost my poor meatball when somebody sneezed.*"

Adam glanced at Jordan, who faked a very good sneeze.

"Ew, ew!" cried Claire. "Cut it out! Germs!"

The boys ignored her. Adam continued his song. "*It rolled off the table and onto the floor, and then my poor meatball rolled out the front door. It rolled down the pavement and under a bush, and now my poor meatball is nothing but mush.*"

Adam looked as if he were going to send his meatball down the spaghetti mountain, and maybe, actually, out the front door, so Mallory leaned over and speared it with her fork.

"Hey!" exclaimed Adam. "Give it! That's mine!"

Meanwhile, Jordan, Byron and Nicky were hysterical at the thought of a travelling meatball and were experimenting with theirs. They rolled meatballs down spaghetti mountains until Dawn told them that if they couldn't behave, she and Mallory would have to separate them.

"We'll behave," Adam spoke up from the other end of the table, "if Mallory will give me my meatball back."

Mallory returned the meatball.

For two minutes, Dawn and the Pikes ate peacefully. The mounds of spaghetti and meatballs were disappearing.

Then, so quietly that Mallory and Dawn weren't sure at first that they'd heard anything, Nicky began singing the worm song. But he was eating at the same time and he looked totally innocent.

"*Nobody likes me,*" he sang, "*everybody hates me. Guess I'll go eat worms.*" He picked a single strand of spaghetti off his plate and held it above his mouth.

"Nicky," warned Mallory.

Nicky dropped the spaghetti into his mouth. "*First one was slimy,*" he sang.

"Mallory, Dawn, make him stop!" cried Margo. "I'm going to be sick."

Margo is famous for her weak stomach. Everything makes her throw up—riding in the car, aeroplane takeoffs and landings, roller coasters. Those are motion sicknesses, of course, but Dawn thought there was a good chance that this would make Margo get sick too. And she certainly didn't want anybody throwing up at the table, especially throwing up spaghetti.

But it was too late. Too late to stop the worm song, I mean.

By then, Byron was holding a strand of spaghetti over *his* mouth. "*Second one was grimy,*" he sang, continuing the song.

"Mallory!" shrieked Margo, looking a little green.

"Oh, no! Oh, no! Not the worm song! Please stop the boys before something goes wrong," said Vanessa Pike, future poet.

Adam sucked in two strands of spaghetti,

pretended to gag, and sang, *"Third and fourth came up."*

At that point, Margo jumped up from the table and headed for the nearest bathroom.

Silence.

Margo stopped, turned around, looked at her brothers and sisters, and said, "Fooled you!"

She returned to the table. All the boys stuck their tongues out at her. Margo looked pleased with herself.

"That may have been a false alarm," said Dawn, "but one more word of the worm song and you will *all* be in trouble. Understand?"

"Yes," mumbled the Pikes.

They finished their dinner. It wasn't until they were clearing the table that the remainder of the worm song escaped from Nicky's mouth. It was as if he just couldn't help himself. He sang in a rush, *"So-I-began-crying-thinking-I-was-dying-eating-all-those squishy-squashy-worms."*

"That does it!" cried Mallory. "Didn't Dawn say no more worm song?"

The Pike kids scowled at Nicky.

"Yes," Nicky replied.

"I meant it, too," said Dawn. "You guys are banished to the playroom. I want you all down there for half an hour. No running, no jumping, no teasing each other. Just *behave* for the next thirty minutes and let your sister and me finish cleaning up the kitchen."

Reluctantly, the seven Pikes headed down the steps to the playroom.

For ten minutes, Mal and Dawn worked in peace, scraping dishes, loading the dishwasher and sponging off the table. They were almost done when they heard a giggle from the playroom. Then another and another.

But there were no crashes or shrieks or yelps.

"Maybe that means they've settled down," suggested Dawn hopefully.

The next thing my friends heard was Vanessa saying, "No, like this!"

"No, I've got it! Like *this*!" exclaimed Nicky. "Wiggle your fingers."

"How about an elephant?" said Margo. "That would be easy. You could make it look like you were flapping big ears."

"What would the sign for 'rabbit' be then?" wondered Byron. "They have big ears, too."

"No, they have *long* ones," Claire corrected him.

Upstairs in the kitchen, Dawn said to Mal, "What on earth are they doing?"

"Let's go and see," she replied.

They tiptoed to the top of the stairs. In the playroom, the Pikes were seated on the floor in a sloppy circle, and their hands were working busily.

"Stupidhead!" Margo announced. She crossed her eyes and pointed to her head.

"Witch!" said Vanessa. She formed her hands into a peak over her head, making a witch's hat.

"Banana-brain," said Jordan. He touched his fingertips together, then separated his hands, indicating the shape of a banana. Then he tapped his head.

Mal and Dawn looked at each other in surprise.

"The secret language," whispered Mallory. "They're making up their own. I don't believe it."

"You're sure it's not the real thing?" said Dawn.

"You really think there's a sign in that dictionary of Jessi's for 'banana-brain'?"

"No," replied Dawn, giggling.

"We'll have to invite Haley and Matt over again," said Mallory carefully. "If my brothers and sisters like secret languages so much, then they ought to be able to learn the real thing."

"And if they did learn it," said Dawn slowly, catching on, "Matt could communicate with the kids in the neighbourhood—with kids who can hear."

When Mallory told me this the next day, my heart leaped. It was more than I'd hoped for. It was like getting the part of Swanilda when I wasn't even sure I could be one of the townspeople.

The Pikes' secret language meant that they were going to accept Matt. I was sure of it. It meant that they wanted to communicate with him. I thought it might even mean that they would want to learn actual American Sign Language.

And it meant one more thing—that the kids would probably get to know and like Haley, just for herself.

I couldn't wait until Haley realized that.

8th CHAPTER

Rehearsal.

My bones ached. My muscles ached. Each and every one of my toes ached.

Being Swanilda was not easy.

It was four o'clock on a Saturday afternoon and the cast of *Coppelia* had been rehearsing for hours.

"We want per-fec-see-yun," said Madame Noelle crisply. "Per-*fec*-see-yun." She banged her club on the floor. "Nothing less. Mademoiselle Parsons" (that was Katie Beth), "you must turn the head faster and start the turn a little later. Just a froction of a second, *non*? Mademoiselle Bramstedt" (that was Mary, one of the townspeople), "higher on the toes. This is a toe-dancing, *en pointe* production. Please to remember. Mademoiselle Romsey, excellent work."

I closed my eyes with relief. Thank goodness. That was all she'd said to me that day.

Of course, I'd been working extra hard—practising longer hours at home and putting every ounce of *me* into my dancing.

The other cast members glanced at me approvingly. I was glad. I needed their approval. I wanted to show them that I could be a good Swanilda even if I was young and new at the school.

"Okay, closs. Our time is ended," said Madame. "This was a good rehearsal. Go change now. I will see you in your closses next week."

As I walked towards the dressing room, a hand touched my shoulder. I looked around. It was Katie Beth. She was with Hilary.

"Good work," said Katie Beth briskly.

"Yeah, good work," agreed Hilary. "Nice job."

They linked arms and walked away.

Not exactly friendly, but a whole lot better than the sarcastic comments they used to make. Katie Beth had almost smiled.

In the changing room, I got dressed slowly. Daddy had said he'd be a little late picking me up. Even though it was Saturday, he was in his office in Stamford. He was working on a special project and had a big deadline coming up. That morning he'd told me that he'd pick me up at 4:30, after some important meeting.

Although I changed my clothes slowly, I was dressed by 4:10. I walked into the lobby of the school to wait for my father. I sat on a bench and watched the other students stream past me, out the front door. When things quieted down, I noticed Katie Beth sitting on the other bench, not far away.

We smiled embarrassed smiles and looked at our hands.

After a moment, I looked up again. Katie Beth wasn't alone. Sitting next to her was a younger girl, about Haley's age. She looked somewhat like Katie, or would have if she'd pulled her long hair back from her face, the way Katie's was fixed.

Were they sisters? If they were, why weren't they talking? When Becca and I are together, we never shut up.

Katie Beth caught me looking at her and said, "This is my sister, Adele."

"Hi, Adele," I said.

Adele didn't answer, but when Katie Beth nudged her, she smiled at me.

I decided to take a big risk. I got up and moved to the bench next to Katie Beth and Adele. "I'm waiting for my father," I told them. "He won't be here until four-thirty." I checked my watch. "Fifteen more minutes."

Katie Beth nodded. "We're waiting for our mum. She's talking to Madame Noelle. She's upset because I need new toe shoes so often."

I nodded understandingly. "My parents

don't like it, either. But there's really nothing you can do about it."

"That's what I tried to tell Mum, but. . ."

Katie's voice trailed off and I knew she meant, "just try to figure out parents."

I smiled.

Just then, Adele touched her sister on the arm. Katie Beth turned to look at her. To my great surprise, Adele signed "bathroom." She was using American Sign Language!

To my even greater surprise, Katie Beth looked at her sister as if she were a cockroach and then turned back to me. She was blushing bright red.

Adele nudged Katie Beth again and signed "bathroom" for the second time. She was getting that look on her face that Becca sometimes gets which means, "This is an extreme emergency. I need the bathroom *now*."

"Hey, Katie," I said, "Adele can use the bathroom down the hall. No one would mind." I signed that to Adele, who gave me the most incredibly grateful look you can imagine, jumped to her feet and ran down the hall. As she passed me, hair flying, I caught sight of the hearing aids in her ears.

Katie Beth glanced at me, puzzled.

"She had to go to the bathroom," I told her.

"You mean you understood her?"

"Yes," I replied. "Didn't you?" I was sure "bathroom" was one of the most popular signs in sign language. It was probably the first one ever made up.

"No," Katie Beth answered in surprise. "I don't know sign language."

"You *don't*? But how do you live with Adele? How do you know wh—"

"Oh, I don't live with her," Katie Beth broke in. "Not really. She goes to a special school for the deaf. It's in Massachusetts. She lives there most of the time. She only comes home for holidays, part of the summer and a few weekends."

"But when she's home," I pressed, "how do you talk with her?"

"Well, I don't exactly. I mean, my parents and I don't. Sometimes if we shout really loudly, she can hear us a little. And she can read lips, sort of."

"Does she talk?"

Katie Beth shook her head. "Nope. She could but she won't. She is so stubborn."

I wondered about that, considering the sounds I'd heard coming from Matt's throat.

Then another thought occurred to me. Boy, was Matt ever lucky. How terrible it must be for Adele. She couldn't even communicate with her own family, unless they wrote everything down all the time, and I didn't think there was much chance of that.

I still wasn't sure that the Braddocks had

done the right thing by teaching Matt only sign language, but I did see that they were a pretty incredible family. They'd kept him at home (Adele must have felt pushed off the face of the earth), and they'd *all* made the effort to learn and use sign language— fluently.

"You know," I said to Katie Beth, "sign language is fun. And in a way, it's like dancing."

"What do you mean?"

"Well, it's a way of expressing yourself using your body."

Katie Beth looked thoughtful. Then she asked, "How come you know how to sign?"

I told her about Matt. "I could show you some signs," I said as Adele returned from the bathroom.

"I don't know. . ."

"Oh, come on. It's fun. Look—this is the sign for 'dance.'" I demonstrated.

"Hey, cool!" exclaimed Katie Beth.

Adele was watching us. She smiled. Then she used her hands to ask me if I was a dancer like her sister.

I nodded. Then I asked her how old she was.

Adele held up one hand and formed her index finger and thumb into a circle, her other fingers pointing upward.

Nine. (There are signs for numbers, just like there are for letters.)

So she *was* Haley's age.

"Do you dance?" I signed to Adele.

She shrugged. Then she signed back that she couldn't hear the music, and she didn't know ballet, but she liked to dance in her own way.

During our signed conversation, Katie Beth had been watching us curiously. I knew she didn't know what Adele and I were saying to each other, and I wondered how she felt being left out of a conversation. At the Parsonses' house, Adele must always be left out.

"What are you saying?" Katie Beth couldn't resist asking.

I told her. Then I showed her the signs for a few more words. Adele was grinning away.

By the time Adele and Katie Beth's mother showed up, it was almost 4:30. I walked outside with the Parsonses to watch for Daddy's car.

"Good-bye!" called Katie Beth as they drove off. "And thanks! See you on Monday!"

"'Bye!" I called back. Adele and I waved to each other.

I felt that something important had happened between Katie Beth and me. We were linked. She would never call me a teacher's pet again. But we probably also would not wind up as best friends. My only best friends were Keisha and Mallory. I was linked to them, too, but those links were much, much stronger.

9th
CHAPTER

saturday

Jessie youre secret langage is a hit. Its catching on everywhere and its the best babysiting game ever invinted. I used it to ix esk entirtane karen Andrew and David micheal.

See I sat at kristys house last night. kristy was at a baketball game with her big borthers Sam and Charlie. I love siting but the house scars me. And karen doesn't help with her gost stories and which stories. So last night when karen started with the ghost stuff I decided to show the kids a litle of the secrit langage. They love it!

73

The secret language sure was catching on, and I couldn't have been happier. The more kids who learned it, even just a few words of it, the more kids Matt could "talk" to. I was really happy about Claudia's notebook entry. Of course, I knew before I read the entry that Claudia was teaching the secret language to Kristy's little brother, stepbrother and stepsister. That was because Claudia and Karen kept calling me and asking me to look up things in the sign language dictionary. But, as usual, I'm getting ahead of myself. Let me start back at the beginning of the evening when Claudia arrived at Kristy's house.

Claudia's mother dropped her off at the Brewer mansion at seven o'clock. Claudia rang the bell, and it was answered by Karen Brewer, Kristy's stepsister. Kristy loves her stepbrother and stepsister just as much as if they were her real brother and sister. She wishes she could see them more often. But Karen and Andrew mostly live with their mother and stepfather. They only stay at their father's house every other weekend, every other holiday, and for two weeks during the summer.

Karen is this bouncy, bold little girl who loves to scare people (including herself) with stories about witches and ghosts. She's even convinced that her father's next-door neighbour, Mrs Porter, is actually a witch named Morbidda Destiny. And she's sure that a ghost named Ben Brewer (some old ancestor of hers, I guess) haunts the third floor of her father's house.

Andrew, on the other hand, is shy and quiet. Karen often scares him, although she doesn't mean to. Usually, she's very protective of him, and he adores her.

That night, Claudia was going to be sitting for Karen, Andrew and David Michael, Kristy's seven-year-old brother. Claudia arrived just as Kristy, Sam and Charlie were running out the door to the Stoneybrook High *versus* Mercer High basketball game.

"'Bye, Kristy! Hi, Karen!" said Claudia.

"'Bye!" called Kristy as the door slammed behind her.

"Hi," said Karen, "I'm going to be very busy tonight. There's a ghost party on the third floor."

"And you're going to it?" asked Claudia, trying to look serious.

"Are you kidding?" replied Karen. "That would be crazy. But I'm in charge of refreshments. All night it's going to be my job to take food to the bottom of the third-floor stairs and leave it there for the ghosts."

"What are you going to feed them?"

"Ghost paté," replied Karen. "It's really the only thing for a ghost party."

"Well, I'm sure they'll appreciate it," said Claudia.

"Hi, Claudia," spoke up another voice. It was Kristy's mother, the new Mrs Brewer. "Thanks for coming. Mr Brewer and I will be home by ten-thirty. And the kids should go to bed at nine."

"Aw, *Elizabeth*," complained Karen. "Andrew's younger than me. He should go to bed before I do."

"But it's Friday, honey," Mrs Brewer pointed out. "He can stay up a little later."

"Then *I* get to stay up even later than he does."

Kristy's mother sighed. "All right. Claudia, Andrew's bedtime is nine o'clock, Karen's is nine-fifteen and David Michael's is nine-thirty."

"Goody!" cried Karen, jumping up and down. "Thank you!" Claudia thought Karen might complain about David Michael's bedtime, but she didn't. Fair was fair.

"Now," Mrs Brewer went on, "Andrew is getting over tonsillitis and needs a spoonful of penicillin before he goes to bed. The bottle is in the kitchen, in the cabinet next to the fridge."

"Okay," Claudia replied.

"I guess that's it. You know where the emergency numbers are. And Mr Brewer and I will just be across the street at the Papadakises'."

The Brewers left, and Karen and Claudia went upstairs to the big playroom, where they found Andrew and David Michael building a space station out of Lego and Tonker Toys.

"Hi, guys," Claudia greeted the boys.

"Hi!" they replied.

"Want to help us?" asked Andrew.

"Sure." Claudia sat down in front of the space station.

"Well," said Karen, "I guess I better go."

"Go where?" asked Claudia vaguely, sifting through a pile of Lego.

"Down to the kitchen, then up to the ghosts."

"Down to the kitchen?" Claudia repeated. "For real food?"

"Sure. That's where the ghost pate is."

"What's ghost pate?" asked Andrew nervously.

"Don't worry about it," David Michael told him. "Karen's just pretending again."

"Am not?" cried Karen.

"Are too!"

"Hold it! Hold it!" said Claudia. (Silence.) "Karen, use pretend food, okay? You don't need to go down to the kitchen."

There were, Claudia thought, a few problems with living in a house as big as the Brewers'. For instance, it was easy for the kids to get out of earshot in the house, and Claudia didn't like that. And when she sat downstairs at night waiting for the Brewers to come home, she sometimes felt terrified.

Then Claudia added, "And Andrew, don't worry. It really is just a game."

"Is not!" said Karen indignantly. She stooped down, pretended to pick something up, and walked out of the room calling, "Here comes the pate!"

When she returned, Claudia decided that it might be a good idea to get Karen's mind off the ghost party. First she tried to interest her in the boys' space station. When that didn't work, she said in a hushed, excited-sounding voice, "How would you guys like to learn a secret language?"

"Huh?" replied Andrew and David Michael. They didn't look up from their work.

But Karen said, "A secret language? What do you mean?"

"I," Claudia began, "can show you how to talk without making any sounds at all. Without even opening your mouth."

Now she had captured even the boys' attention. "That's impossible," said David Michael.

"No, it isn't." Claudia made the sign for "dance," which I had shown the members of the Babysitters Club. "That means 'dance,'" she informed them.

She showed them three other signs. "Some deaf people," she told the kids, "know thousands of signs. They can have whole conversations with their hands."

"Is there a sign for 'ghost'?" asked Karen.

"Probably," Claudia replied. "But I don't know what it is."

"Oh." Karen looked disappointed.

"I know how we can find out, though," Claudia said, brightening. "We'll call Jessi Ramsey. She has a dictionary with all the signs in it. She can look up 'ghost'."

The four of them trooped into the hallway, and Claudia dialled my number. Becca answered the phone and called me into our kitchen. When Claudia had explained what was going on, I said, "Just a sec. I'll go get the book."

I ran to my room, grabbed the dictionary off my desk and tried to look up "ghost" as I was running back to the kitchen. "Here it is!" I exclaimed. (I was pleased to be able to help Claudia. Sometimes Mal and I feel like the babies of the Babysitters Club, since we're younger and have been members for such a short time.) "There *is* a sign for ghost. Only it's going to be kind of hard to describe."

I did my best.

Then Karen wanted the sign for "witch." That one was almost impossible to explain over the phone. After "witch," she wanted "cat," "storm," "night," and "black."

I thought that was the end of things, but no sooner had I put the dictionary away than the phone rang again. This time it was Karen herself.

"I forgot the sign for 'night,' " she said.

I tried to explain it again.

"And is there a sign for 'afraid'?"

"What are you going to do?" I asked Karen. "Sign a ghost story?"

"Yes," she replied seriously.

I smiled. "Okay." (The sign for "afraid" is covering your heart in fear with both hands. I love it, I just love it.)

Meanwhile, back at Kristy's house, Karen was trying to sign her ghost story. She didn't know nearly enough words, though, and soon gave up.

"Let's make ourselves a snack and then you guys will have to start getting ready for bed," Claudia told the kids.

"What kind of snack?" asked Karen.

"Whatever you want," Claudia replied. "But if you have the right ingredients, I'll fix *you* ghost pate."

Luckily, Claudia found what she needed—crackers and liverwurst. She spread a cracker with liverwurst and handed it to Karen. "There you go," she said. "Ghost pate."

"Yick," said Andrew.

But Karen ate her snack eagerly. "*Thank* you, Claudia," she said several times, glad that someone was taking her game seriously.

When the snacks were eaten and the

kitchen was clean, Claudia gave Andrew his medicine, and then took the kids back upstairs. "Time to get ready for bed now," she said. "Andrew, you first."

While she was giving Andrew a hand, she thought she heard Karen on the phone in the hall, but she didn't think anything of it. Andrew's room was a mess and he couldn't find his pyjamas. Then he got worried about the ghost party again.

"Honest. It's not real," Claudia told him. "Karen made it all up."

"Then why did you make the ghost pate?" he asked.

Oops.

"That was just silly," said Claudia. "It was pretend."

Andrew found his pyjamas, put them on, and went into the bathroom to brush his teeth. When he returned, he climbed into bed.

"I won't be able to fall asleep," he announced. "I'm scared."

"Sure you will," Claudia told him. "You'll fall asleep. Count something, like sheep."

"I'll have to count ghosts," Andrew said.

"Well, at least count friendly ones. There *are* friendly ghosts, you know."

"There are?"

"Yup."

"How do you tell them from the spooky ones?"

"The friendly ones are the ones who smile and call, 'Hi, Andrew!' The spooky ones just say, 'BOO!'"

"Oh."

"Call me if you need me."

"Okay. Night, Claudia."

"Night, Andrew."

Click. Light off.

Creak. Door open a crack.

Claudia tiptoed down the hall to Karen's room, where she found her sitting on her bed holding Tickly, her blanket, in one hand, and Moosie, her stuffed cat, in the other.

"We have time for a story, don't we, Claudia?" she said. "We have until nine-fifteen. Fifteen more minutes."

"Right," replied Claudia. "What do you want to hear?" And then she went on in a rush, "How about *The Cat in the Hat*?" She suggested that because Karen always suggests *The Witch Next Door* or one of her other witch stories, and Claudia had had enough ghost and witch tales for one night.

"Okay," agreed Karen.

So they read the book, lying side by side on Karen's bed.

When they were finished, Claudia returned the book to its shelf while Karen snuggled under the covers next to Moosie and Tickly.

"Good-night," said Claudia.

Karen didn't say anything, but she

pulled her arms out from under the covers. She signed something to Claudia.

"What was that?" asked Claudia.

"It was 'good-night'! I called Jessi again while you were helping Andrew get ready for bed."

Claudia signed "good-night" back to Karen.

Then Karen made another sign. "I love you," she said.

Claudia smiled and signed back. She switched on Karen's nightlight and quietly left the room, remembering to crack her door open like Andrew's.

Then she tiptoed down the hall to David Michael's room, thinking that signing was the nicest language she had ever seen.

10th CHAPTER

I was babysitting regularly at the Braddocks' now. I loved it, but my schedule was tough. On Tuesday and Friday I went to my dance class and sometimes stayed later than usual, trying to keep in shape for rehearsals. Rehearsals were held on the weekends, and often on Thursday as well, which *had* been my only free afternoon of the week. But every Monday and Wednesday afternoon I went directly from school to Matt and Haley's house. Then Mrs Braddock would leave for her part-time job. She was working with deaf adults at the Stoneybrook Community Centre.

The Braddocks and I had a routine. I would reach their house at three o'clock, just a few minutes after Haley got home from Stoneybrook Elementary. Then Mrs Braddock would leave and I would fix a snack for Haley and me. After we'd eaten, we'd sit on the front step and wait for Matt's bus to drop him off. Then *Matt* would eat a snack, and when *he* had finished we'd go outside to play. We'd play with the Pikes, the Barretts, and sometimes even Jenny Prezzioso, who seemed to accept Matt a little more than she had the first time she'd met him. On rainy days we had to stay in, of course, but we invited kids over, or went to somebody else's house. We were always with other kids, and Matt and Haley were eating it up.

Plus, the secret language was spreading fast. Learning signs was a game, and the kids, especially Vanessa and Nicky Pike, learned them quickly. This was great, because Vanessa and Haley were getting to be friends, and Nicky, Matt, and Buddy Barrett were getting to be friends, too. They often needed Haley (or me) to translate for them, but the friendship was growing anyway.

One day, the weather was warmer than usual.

"Summer!" Matt signed to me excitedly. He crooked his right index finger and imitated somebody wiping a hot forehead.

I smiled at him. It wasn't summer, though, so I signed, "It *feels* like summer."

Matt nodded. He had just finished his snack and we were heading outside to play. We opened the front door and found the

Pike triplets, Buddy Barrett and Nicky crossing the Braddocks' lawn.

"Hi!" Matt waved eagerly.

The boys waved back.

"Where's Vanessa?" Haley called.

"She had to go to the dentist," Nicky answered.

"Oh." Haley sounded disappointed.

The boys began a game of six-person baseball. They didn't need to talk much to play that.

Haley and I sat down on the steps and watched them.

Buddy hit the ball out into the street, ran the bases and jumped up and down as if he'd scored a home run.

"Not fair!" Nicky shouted angrily.

"The ball was out!" Matt added.

I was about to remind the boys to sign when suddenly they remembered on their own. Nicky signed, "Not fair!", Matt signed "The ball was out," and then Jordan jumped in.

"No!" he signed. "Safe."

Haley and I looked at each other.

"They're not bothering to talk at *all*," said Haley, awed.

"Nope," I replied. "They've learned every sign that could possibly have anything to do with football or baseball."

Haley grinned. "It's a good thing Matt plays sports so well. If he didn't, I don't know what I'd do."

86

"What do you mean?" I asked.

"Well, it's sure helped him make friends here."

"I know," I said, "and that's great. But what does that have to do with you? You said if *he* wasn't good at sports, you didn't know what *you'd* do."

"I have to help him," Haley said simply. "I have to watch out for him."

"You do? I'm the babysitter," I teased.

Haley smiled. Then her smile faded and she looked sort of sad. "You're not Matt's sister," she told me.

"No, I'm not."

"You don't know what it's like."

"That's true. . . What *is* it like?"

"You have to stand up for him when kids tease him. But while you're doing it, you wish you weren't."

"How come?"

"Because it makes you as weird as Matt. And that makes you hate Matt some-times." Haley paused and corrected her-self. "Well, not hate him. But . . . oh, what's the word?"

"Resent?" I suggested. "You resent Matt?"

"Yeah." Haley looked ashamed.

"Don't feel bad about it," I said. "I resent my brother and sister sometimes, too. Like when Mama asks me to give Squirt a bath or something and I want to practise my ballet."

Haley nodded. "But your brother and sister aren't deaf."

"So? Why should you have to be a perfect person just because your brother *is* deaf?" I asked Haley. "That doesn't make any sense to me. Matt's not special, he's just different."

"He *is* special!" cried Haley.

I smiled. "I'm glad you think so. What I meant was that basically, Matt's like most other seven-year-old boys. Except that he's deaf and you have to use sign language to talk to him. But look. Look at Matt right now."

Matt, Nicky and Adam were jumping up and down because their team had earned another run. Matt stuck his fist in the air like a proud athlete. Nicky and Adam imitated him.

Haley couldn't help grinning. "I really love him," she said. "And I'm proud of him. He's smart, he works hard, and even though he's different, he tries to make himself as *not* different as possible. And he's only seven! But boy, sometimes I wish . . . I know this is really, really awful, Jessi, but I guess I can tell you. I've never told anyone else, though."

"What?" I asked her.

"Sometimes I wish he'd never been born."

I was a little surprised at what Haley had said, but when I thought about it, it made sense. I tried to be matter-of-fact. After all, her feelings were her feelings. They didn't make her a bad or a good person. Still, she had surprised me.

"Well," I said slowly, "I can understand that. I really can. I've wished the same thing sometimes about Becca and Squirt. More with Becca, maybe, since she's so close to my age. But I've felt it with Squirt, too. Sometimes I think, boy, wouldn't it be great to be an only child. I'd have Mum and Dad all to myself, and no one would ever interrupt me while I was practising or trying to do my homework, and no one would ever snoop in my room or take my things without asking. But then I think, if I didn't have Becca, who could I giggle with late at night? And who could I complain to? Sometimes the kids at school tease me because I'm black, and *no one* knows how that feels the way Becca does."

Haley nodded thoughtfully. "I guess you do understand," she told me. (She sounded very grateful.) "You know, all I really want is a family who talks with their mouths, not their hands. A little brother who doesn't make wild animal noises, who walks to Stoneybrook Elementary instead of riding that dumb van to Stamford everyday."

"Who doesn't embarrass you," I added.

"Right. And then sometimes . . . sometimes I don't know what I'd do without him. Look at this." Haley reached under her blouse and pulled out a gold chain. Hanging from it was a wobbly-looking round pendant painted red with an H scratched in it. You could tell the pendant had been made from clay. "Matt made this for me in art class," she said. "He gave it to me for Christmas last year. I always wear it. This is really weird but, like, I'll be totally mad at Matt for embarrassing me or something, and then I'll remember the necklace and I can't feel mad at him at all. I'll just want to, you know, protect him and stuff."

I did know. "Yup," I said. "Once I was mad because Becca got sick and Mama made me miss a ballet class to watch Squirt while she took care of Becca. I wanted to kill Becca . . . and Squirt. Then Squirt put his arms around me and said, "Dur-bliss?" and I started laughing and wasn't mad at all."

Haley giggled. We stopped talking for a while. I felt like I was finally beginning to understand the Braddock kids.

We watched Matt hit a home run and that was when Haley said to me, "You know, if Matt had to be handicapped, I'm glad he was made deaf. If he was crippled or blind he probably wouldn't be playing baseball right now. I think he'd be able to do a lot less. Being deaf, well, maybe he can't talk or hear, but think what he *can* do.

Almost anything. He can even watch TV. With closed-captioned TV you get this special decoder and then you can *read* some shows. The words the people are saying are written on the screen. It's like watching a film with subtitles. So really the only thing Matt can't do is go to a concert or a play or something."

I'd been thinking about something I'd read recently. Someone, Helen Keller, I think, had noted that blindness only separates you from *things*, while deafness separates you from *people*. So I was about to disagree with Haley, but what she had just said caught my attention.

"Matt's never been in a theatre?" I asked. "He's never been to any kind of performance?" How awful.

"Well, sometimes his school puts on plays in sign language," said Haley.

"But imagine," I murmured. "Never been to a ballet or a musical. . ."

"Well, he couldn't hear the music," Haley pointed out.

"I know," I replied, remembering my conversation with Adele. I was also remembering Mme Noelle's club. I was thinking about when we do warm-ups and Madame roams around the ballet studio saying, "And *one* and *two* and *three* and *four*," banging that club. When she walks by you, you can feel the vibrations of the club hitting the floor. You can also feel the

91

vibrations of the piano music Madame's assistant sometimes plays. If you stand with your hands resting on top of the piano you can feel soft and strong hums.

I thought about *Coppelia*. I thought about how much more there was to a ballet than the music. There was plenty to see — the dancing and the costumes and the scenery. Plus, it was just plain exciting to be in a theatre — to look at the rows and rows of red seats and watch the ushers showing people up and down the aisles and hold your breath when the lights go down and the curtain goes up.

I was getting an idea. It was a really terrific idea, but I didn't say anything about it to Haley then, just in case I couldn't pull it off.

Still, as soon as I got home that evening, I began working on the idea. I decided that the first thing to do was to have a talk with Mme Noelle.

11th CHAPTER

My plan was working! It really was. I was very excited. I'd spoken to Mme Noelle, to Mrs Braddock and even to the head of my whole dance school. Nothing was settled, but everything was "in the works" (as Daddy would say).

One Friday, I got to Claudia's house for a club meeting a couple of minutes after five-thirty. I charged up the Kishis' walk, skidded to a stop, rang their bell, heard Claudia yell, "Come in!" and charged up to her room. As usual, I was the last to arrive. I hadn't even had time to change completely after ballet class, so I was wearing my leotard and a pair of jeans. My hair was still pulled back tightly, the way Madame says we must wear the hair during closs.

"Hi," I said when I entered the head-quarters of the Babysitters Club. Even though I was only two minutes late and everyone knew I had a tight schedule because of dance class, I felt a little nervous. After all, Kristy could be sort of strict. Besides, Mal and I, as the newest and youngest club members, felt that we better not make any mistakes. We didn't want to stir up trouble, and we felt we had to prove ourselves.

"Sorry I'm late," I apologized.

I checked out Claudia's room. People were in their usual places: Kristy was in the director's chair, Mary Anne, Dawn and Claudia were sitting on the bed, and Mal was on the floor. She and I always end up down there. The room was a cluttered mess, but I could see that Mal had cleared a space for me next to her.

Claudia's room is always a mess—for two reasons. 1. She's a magpie. She's a really good artist and likes to keep all kinds of stuff on hand—bottle caps, interesting pebbles, scraps of fabric, bits of this and bits of that, not to mention her paper and canvases and paints. She never knows what she might need for a sculpture or a collage. 2. Claudia is also a junk-food addict. She likes anything that's sweet, but her parents don't approve of this habit, so Claudia has to hide the stuff around her room. Then sometimes she forgets where she's hidden it and has to go rooting through all her stuff to find it.

Anyway, Kristy accepted my apology with no problems.

I plopped down next to Mal.

"Biscuit?" asked Claudia, holding one out to me.

I smiled, but shook my head. "No thanks."

"Cake?" she tried again.

"I better not. I'd love one, but I think I'll wait for dinner." I like junk food as much as Claudia does, but I try not to eat too much of it. Ballerinas have to be strong and agile and in good shape. Junk food doesn't help you to be any of those things.

"Okay," said Kristy, clapping her hands together. She swallowed the last of a biscuit. "Any club business? Anything urgent?"

"The treasury's low," spoke up Dawn.

"How'd it get low?" asked Kristy.

"Mostly paying Charlie to drive you to and from the meetings."

"Well, subs day is coming up," said Kristy. We all put in some money from our babysitting jobs to keep our club running. We use the money to pay Charlie, to buy stuff for a party or something every now and then, and to buy things to put in our Kid-Kits. (Kristy thought up Kid-Kits. They're boxes full of games and books— our old ones—plus new colouring books, activity books and sticker books which we sometimes take with us when we sit.)

"One day of subs isn't going to do it," said Dawn worriedly.

"Well," Kristy went on slowly, "could all of you put in double next time—just this once?"

We grumbled but agreed to. Nobody wanted to pay double, but we could afford it, since we earn so much money sitting.

The phone rang then and Claudia answered it and lined up a job for Dawn.

"Any other business?" asked Kristy.

Mallory and I glanced at each other. We had decided that we should talk more at the meetings—at least about business. At first we had wanted to keep a low profile; now we were worried that we weren't joining in enough.

I can't believe what I did next. I actually raised my hand—like some dumb first-grader.

"Yes?" said Kristy, looking surprised. (About the hand-raising, I guess.)

"Well, I—I—I mean, I, um . . . um—"

Luckily the phone rang again.

I stopped talking as Mary Anne reached for the receiver and lined up a job for Kristy. As soon as Mary Anne was done, Kristy said, "Yes, Jessi?"

This time I managed to speak like a human. I thought the club members should know about Matt and his progress, since any one of them might babysit for him and Haley sometime. I told them that Matt and

Haley were both making friends. Then I told them about the conversation Haley and I had had about what it was like to be Matt's big sister. Finally I said, "Is anyone interested in learning more about signing?"

I was surprised at the answer. "Yes!" chorused Kristy, Claudia, Dawn, Mary Anne and Mallory.

"You *are*?"

"Sure," replied Claudia. "All the kids around here are learning to sign. We better learn how, too. Besides, us babysitters have to be prepared for anything."

"Right," agreed Kristy, who sounded as if she wished *she'd* said that.

So in between phone calls I showed the other club members how to finger spell. I thought that would be helpful because if they were sitting at the Braddocks and didn't know the sign for something, they could always spell the word out. (Finger spelling is somehow more personal than writing stuff on paper. At least you can *look* at the person you're talking to.)

We were up to the letter J when the phone rang. Dawn answered it, listened for a moment, and then put her hand over the mouthpiece and said with a grin, "Hey, Mary Anne, it's *Logan*!"

(Logan is one of our associate club members, but he's also Mary Anne's boyfriend, remember?)

Mary Anne took the receiver, faced herself into a corner of the room, and began talking so quietly that none of us could hear her, no matter how far we leaned over. Every so often a little murmur would come from her direction, but no actual words.

When she finally hung up, she turned back to us, blushing, and said, "Logan says hello. He just wanted to know what was going on. He said he might want a signing lesson sometime, Jessi. In case he ever sits for the Braddocks."

"What *else* did he say?" Claudia teased, looking at Mary Anne's red face.

(I feel sorry for anyone who blushes so easily.)

"Oh . . . not much."

We started talking about our families then. We do that sometimes, when we're not lining up jobs or talking about club business. We sort of take turns saying what's going on in our lives.

"My brother called from California last night," said Dawn. "He's still really happy out there."

"You think he'll stay?" asked Kristy.

"I'm pretty sure. When the six months are up, the lawyers and everyone have to get together again to discuss the trial period—but I know he'll stay."

I couldn't imagine my family being torn in half like Dawn's had been. I just couldn't. What would I do if Squirt and Daddy were living in California?

"Tigger learned how to fetch yesterday," said Mary Anne. "Have you ever known a kitten that could fetch?"

"You're just trying to distract us from Logan," said Dawn with a smile.

"You're absolutely right," agreed Mary Anne.

"Well, here's something that's been going on at my house," said Kristy. "I find this hard to believe, but Mum has been mooning around saying she wants a baby."

"A *baby*?!" the rest of us shrieked.

Kristy nodded, looking puzzled.

"Is she pregnant?" asked Claudia.

"Nope," said Kristy. "I know that for a fact because she's also been saying she wishes she were pregnant, but she thinks she's too old. After all, Charlie is seventeen."

"Yeah, but how old's your mum?" asked Dawn.

"I don't know. Thirty-seven or something."

"Then she could still get pregnant."

"Really?"

"Sure."

"Hmm."

Ring-ring.

"Hey, one of you guys want to get the phone?" asked Kristy, looking down at Mal and me.

"Sure!" we cried. We both leaped up.

"Only one of you can answer it," said

Claudia. "Trust me. In the old days, the four of us always used to try answering the phone at the same time and it never worked."

I might be more agile than Mal, but she'd been sitting closer to the phone, so she reached it before I did. I plopped back down on the floor with a disappointed "Hmphh."

"Hello, Babysitters Club," said Mal professionally. She sounded good and she knew it. "Oh, yes. Hi, Mrs Braddock. . . Tell her what? . . . Oh, okay. Sure. . . 'Bye."

Mallory hung up the phone and turned to me quizzically. "That was Matt's mother. She said to give you a message: Everything is arranged."

"It is?" I cried. "Oh, that's great. Really great!"

"Are you going to let us in on this?" asked Kristy.

"Yeah," said Mary Anne. "What's arranged?"

I hesitated. "I can't tell you. I mean, I can't tell you yet. But I'll be able to soon . . . Really, I promise," I added when I saw their frowning faces.

"How come you can't tell us now?" asked Mal.

"I just can't, that's all. But I do want to ask you something—all of you. I was wondering if you'd like to come see *Coppe-*

lia. Everyone in the cast gets ten free tickets to opening night, so I'm inviting Mama, Daddy, Becca, Grandma, Grandpa and you guys."

The club members began shrieking, "Opening night! . . . The ballet! . . . Going to Stamford!"

I'd never heard them so excited.

I took their reaction as a yes.

12th CHAPTER

My personal feeling about the principal's office is that it's better not to be in it. For any reason. What could happen is that someone passes the office, sees you there, and spreads rumours about you being in big trouble, when in fact you're just handing in a late form or something.

Despite my thoughts, I had to go to the principal's office early one Thursday afternoon. I had a note from my mother giving me permission to leave Stoneybrook Middle School an hour early that afternoon. When the school secretary read Mama's note and saw why I was leaving early, she started gushing. "Oh, what a lovely thing to do! Why, I think that's wonderful. Simply wonderful." She made out a pass and handed it to me saying, "You kids today! You're so nice and thoughtful. No one gives you enough credit."

I had to agree with her on that one.

At 1:25 that afternoon I was waiting on the pavement in front of school. At 1:30, Mrs Braddock pulled to a stop in front of me, and I climbed into the front seat.

"Ready?" she asked, smiling.

"Ready as I'll ever be." I began rehearsing a speech with my hands. "What's the sign for costume?" I asked. I realized that this was not a good question to ask a person whose hands were gripping the steering wheel of the car you were riding in, but I asked anyway.

"I'll demonstrate at the next red light," Mrs Braddock replied. And she did.

The ride into Stamford took a while, and we talked and rehearsed the entire time. At last we were driving into the city. Tall buildings everywhere. I recognized the street my ballet school is on, and the street Daddy's office building is on. Finally we pulled into a car park with a big sign in front that said PARKING FOR SCHOOL FOR THE DEAF. We found a space and parked, and then Mrs Braddock led me inside an old, old building that looked like it might once have been a mansion, somebody's home.

"It's run pretty much like any other school," Mrs Braddock said as we walked slowly down a brightly lit corridor. "The kids go to art lessons and gym classes. They eat in a dining room. The differences are that the classes are quite small—usually not more than eight students, at least in the younger classes, and that the children start here at a very young age. Matt was two when he entered, and the teachers began lessons in signing right away. His classes were much more intense than normal nursery school classes."

We were walking slowly because I kept trying to peek into classrooms each time we passed a doorway.

"The younger classes are on this floor," said Mrs Braddock. "Matt's is at the very end of the corridor."

We reached the last door in the hallway and paused beside it.

"This is one of the two second-grade classes," Mrs Braddock told me. "The children here are all seven years old, but they have different degrees of hearing difficulty. Some are profoundly deaf, like Matt. A few have some hearing. Several of them can speak. The children receive lots of individual attention. They all know how to sign, but those with speech are also given speech lessons. A few are learning lipreading. Matt may try that when he's older, if he wants to."

I nodded, trying to peek into the classroom.

"Since some of the children can hear, and some are learning speech and lipreading," Mrs Braddock went on, "make sure you speak—slowly and loudly—while you're signing, okay?"

104

"Right," I replied. (Mrs Braddock had mentioned that before.)

"Well . . . are you ready, Jessi?"

"I hope so."

"Don't be too nervous. It's just a bunch of seven-year-olds who *love* visitors. And Matt's teacher and I will help you if you need it."

"Okay." I took a deep breath and let it out slowly, just like I do before I go onstage during a performance.

Mrs Braddock opened the door and I entered Matt's classroom. Eight excited little faces turned to me and a young woman rushed over to us.

"Hello, Mrs Braddock," she said, shaking her hand. Then she turned to me and shook my hand. "You must be Jessi. I'm Ms Frank, Matt's teacher. Thank you so much for coming. I'm glad this visit could be arranged." (This visit was what Mrs Braddock's mysterious phone call had been about at our club meeting.) "The children are thrilled, even though they don't know why you're here. All I've said is that you have a surprise for them. Before I introduce you, though, I just want to say that your idea is marvellous. It'll be a great experience for the children and I really want to thank you."

I was beaming. Everyone, at least once in his or her life, deserves such praise.

The children were still looking at me

eagerly. You might have thought that eight deaf children would make a pretty quiet class, but no way. First of all, the talkers Mrs Braddock had mentioned were talking—loudly. (Matt's mother had said that since deaf children can't always hear themselves, they don't know how loudly they're speaking and have to learn to modulate their voices.) Some of the others made sounds as they signed to each other. And one child, finishing up an assignment, was listening to a cassette at top volume.

While Ms Frank gathered the children into a circle on the floor, I took a quick look around. Matt's classroom seemed pretty much like a classroom in any elementary school, except that I felt bombarded by all the things there were to *see*. I guessed that Ms Frank's idea was that if her kids couldn't learn by hearing, they'd learn by seeing. Every inch of wall space and table space was covered—with displays about the months of the year, telling time, using money, colours and shapes, insects and animals, you name it. Across the top of the blackboard was a long chart showing the alphabet. Underneath it was the finger spelling alphabet, a hand demonstrating each letter.

The other difference between Matt's room and most second-grade classrooms was the audio equipment—tons of headphones and tapes for the kids who could hear and talk.

106

Mrs Braddock took a seat in the back of the room, and Ms Frank led me to the front of the room.

"Why don't you sit on the floor with the kids?" she suggested. "You'll all feel more at ease."

(Good thing I was wearing jeans.)

Ms Frank, also wearing trousers, sat right down on the floor next to me. (Now that's my kind of teacher.)

"Boys and girls," Ms Frank said, speaking loudly and clearly, and always facing the kids (so the lip-readers could watch her mouth), "this is Jessi Ramsey." She signed as she spoke, and of course spelled out my name, J-E-S-S-I R-A-M-S-E-Y.

Matt took his eyes off Ms Frank's hands long enough to grin at me. I smiled back.

"Jessi is here," Ms Frank went on, "because she knows Matt Braddock and has a very special surprise for you. Jessi?"

"Thanks," I said. Then I began speaking and signing. Ms Frank stayed where she was, in case I needed help. "I am a dancer," I began. Then I finger-spelled the word *ballet*, for which I hadn't been able to find a sign. "I like dancing because I can tell a story with my body. I don't need to talk."

A few faces perked up at this idea.

"A ballet," I went on, "tells a story without any words—just dance and music. I know some of you can't hear music, but did you know that you can feel it?"

The children nodded.

"We've talked about that," Ms Frank told me. "We've been experimenting with vibrations—with rhythm and drumbeats and the piano."

"Oh, good." I began signing and talking again. "My dance school," I said, "is going to perform a ballet called *Coppelia*." (More finger spelling.) "I'll be dancing in it. It's about a toymaker and a big doll that he creates. Everyone will wear costumes—" (luckily I remembered the sign for that word that Mrs Braddock had shown me in the car)"—and the stage will look like a village."

The children were hanging on my every word and sign.

"I would very much like for you to come and see *Coppelia*, to come to the theatre." (The invitation was for opening night, but I decided not to try to explain what that meant.) "I know you might not be able to hear the music, but you can watch the dancers tell their story. Do you want to come?"

"Yes! Yes!" cried the kids who could speak. The others nodded eagerly. Matt was so excited he looked like he might explode.

Ms Frank spoke up then. "The story of *Coppelia* is a little complicated," she told Matt and his classmates, "so I'll tell it to you before you go to the show. Some of you might want to read about the story, too."

The boy sitting next to Matt raised his hand. "When is the show?" he signed.

"Next Friday," I told him with Ms Frank's help. "Eight days from now."

"What should we wear?" signed another boy, and everyone laughed.

"Whatever you want," I told him, "but it might be fun to get dressed up."

The school bell rang for the end of the day, and I noticed that a big light flashed next to the door. I guessed that was the signal for the kids who couldn't hear the bell.

Even though school was over, none of the kids got up. Two more had questions. Finally Ms Frank had to send them on their way. Soon the classroom was empty except for Ms Frank, Mrs Braddock, Matt and me. While the adults were having some important looking conversation, Matt showed me his desk and something (I wasn't sure what) that he'd made in art class.

I oohed and ahhed. And smiled a lot.

Then—quite suddenly—Matt threw his arms around me and gave me a big hug. He leaned back and signed, "I love you. I can't wait to see a ballet. Thank you. You're my best grown-up friend."

At first I wasn't sure what to react to— Matt's enthusiasm or being called a grown-up. It didn't take long to decide. I signed back, "I love you, too."

13th
CHAPTER

Wednesday

Hey, everybody, Jessi's brother and
sister are adorable! Especially Squirt. I
mean -- not that Becca isn't cute, but
Squirt is a baby after all, and there's
something about babies.... Oh, well.

Anyway, while Jessi was at the
Braddocks' I had a great time sitting
at her house. I love taking care of
babies, and Becca was a lot of fun.
We had a good talk, too.

Then Charlotte Johanssen came over
to play and suddenly I got the feeling
that something was going on. Becca
and Charlotte have a secret. But they
wouldn't say a word about it. What's
going on?

When Kristy babysat for Becca and Squirt, it was the first time she'd been over to my house—at least, the first time she'd been there since Stacey McGill moved out of it. She went over after school to watch my brother and sister while Mama went to Stamford to run boring errands that Becca and Squirt wouldn't want to be dragged along on.

When Mama left, Squirt was taking a nap, but Becca was bouncing around. She loves new babysitters because she can show off all her stuff to them, stuff the rest of us have seen a billion times. The first thing she showed Kristy was her rock collection. Now let me set you straight about something. What Becca knows about rocks and minerals you could fit on the head of a pin. She doesn't know shale from quartz. She just collects rocks she thinks are interesting. For example, she has a flat pebble that is almost exactly round and has a yellow splotch in the middle so that it looks sort of like a fried egg. And she has a rock that looks exactly like Mr Millikan's nose. Mr Millikan is the principal of the school Becca went to in New Jersey. The resemblance of the rock to his nose is really amazing. In Oakley, if you asked *any*body what that rock looked like, they'd say right away, "Millikan's nose." Here in Stoneybrook, people just say, "A nose?"

When Becca had shown Kristy every last

one of the rocks, she moved on to her dolls and then her stuffed animals. Becca has so many of both, that when she sleeps with all of them, sometimes it's hard to pick Becca out of the crowd.

"Want to see my books about cats?" Becca asked Kristy next. "I have *The Christmas Day Kitten* and *Pinky Pye* and *Millions of Cats* and—"

"Bloo-ga!" Squirt suddenly called from his room.

"Oops! There's your brother!" said Kristy. I'm sure she was relieved that she didn't have to look at another collection. "Let's go and get him up."

"Yeah!" cried Becca.

Kristy and Becca opened the door to Squirt's room, where their noses were met by baby smells—powder and Baby-Wipes and a wet nappy.

"Oh, you need to be changed," said Kristy, bending over the crib and feeling Squirt's nappy.

Squirt burst into tears. He wasn't expecting a strange face to peer over the side of his crib. He was expecting Mama or Daddy or Becca or me.

Becca was pulling up Squirt's blind and opening the curtains.

"Hey, Becca. Come here," Kristy said. "Show Squirt your face."

Becca obliged and Squirt stopped crying. "Ga-ga?" he asked.

"I think that means he wants milk," said Becca.

Kristy dressed Squirt, and she and Becca and the baby went downstairs and all had some milk.

As they were sitting around the table (well, Squirt wasn't at the table; he was in his high chair, chewing some biscuits), Becca looked at Kristy and said, "You're really nice."

"Thanks!" replied Kristy, flattered.

"And I mean *really* nice. Not fake nice. Nice like you mean it."

"Of course I mean it."

"Some people don't."

"Who doesn't?" Kristy wanted to know.

"A lot of people in Stoneybrook. When we first moved here, either no one would play with me or people just pretended to like me."

Ah, thought Kristy. She knew what was coming. I've talked with the girls in the Babysitters Club about being black and trying to fit in in Stoneybrook. It hasn't been easy.

"Some people," Becca went on, "were just plain mean. Other people pretended to be nice, but they really weren't . . . I don't know why they bothered pretending."

"You know what?" said Kristy. "Everyone has trouble fitting in sometimes."

"Everyone?"

"Everyone. You know Matt? The boy your sister is sitting for now?"

"The deaf one?" asked Becca.

"Yeah. Well, at first the kids in his new neighbourhood didn't like him because he's deaf. And last summer I moved to a new neighbourhood where no one liked *me*."

"Didn't like *you*?" Becca repeated, mystified. "But there's nothing wrong with you. I mean, you're not deaf or anything. And you're white."

"But I'm not rich. My mother married this millionaire and he moved Mum and my brothers and me into his mansion on the other side of town. The kids all knew where I'd come from, and they made fun of me. . . Of course, I didn't help things by calling them snobs. But what I'm saying is that everyone is the odd one out sometimes. You're the only one in jeans at a fancy party, or the only Japanese kid in school, or the only diabetic in your class. See?"

"Yeah. Being called names still hurts, though."

"Oh, tell me about it. But doesn't it help to know that you're not the only one who doesn't fit in sometimes?"

"A tiny bit. It helps a tiny bit."

"I guess a tiny bit is better than nothing," said Kristy, and she and Becca grinned at each other.

"Kristy, can I invite Charlotte over?" asked Becca.

114

"Charlotte Johanssen? Sure."

"Oh, goody," said Becca, and she made a dash for the phone.

Charlotte is a kid the club sits for a lot. She's exactly Becca's age, but she's a year ahead of her in school since she's really smart and skipped third grade last year. Charlotte's favourite sitter used to be Stacey McGill, and she was crushed when Stacey moved away. In fact, it even used to be hard for her to come play with Becca, knowing she was in Stacey's old house. Luckily, she got over that, because Becca needs friends desperately. Charlotte was the first kid who didn't automatically avoid her or tease her just because she's black. She didn't seem to notice or care.

Becca and Charlotte were slowly getting to be good friends when something happened that totally cemented their relationship—the Little Miss Stoneybrook contest, which was a sort of beauty show for little girls. Becca refused to be in it because she has terrible stage fright, and ordinarily Charlotte (who's on the shy side) wouldn't even have considered something like that. But she let herself get talked into being a contestant—and then blew it once the contest started. She actually ran off the stage in tears and asked to be taken home.

Well, that did it. Becca sympathized completely. The two of them have been like Siamese twins ever since.

Kristy said that Charlotte reached our house less than five minutes after Becca called her.

"Hi, Kristy!" Charlotte said. (She isn't shy around the members of the Babysitters Club anymore.)

"Hi, Char. I'm glad you came over. What are you guys going to do?"

Becca and Charlotte looked at each other and raised their eyebrows.

"We're going to pretend we're ballerinas," said Becca. "Just like Jessi."

"Yeah," said Charlotte. "We're going to be the famous dancing team, the Polanski Sisters."

"We're going to dance in Jessi's practice area in the basement," Becca added.

"Is that okay with Jessi?" asked Kristy. "Are you sure you're allowed to do that?"

"Positive. She lets us all the time." (It's true. I do.) "Anyway, we have to rehearse for the big performance."

"What big performance?"

"The opening of *Copernicus*," replied Becca.

"*Coppelia*?" asked Kristy.

"Yeah, that."

"Okay. Just be careful with Jessi's things. Squirt and I will be playing upstairs."

"Okay!" Becca and Charlotte ran down to the basement.

Kristy looked at Squirt, who was an enormous mess. He had a milk moustache, and soggy biscuit was everywhere—all over his face, in his hair, on his hands, covering the tray of his high chair.

It took Kristy quite a while to clean him up and after she'd finished, she realized his nappy was wet again.

How do parents do it? Kristy wondered. How do they run a house, take care of their kids and go to work, too? It seemed impossible. She decided not to worry about it. At least not for several more years. Maybe by the time she was a parent there would be automatic nappy changers or something.

When Squirt was clean and dry, she carried him down to the sitting room. She was going to show him some of his board books, but she decided to see what the girls were up to instead. She didn't hear a sound from the basement, which worried her.

Kristy stood with Squirt at the top of the steps. She could hear murmurings from the girls, but nothing more. She tiptoed downstairs. What *were* they doing?

"Becca? Char?" She found them sitting on one of Jessi's exercise mats. "What happened to the Polanski Sisters?" she asked.

Becca smiled. But she didn't answer the question. Instead she said, "We know a secret!" She didn't say it in a way that made Kristy cross. She said it as a point of interest, something she was excited about.

"Ooh, what?" asked Kristy.

"Can't tell." (Now *that* was annoying.)

"Can't tell *yet*," added Charlotte.

"You mean I'll find out?"

"Yup."

"When?"

"Can't tell." Becca and Charlotte grinned at each other. "But it's a good secret," said my sister.

Kristy remembered the mysterious phone call I'd got from Mrs Braddock. Something was going on. She knew that for sure. But what?

Kristy Thomas does not like to be left out of things.

14th CHAPTER

Opening night!

Oh, my lord!

I can't believe it!

The opening night of anything (if you're in the cast, that is) is the most exciting and also the most scary part of a production. It's even scarier than auditioning. Opening night is when you know whether your work has paid off. It's when you know whether you've worked hard enough. And it's the first time you perform your new role in front of a whole theatre full of faces.

So I was nervous about the opening night of *Coppelia*.

But I wasn't *too* nervous. There have been other opening nights in my life, and there will be more. I hope.

This opening night would be special, though. It would be different from any other. This was because, thanks to the

119

Braddocks, Mme Noelle and Ms Frank, Matt and his class would be in the audience. That was part of the secret Becca had told Charlotte.

I'd kept the secret for as long as I could. I didn't hit the members of the Babysitters Club (even Mallory) with the news until two days before opening night. (Kristy cancelled our regular Friday meeting on the afternoon of that first performance so that everyone could have time to get ready for the big trip to Stamford.)

The girls were really excited when I gave them the news.

"You did that for Matt?" asked Mary Anne with an awed smile.

"You *arranged* all that?" added Kristy.

I nodded.

Everyone looked impressed.

I felt great.

And now it was opening night. As I had promised, I'd given my ten free tickets to Mama, Daddy, Becca, Grandma and Grandpa (they'd travelled all the way from New Jersey just to see the show), and Kristy, Dawn, Mary Anne, Claudia and Mal.

Guess who was going to babysit for Squirt? Logan Bruno, Mary Anne's boyfriend, one of the associate club members.

One other important person was also in the audience—Mr Braddock, Matt's father. Where were Mrs Braddock and

Haley? That's the rest of the secret, and you'll find out about it soon enough.

The performance was to start at eight o'clock. Now it was ten minutes to eight. My stomach was jumping around as if I'd swallowed grasshoppers. When the curtain rises on this ballet, Coppelia herself is already on stage. Dr Coppelius has seated her on the balcony of his workshop. I, Swanilda, am the first to actually enter the stage.

But tonight—and only tonight—I would be onstage *before* the curtain rose.

Now it was five minutes to eight. My hair was fixed, my costume was on, my make-up was finished, I had shaken myself out and warmed myself up.

Five more minutes crawled by.

"Ready?" A hand touched my shoulder.

I jumped a mile.

"I am sorry," said Mme Noelle, "but it is time to begin. The house is packed. Oh, and your friends, the deaf children, they are sitting in the fourth row—centre. Excellent seats."

"Oh, thank you so much, Madame," I said. "That's wonderful."

"Are you ready?"

"Yes. Yes, I am."

"All right then. Go ahead."

The audience had been noisy. They were chattering and rustling their programmes and opening packets of sweets. Suddenly they fell silent. I knew the lights had dimmed, the audience lights anyway. But the stage was still lit, and the curtain was down.

"Jessi?" asked another voice. It was Mrs Braddock. She and Haley had appeared beside me, both very dressed up—and both very nervous.

"Okay," I said. I squeezed Haley's hand. "Let's go."

I was the first to walk onto the stage in the theatre. I was followed by Haley and Mrs Braddock. When we reached centre stage, standing in front of the curtain, we stopped and looked out at the sea of faces.

"Good evening," I said, and Mrs Braddock signed, "Good evening."

"Tonight's performance," I continued, "is a special one. In the audience are eight students from the school for the deaf here in Stamford." (Mrs Braddock was still signing away—my translator.) "This," I said, "is Carolyn Braddock, the mother of one of the students, and Haley, his sister. So that the students can get as much as possible out of the performance, Haley is going to narrate the story before each act and her mother will translate the narration into sign language. This is not usually part of a performance of *Coppelia*, but we hope you enjoy it anyway. Thank you."

I walked offstage then, to prepare for my real entrance, and behind me I could hear

Haley speaking in a small, scared voice. "Louder!" I whispered, as soon as I was out of sight of the audience.

Haley spoke up. Her mother signed away. The audience liked them. I could tell.

The next thing I knew, the curtain was rising and the ballet was beginning for real. You might think that I was aware of the fact that my friends and family and Matt and his classmates were in the audience, watching me. But I wasn't. When I'm onstage, I *am* the dance. I'm the steps and turns and leaps. I'm Swanilda telling my story. Nothing less. For me, that's the only way to handle a performance.

Backstage, between acts, I paced around nervously.

"You are doing fine," Mme Noelle said to me several times. "A fine job."

Katie Beth, hearing Madame's praise, even added, "You really are. You're a perfect Swanilda."

I smiled and thanked her.

There was no way Swanilda could have been black, so I wasn't *perfect*, but I knew I was dancing very well. And I knew the show was going well. After all, we had rehearsed and rehearsed and rehearsed. It was paying off.

"You know something?" Katie Beth spoke up.

"What?"

"Adele's here tonight. She's in the audience. I told my parents about the special show, so we asked her to come home for the weekend."

"Hey, that's great!" I cried. "It really is. So the signing is for her, too."

"I think she wants to see you after the show. She really likes you. I mean because of the signing and tonight's performance and everything."

"I'd like to see her, too. Maybe she could meet Matt."

"Guess what. I'm learning how to sign," said Katie Beth. "There's a class at the school Matt goes to. I found out about it all by myself. Mum and Dad aren't taking it, but I started anyway. Adele is my only sister. She's not around much, but when she is, it'd be kind of nice for us to be able to talk like normal sisters do."

"That's great," I said again. "If you ever need any help, let me know. Better yet, maybe I should join the class. I might learn even faster."

"It meets on Mondays," said Katie Beth.

"Oh. That's a problem. I always babysit on Mondays. Well, anyway, I'm glad you're taking it."

Act II had ended and from the other side of the curtain I heard Haley say, now in a much more confident voice, "Act Three is the last act of the ballet. You will see the dancers in the village square again. Franz and Swanilda aren't mad at each other any-more, so they decide to get married, and they go to the Burgomaster for their dowr-ies." (I had no idea how Mrs Braddock was signing all this stuff, but I didn't bother to worry about it.) "But just then, Dr Coppelius runs angrily into the square. He accuses Franz and Swanilda of wrecking Coppelia, which was his life's work. Since they did destroy the doll, Swanilda gives her dowry money to Dr Coppelius. He is pleased by that, and after he leaves, Franz and Swanilda get married. And I guess they live happily ever after."

I smiled. Haley had added that last line herself.

Haley and Mrs Braddock left the stage and the curtain rose. I became Swanilda again.

It's hard to describe how I feel when I'm onstage. But I think a bomb could have dropped and caved in the theatre, and I'd still have been Swanilda, dancing.

I couldn't believe it when the final cur-tain came down. It felt as if no time had passed since I'd stood onstage with Haley and Mrs Braddock. Yet I'd told Swanilda's story.

The audience was clapping loudly.

The cast assembled backstage. We held hands in a long line. When the curtain rose we stepped forward and bowed.

The audience clapped more loudly.

Christopher Gerber (who was playing Franz) and I let go of the people on either side of us and stepped forward to take our own bows. As we straightened up, I saw a figure climbing the steps to the stage.

It was Matt. His arms were full of roses. He walked timidly across the stage and handed them to me. Then he signed, "Thank you from all of us."

The audience had grown silent. I translated for them. Then, cradling the roses in one arm, I signed to Matt, "You're welcome. This is the best night of my life."

Matt signed, "Mine, too," and when I translated that, the audience laughed gently. Well, some people laughed. I heard a few sniffles, though, and saw a woman in the front row dig through her purse for a Kleenex.

Matt turned to leave and Christopher and I stepped back into the line. That was when another figure, this one with flowing blonde hair, climbed the steps to the stage. The girl was also carrying flowers, a smaller bouquet, and was walking even more timidly than Matt had been.

It was Adele.

She stopped in front of Katie Beth and handed the flowers to her. Katie looked at her sister for a moment and both of them began to cry.

Oh, *no*, I thought.

But they recovered quickly. And Katie

126

Beth said the last words I'd have expected her to say: "This is my sister, Adele. She's deaf, too."

I handed my flowers to Christopher in a rush, stepped over to Katie Beth, and translated what she'd just said into sign language. This was partly so Matt and his friends would know what was going on, but mostly so that Adele would know.

It was cause for more tears.

So I looked out at the audience and said, signing, "Any more flowers?"

Everyone began to laugh and the curtain came down. Applause rang in my ears. The show had been a success.

15th CHAPTER

The cast drifted offstage to change and to remove their make-up. We were elated—the show had gone very well—but we were also exhausted. I stayed behind with Katie Beth and Adele.

"I'm really glad you came," I signed to Adele. "I didn't know you were going to."

Katie Beth smiled at her sister.

"Surprise!" signed Adele. "I wanted to see you dance."

"She wanted to see us dance," I translated for Katie Beth, just in case she hadn't understood. I wasn't sure how much signing she'd learned.

"You never asked me to come to a show before," Adele went on, looking sad suddenly. "I thought you didn't want your friends to know me. You never even tried signing—until you met Jessi."

I translated for Katie Beth, who melted.

The sisters began to cry *again*. Before I left them alone, I said to Katie, "Tell her about the class you're taking. You know she'll be happy." And, I thought, then the two of them can cry some more.

For about five minutes, I had peace in the dressing room. I had just changed out of my costume and into my jeans and a sweater when—BOOM. Everyone piled backstage. And I mean everyone.

"Hi, honey!" That was Mama.

"Hi, babe!" That was Daddy.

"Hi, Jessi! Hi, Jessi!" That was Becca.

"Hello . . . hi . . . congratulations . . . fabulous show . . ." That was Grandma, Grandpa, Mr and Mrs Braddock, Haley, Kristy, Claudia, Dawn and Mary Anne. Matt was there, too. He signed "congratulations"—a big grin as he clasped his hands in front of his face and shook them back and forth.

"Jessi! I am so impressed!" *That* was Mal.

Everyone was standing around me in a bunch, but Mal pushed her way through the crowd and threw her arms around me.

I hugged her back.

"Do you know how glad I am that you're my best friend?" she said, pulling away and taking my hand. "I mean, not just because of this. You were already my best friend. But now you're a ballet star, too. That's amazing. I can't believe it!"

I grinned. "Thanks," I said. I didn't know what else to say, even though inside I *felt* lots of things to say. Sometimes I think I like ballet because it's easier for me to express myself with my body than with words.

Mal and I were still standing in that crowd when another voice spoke up. "Hi, Jessi," it said softly.

I must have been dreaming. I really must have. Had the whole evening been a dream? I guessed so, and felt disappointed.

The voice was Keisha's.

Just in case I wasn't dreaming, I turned around very slowly.

Keisha was standing behind me, smiling shyly.

"I don't believe it," I whispered. "I'm dreaming, right? This is a dream."

Keisha shook her head slowly. Then she glanced at Mal, and I realized that Mal and I were still holding hands. That awful guilty feeling came over me again.

Did Keisha think I'd betrayed her? I dropped Mal's hand.

"I came with Grandma and Grandpa," Keisha said. "Your parents sent me a ticket."

"Did you like the show?" I asked.

"It was wonderful. Your shows are always wonderful."

"Oh, Keisha," I said. And the next thing I knew, Keisha and I were hugging and crying. We were a re-enactment of Katie Beth and Adele.

When we calmed down, I noticed that my family was smiling at me. How long had they been keeping the secret about Keisha's visit? I realized that there'd been a lot of secrets lately—getting Matt and his class to the performance, preparing Haley and Mrs Braddock to take part in the show, Katie Beth and her signing class, and of course, Keisha's surprise.

Keisha and Mal and I stood around awkwardly.

"Are you Jessi's cousin?" Mal asked finally.

"Oh!" I exclaimed. "Sorry. I guess I should introduce you. Mal, this is my cousin Keisha from Oakley."

"The one who has the same birthday as you?"

I nodded. "And Keisha, this is Mallory. She. . ." I trailed off. How could I tell Keisha that Mal was my new best friend?

Mal saved the day. "I've heard a lot about you, Keisha. Jessi and I have tons of things in common, but not the same birthday. That's really special. I wish *I* had a cousin my age who was *my* best friend."

That did it. Keisha beamed.

Oh, thank you thank you thank you, I said silently, wishing I could send thought waves to Mal.

"Hey!" exclaimed Mal, "look who's here."

Matt had joined us. He signed that he had loved the ballet and so had his friends. But, he wanted to know, why were the men wearing tights?

I translated for Mal and Keisha, who managed not to laugh. Then I tried to explain about ballet costumes, which wasn't easy.

"Honey," said my mother then, "we better get going. How would you like to go celebrate somewhere?"

"Like an ice-cream parlour?" I asked.

Mama laughed. "Or like a restaurant."

"Great," I said, even though I'd rather have gone out for ice-cream. "Are we all going?"

"Every last one of us—if your friends call their parents to tell them they'll be home a little late."

"There's a pay phone out in the hall," I said.

My friends left, searching their purses for change on the way.

I was just putting on my coat when Adele and Katie Beth walked over to me. I introduced them to Keisha, signing.

From a little distance away, I saw Matt watching us. He ran to Adele when he saw her signing. Then they began signing away. They went so fast I couldn't follow them.

"Just when I think I'm really getting

132

good," I said to Katie Beth, "I see deaf people who are *fluent* in sign language. Then I know how far I have to go."

Katie Beth nodded. "I feel like I've got miles to go before I catch up with *you*. . . Listen, Jessi, I want to, um, to tell you s-something," she stammered.

I glanced at Keisha, who took the hint. "I better put my coat on," she said in a rush. "I'll see you in a few minutes." She hurried off.

"What is it?" I asked.

"You were—you were good tonight, Jessi. Really good. I know Madame made the right decision when she picked you to be Swanilda. I was jealous before. But I've got to learn that not everyone can have the lead."

"If they did," I said, giggling, "there wouldn't be any story. Just a bunch of dancing Swanildas and a bunch of dancing Franzes—or whatever you'd call more than one Franz."

Katie Beth giggled, too.

"You know," I told her. "I'll confess something. I know this sounds sort of, um, goody-goody, but when I was rehearsing Swanilda's role, part of me felt really happy and another part felt really guilty."

"Guilty? Why?" asked Katie Beth.

"Because since *I* got to be Swanilda, no one else did. I felt terrible about that. Isn't that weird?"

"I think it's nice. Goody-goody, maybe, but nice."

Katie Beth and I laughed.

Then we heard someone calling her name.

"Oh," said Katie Beth. "That's my mum. Adele and I better go."

"Okay," I replied as Katie Beth dragged her sister away.

Adele and Matt waved to each other.

Then *my* mother was calling. "Jessi, let's get a move on. Everyone is ready to go."

Mama, Daddy, Becca, me, Grandma, Grandpa, Keisha, Mal, Kristy, Dawn, Mary Anne, Claudia, Mr and Mrs Braddock, Matt and Haley climbed into four cars—the Braddocks', my grandparents', Mama's and Daddy's. We drove to this place called Good-Time Charley's, which was sort of a compromise on the restaurant/ice-cream parlour question. It was a place that served hamburgers, quiche and salads, but was famous for its desserts. The adults told the kids we could order whatever we wanted.

"All *right*!" said Haley.

"I'll say," agreed Claudia, the junk-food nut. I bet she was hoping for a butterscotch sundae.

Since there were sixteen people, we had to sit at two tables. We managed to divide it up unevenly, though—the ten kids at one table, the six adults at another. I just love being in a restaurant and not sitting with the grown-ups.

When the waiter brought the menus around, all us kids looked at the food side for about half a second, then turned the menus over and looked at the desserts.

Claudia ran her finger down a column, stopped abruptly, and said, "That's it! A butterscotch sundae!"

It took me a while to choose something. When I'm dancing in a show I really watch what I eat. I was dying for cherry cheesecake, but I ordered ambrosia instead. Ambrosia is sliced-up fruit with coconut on it. I asked the waiter for whipped cream with it, though. I didn't want to be a total nerd.

"Boy," said Kristy when our food arrived, "what a treat. This has been a great evening. I wasn't sure I'd like ballet, but I did. I especially liked seeing you, Jessi."

"Thanks," I said.

Claudia began smushing her sundae around. She likes to mix it up thoroughly before she eats it.

"Claudia, that is so gross," said Mary Anne. She glanced at Matt. "Is there a sign in the secret language for 'gross'?" she wondered.

"There's one for 'grotesque,'" I said.

"And for 'disgusting,'" added Haley. She made the sign, looking as if she were about to puke or something.

135

Matt looked at her in alarm.

Haley giggled, then tried to explain what we were talking about.

Matt just shook his head. He glanced around at all of us, with our sundaes and cakes and shakes and ambrosias. Then he patted his hand over his heart.

"Happy," he signed. "Very happy."

MARY ANNE'S
BAD-LUCK MYSTERY

1st
CHAPTER

"You know," said Kristy Thomas, "I've been thinking. If I took a bunch of these old wilted peas and put them in the mashed potatoes—evenly spread out—and then took my fork and smushed them all down, my lunch would look almost exactly like—"

"Stop!" I cried. "Stop right there. I don't want to know what you think it would look like."

"Do you want to know what I think it would smell like?" Kristy asked.

"Absolutely not." I replied, turning green. "Please. Don't say another word about the lunch. Why do you buy the hot lunch every day, anyway? Why don't you buy a salad or something?"

"Because," replied Kristy, "it's so much more fun to say disgusting things about the hot lunch."

Everyone laughed. We couldn't help it.

"We" were five of the members of the Babysitters Club—Kristy, me (Mary Anne Spier), my friends Dawn Shafer and Claudia Kishi and Logan Bruno. (I guess you would call Logan my boyfriend.) It was a Monday and it was eighth-grade lunchtime at Stoneybrook Middle School. That meant we were sitting around our usual table. In front of Kristy and Logan and me were hot lunches; in front of Claudia was a tunafish sandwich; and in front of Dawn, the health-food nut, was a lunch from home—an apple, some cottage cheese, a plastic container of this brown-rice casserole, and something Dawn called trail mix, which really looked more like birdseed.

Dawn is from California, which explains a lot.

"Just out of curiosity," spoke up Logan, "what *would* the peas and mashed potatoes look like, Kristy?"

"Oh, please! Oh, please! Don't egg her on," I exclaimed. "Logan, why are you doing this to me?"

"It's fun watching you turn green," Logan replied.

The five of us began to laugh again. We really are great friends. And we always sit together. Well, at any rate, us girls always sit together. Logan only sits with us about half the time. The rest of the time, he sits with his other friends. Understandably, those other friends are boys. If you were a thirteen-year-old guy, do you think you could sit with a table full of girls every lunch break?

No.

Kristy is my oldest friend in the world. She used to live next door to me. In fact, we lived next door to each other all our lives—until last summer. Last summer, Kristy's mum, who was divorced, got remarried. The man she married lives in a gigantic house, a mansion really, on the other side of our town, which is Stoneybrook, Connecticut. So Kristy and her mum and her three brothers (Sam and Charlie, who are in high school, and David Michael, who's just seven) moved into Watson Brewer's house. Now Kristy also has a little stepbrother, Andrew, who's four, and a little stepsister, Karen, who's six. (They live with Kristy's family every other weekend. The rest of the time they live with their mother and stepfather.)

I miss Kristy a lot, even though a very nice family moved into *her* house, and even though I've become really close to Dawn. Dawn moved to Connecticut from California last January, about ten months ago. She and I hit it off right away, and now she and Kristy are both my best friends, even though they are very different people. Here's a comparison of the three of us:

Kristy is outspoken. "Big Mouth" might be a better way to describe her. She's sort of a tomboy, is full of ideas, and acts like a blender on high speed. By that I mean she's going, going, going all the time. Sometimes I just want to say to her, "Give it a rest, Kristy!" Kristy doesn't care much about how she looks (she *always* wears jeans, a sweater if necessary, and trainers) and she is not interested in boys. In fact, she doesn't like most of them. (Logan is an exception.) Kristy basically thinks that boys are like flies— pests. That's because she's been unfortunate enough to know mostly the annoying ones. Kristy likes sports and children and is the founder and chairman of the Babysitters Club, which I'll tell you more about later. She has brown hair and brown eyes. She and I are the two shortest girls in the entire eighth grade.

Dawn is, well, she's *Dawn*. She's this California girl who's trying to get adjusted to life on the East Coast—to cold weather and to people who'd rather eat a beefburger than soyabeans. Like Kristy, she's also adjusting to some changes in her family. The reason she moved here was that her parents got divorced. Her mother had grown up in Stoneybrook, so she brought Dawn and her younger brother, Jeff, back to her hometown. Only it didn't exactly work out. Jeff was really unhappy, and finally, a few weeks ago, went back to California to live with his dad, so now it's just Dawn and her mother. (They're very close.) Unlike Kristy, Dawn does care about how she looks—and she's pretty good-looking. She has waist-length hair the colour of wheat. Actually, it's almost white. And piercing blue eyes. And she wears trendy clothes, but she's very individualistic about it. In fact, she's just generally an individual. Dawn does things her way and doesn't care what other people think. She isn't snobby, she's just very sure of herself.

Now I, on the other hand, am not self-assured like Dawn, and I'm not outspoken like Kristy. I'm quiet and shy. So why am I the only one of my friends with a steady boyfriend? I don't know. Maybe it's because I'm sensitive. People are always telling me I'm sensitive. When I was younger they meant it as *too* sensitive—in other words, a baby. Now they mean it as caring and understanding. I must say that when my friends are upset or having problems, they come to me quite often. They don't always come for advice. Sometimes they just come to talk, because they know I'll listen. Like Kristy, I don't care too much about the clothes I wear, although lately I'm taking more of an interest. It's fun to dress in baggy sweaters or short dresses, or to put on bright jewellery or hair clips or something. (I used to go to school in boring old dresses and shoes.) Like Dawn, I live with just one parent—my dad. My mum died when I was really little and I don't have any brothers or sisters. I do have a pet, though. He's my grey kitten named Tigger. I don't know what I'd do without him.

So, that's Dawn and Kristy and me. Now let me tell you about Claudia and Logan. Talk about people being different, wait until you hear about Claudia. Claudia Kishi is the most exotic, interesting person in the eighth grade. Honest. First of all, she's Japanese-American and has this long, silky, jet-black hair, these dark eyes and a perfect complexion. Then there's the matter of her clothes. Nobody, but nobody, dresses like Claudia. At least, nobody in our year. (We used to have a friend, another member of the Babysitters Club, named Stacey McGill, who dressed kind of like Claudia. But Stacey moved back to New York, where she used to live. And anyway, trust me, Claudia is unique.) The best way to get this point across is to describe to you what Claudia was wearing at lunch that day. It was her vegetable blouse, an oversized white shirt with a green vegetable print all over it—cabbages and courgettes and turnips and stuff. Under the blouse was a *very* short denim skirt, white tights, green ankle socks over the tights, and lavender trainers, the kind boys usually wear, with a lot of rubber and big laces and the name of the manufacturer in huge letters on the sides. Wait, I've not finished. Claudia had pulled the hair on one side of her head back with a yellow clip that looked like a poodle. The hair on the other side of her head was hanging in her face. Attached to the one ear you could see was a plastic earring about the size of a jar lid.

Awesome!

Some more things about Claudia: She is not a good student. She loves art and mysteries. She's addicted to junk food.

On to Logan. It's a little hard to describe him because I like him so much. Do you know what I mean? I mean that I think everything about him is incredible and handsome and wonderful, and that probably isn't entirely true. So I'll have to try hard to be realistic. In terms of looks, Logan is perfect. Well, maybe not perfect. Maybe more like unbelievable. No. Let's just say he has blondish-brown hair . . . and he looks exactly like Cam Geary, the most gorgeous boy TV star I can think of. In terms of personality he's understanding and funny and likes kids, which means a lot to me. Logan used to live in Kentucky, so he has this interesting southern accent. For instance, he pronounces my name "Mayrih Ay-on Speeyuh." And he says "Ahm" instead of "I'm" and "Luevulle" instead of "Louisville" (which is the city he lived in). It is simply too hard to describe Logan anymore. Really, all you need to know is that we understand each other completely, and we like each other a *lot*.

"So," Claudia said, after we'd stopped looking at Kristy's disgusting lunch tray, "who's going to the Halloween Hop?"

The *Halloween* Hop?" said Kristy disdainfully. "Is it time for *that* again?"

"Halloween is coming up soon," Dawn pointed out.

"I really love this time of year," Claudia said dreamily.

"Why?" asked Kristy. "*You* get dressed up every day."

"Ha, ha," said Claudia.

"Oh, come on. I'm only teasing."

(Kristy's mouth gets her in trouble a lot.)

"Well," I said, hoping to calm Claudia down, "Logan and I are going to the Hop."

"In costume?" Dawn wanted to know.

Logan and I looked at each other and shrugged. "We can't decide," I told my friends. It might be fun to get dressed up, but sometimes you can feel pretty silly. Especially if a lot of kids don't wear costumes.

It was right then that I got the creepy feeling that someone was staring at me. You know? When the skin on the back of your neck begins to crawl? It's as if you can feel each individual hair back there.

It is not a pleasant feeling.

Was I spooked because we were talking about Halloween, or was someone really staring at me?

146

Very slowly I looked over my left shoulder.

Two tables away, Grace Blume, Cokie Mason and two other girls were pointing in our direction and snickering. It was hard to tell who they were pointing at, but I think it was Kristy. Probably because she was wearing the same clothes she'd been wearing for the last seven weeks.

Or was it me? Quickly, I checked to see if there was mashed potato on the end of my nose, or if my sweater was on backward or something. I looked okay . . . didn't I? This is what I mean about not being self-assured like Dawn. At the slightest sign of trouble, I assume that whatever is going wrong has something to do with me, or is my fault.

I glanced back over at Grace and Cokie. (Just in case you care, Cokie's real name is Marguerite. Who knows where "Cokie" came from.) Grace and Cokie and their friends were still staring at us.

I heard Grace say something about "stuck up". Okay, so I know some people think our club is snobby because we sit together all the time. At least, we had done lately. Last year, Kristy and I used to sit with other friends—the Shillaber twins, mostly. And Stacey (who was still in Stoneybrook then) and Claudia used to sit with a big group of kids, boys and girls—Rick Chow, Dorianne Wallingford and

Pete Black, to name a few. (Dawn, being an individual, would go back and forth between our group and the other one.)

If you want my honest opinion, I think there are some hurt feelings this year. The people we used to spend time with feel left out because the Babysitters Club is our new group. I feel kind of bad about that, but I don't know what to do. I guess the twins and Rick and Dorianne and everyone will have to be their own groups.

"Hey," Kristy whispered. (We all leaned over to hear her better.) "If Cokie took a picture of Logan it would last longer. Right now she's boring holes in the back of his head with her eyes."

"That does it," said Logan. "I'm going to the boys' table. I'm tired of being teased for sitting with you guys."

"You mean with us *girls*," I corrected him. I understood Logan well enough to know that he wasn't mad, just annoyed. Sometimes he does take flak for being the only boy in the Babysitters Club.

"Too late," Kristy announced as the bell rang, signalling the end of lunch. "You can abandon us tomorrow, Logan."

Logan grinned.

We all got to our feet.

"Hey, don't forget," Kristy said as we began to scatter. "Club meeting today. See you at five-thirty!"

2nd CHAPTER

I just love checking our mailbox. There is something about getting mail that is exciting. Going out to the box each afternoon is sometimes the highlight of my day. You never know what will be in it. There could be anything—letters (they're best, of course, but only when they're addressed to me), catalogues, coupons, the *Stoneybrook News* (I like to read about crime—burglaries and mysteries and stuff) and interesting magazines. Plus, around holidays and your birthday, you can start watching for parcels and greetings cards.

The only problem with our mail is that it isn't delivered until about five o'clock in the afternoon. That's all right on a school day, but during the summer you could die waiting for that blue-and-white van to come down the street.

Anyway, on the afternoon of the day that

Kristy was being so disgusting about her lunch, I babysat for this little kid named Jimmy Newton until almost five-thirty. Then I rushed over to Claudia's for our meeting of the Babysitters Club. But on the way, I just couldn't resist a quick peek in our mailbox.

When I opened it, it was stuffed! Just the way I like it. I sorted through bills (boring), some ads (kind of interesting), two magazines (yea!), and then I saw it—a letter addressed to me! Oh, wow! I was ecstatic.

Since it was five-thirty by then, I grabbed the letter, stuck it in my pocket, shoved everything else back in the box, and ran across the street to Claudia's. I didn't want to be late for the meeting.

Maybe now would be a good time for me to tell you just what the Babysitters Club is. Well, as I mentioned earlier, it was Kristy's idea and she started it. She got the idea a little over a year ago (when she still lived next door to me), after she noticed how hard it was for her mum to get a sitter for David Michael if Kristy wasn't available. Sometimes Mrs Thomas would have to make four or five calls before she found a person who was free. So Kristy thought there must be other parents around here with the same problem. Then she thought how terrific it would be if a parent could make just one phone call and reach several sitters at the same time. So she got together with

Claudia, Stacey and me, since we all did a lot of babysitting, and we formed the club.

Here's how the club works. Every Monday, Wednesday, and Friday afternoon from five-thirty until six o'clock, the members gather in Claudia's bedroom. Claudia has her own private phone and private phone number, and parents call us at Claudia's when they need to line up a sitter. There are six of us in the club now, plus two associate members (I'll explain all that later), so our clients are bound to wind up with a sitter. With eight of us, somebody is always free.

How do our clients know when and where to reach us? Because we advertise, that's how. Kristy's busy brain is always clicking along, thinking of important stuff like advertisements. That's one reason she's club chairman. (Also, the club was her idea, so who would you expect to be chairman?)

Claudia is the vice-chairman. We felt that was only fair, since we were going to be meeting in her room and using her phone.

I'm the secretary. I suspect that this is mostly because of my neat handwriting, but I would like to think that it's also because I'm organized and can manage things well. As secretary, it's my job to keep our club record book up to date. The record book is where we keep track of our job appointments, our clients, and their names and addresses and stuff.

Dawn is our treasurer. That used to be

Stacey McGill's job, but when she moved back to New York, Dawn took over. (Dawn had joined the club several months after it started, and she became our alternate officer. She could take over the job of anyone who couldn't make a meeting, sort of like a substitute teacher.) Anyway, as treasurer, it's up to her to keep a record of the money we earn, and to collect club subs and see that our treasury doesn't get too low. We use the treasury money to pay Charlie to drive Kristy to and from the meetings, since she now lives too far away to walk; to buy food for club parties; and to replace the stuff in our Kid-Kits. (Kristy invented Kid-Kits. They're boxes that we sometimes take along when we babysit. We keep them filled with our old games and toys, plus new colouring books and crayons and things. Kids love them, and their parents love *us* for bringing them!)

Now, I said before that the club has six members plus two associate members. Logan is one of the associate members. The other is a girl named Shannon Kilbourne, who lives across the street from Kristy in Kristy's fancy new neighbourhood. The associate members don't come to the meetings; they're people we can call on in a pinch—when none of the regular club members is free to take a job. This way, we never have to disappoint a client.

The two *other* girls in the club are junior

members. They're eleven years old and in the sixth grade, so they're only allowed to sit after school and on weekends, not at night (unless they're taking care of their own brothers and sisters). Their names are Mallory Pike and Jessica Ramsey, and they joined the club quite recently, right after Stacey left, as a matter of fact. I really like both Mal and Jessi, even if they are a little young. What's important is that they're good, responsible babysitters, and furthermore, they're just plain *nice*.

Mallory used to be someone our club sat *for*. She's the oldest of eight children, so she knows a lot about taking care of kids. Mal is going through sort of an awkward stage. She has freckles and curly hair, neither of which Mrs Pike will let her do anything about. She wants pierced ears but isn't allowed to have them yet; wants contact lenses but isn't allowed to have *them* yet, either; and doesn't want braces for her teeth but is getting them, anyway. Mal loves to read and write and draw, and she might become an author when she grows up.

Like Kristy and me, Jessi and Mal are best friends who are alike in a lot of ways and different in a lot of ways. They're alike in that it's just plain awful to be eleven. Jessi also wants pierced ears but isn't allowed to get them yet, and is facing a mouthful of metal. And she also loves to read, especially horse stories. She's not a writer, though.

Instead, she's a *very* talented ballet dancer. (As well as a good joke-teller.) Jessi has a younger sister, Becca, and a baby brother, Squirt. The Ramseys moved to Stoneybrook very recently. (In fact, they moved into Stacey's house after the McGills moved out of it.) And, boy, did they have a tough time at first. The Ramseys are black, and there aren't many black families around here at all, and none in Jessi's neighbourhood. Jessi is the only black kid in the sixth grade, if you can believe it. However, things are settling down and getting easier for her family. I think the Babysitters Club is important to Jessi because it gives her a feeling of belonging.

Before I tell you about the memorable meeting we had that day, there's just one other thing you need to know about the running of our club: the club notebook. This is a sort of diary that Kristy makes us keep, which no one likes writing in except Mallory and maybe Kristy. In it, we describe every single babysitting job we go on—which kids we sit for and what goes on. Once a week we're supposed to read the past week's entries so that we all know what's happening with our clients. I have to admit, it's pretty helpful, even if writing in it can be a great big bore.

All right. Back to the meeting.

I rushed to Claudia's front door with the letter tucked in my pocket. I rang the bell but went right on inside. I've lived across the street from Claudia forever, so it's okay to do that.

"Hi, Mimi!" I called to Claudia's grandmother as I ran upstairs. Ordinarily, I would have stopped to talk to her, but I was on the late side that day, and Kristy likes us members to be on time.

When I reached Claudia's room, I saw that I wasn't the last person to arrive. Jessi was still missing. She's usually late because after school she either goes to her ballet class, which is all the way over in Stamford, or goes to her steady sitting job for this family, the Braddocks.

I joined Claudia and Dawn, who were draped across Claudia's bed, looking through our seventh-grade yearbook. The six of us almost always sit in the same places during meetings. Claudia, Dawn and me on the bed; Jessi and Mal on the floor, and Kristy in the director's chair.

Get this. Our chairman holds meetings with a pencil stuck over one ear, wearing a visor. She says she feels more official that way. I haven't mentioned this to her, but I've never seen the President of the United States sitting in a director's chair, wearing a visor.

As I was settling down on the bed, Jessi ran into the room.

"Good. We're all here," said Kristy. "Let's begin."

Darn. I was just about to open my letter.

I didn't get a chance to do that until about fifteen minutes later, when we hit a lull. All official business had been conducted and the phone wasn't ringing, for a change.

I pulled the letter out of my pocket and tore it open.

"What's that?" asked Kristy.

"I got a letter today!" I said. "But I don't know who it's from. There's no return address."

I unfolded the paper that had been in the envelope.

"Oh, darn!" I exclaimed. "Darn, darn, boring *darn*."

"What?" asked Mallory.

"It's a dumb old chain letter, that's what. I *hate* chain letters. You have to send them to everyone you know, and then *they* have to send them to everyone *they* know."

"What kind of chain letter is it?" Dawn asked. "The kind where you send a postcard to the name at the top of the list and a few weeks later you supposedly get a million cards yourself?"

"I don't think so," I replied. "There's no list of names on this letter."

I read the letter quickly. I began to feel chills. Then I read the letter again, more slowly. When I finished, I was covered with goose bumps.

"This is really weird," I told my friends. "With this letter, you don't get anything for not breaking the chain—except good luck. But if you *do* break the chain, the letter says, 'Bad luck will be visited upon you, the recipient of this letter, and your friends and loved ones. Harm will come your way.'"

"Yikes," said Mal.

"Ho-hum," said Kristy.

"I wish I knew who sent it," I mused.

"Do you recognize the handwriting?" asked Claudia.

"There's no handwriting. The letter's typed." I looked at the envelope. "So's the address."

"Oh, well," said Kristy. "That stuff's just stupid, anyway. Who believes in causing bad luck by not mailing out a bunch of letters? How many are you supposed to send anyway, Mary Anne?"

"Twenty," I said.

"Well, don't bother sending one to me. I'll just break the chain.

"Don't worry," I told Kristy. "I'm not going to send *any*. Everyone would hate me because then they'd have to send out twenty letters, and besides, I don't think I even *know* twenty people."

"What?" screeched Mallory. During all this, Mal and Jessi had been staring at me, terrified. "You mean you're going to break the chain? That's crazy! Thanks a lot!"

"Yeah!" exclaimed Jessi. "If *you* break it, bad luck will be visited upon *us*, our friends and loved ones."

"Oh, it will not," said Claudia. "At least, I don't think so. Do you, Dawn?"

"Of course not. . . I mean, I guess not."

"Well, do you want me to send letters to you?" I asked Claudia and Dawn.

They looked at each other. Finally Dawn said, "We want you to send the letters— but not to us."

I giggled. "See? You don't want to have to deal with them. And neither do I. You know how much it costs to use the Xerox at the library? Fifteen cents a page. I'd have to have, um, let's see . . . well, a lot of change. Plus twenty stamps, plus twenty envelopes. And what would I wind up with? Twenty enemies."

"I wouldn't mind getting the letter, Mary Anne," said Mallory.

"Me neither," said Jessi nervously.

"Oh, you guys," Kristy admonished them. "It's just superstition. Forget it. But if you're so worried, why don't you take care of Mary Anne's letter for her?"

"It doesn't work that way," Mallory replied. "The letter was addressed to Mary Anne. She's the one who has to answer it.

"Well, anyway," I said. "Kristy's right. This is just superstition. I think."

I wasn't positive about that, but I was pretty sure. In fact, I was so sure that when the meeting was over, I tossed the letter in Claudia's wastebasket as I left the room.

3rd CHAPTER

I may be clumsy sometimes, but I swear, I haven't fallen out of bed since I was four years old. However, that was exactly how I began the next day.

It was 6:45. I was dreaming about climbing a mountain (I haven't been mountain climbing in my entire life), the alarm clock rang and I fell off the mountain.

How embarrassing.

What was even more embarrassing was that my father heard the crash and rushed into my room. He found me on the floor, tangled up in the blankets. Plus, I scared Tigger. He slunk underneath my desk and wouldn't come out.

"Mary Anne?" said my dad. "Are you all right?"

A reasonable question.

"Yeah," I replied, shaking my head and wishing for the floor to swallow me up. Or

159

at the very least, wishing to die, which would put an end to the embarrassment.

I stood up. "I was having this dream," I tried to explain. "I was climbing a mountain, and then the alarm rang—"

"And you fell off the mountain?" asked Dad.

"Yes! How did you know?"

"I've had some strange dreams myself," he replied. "Okay now?"

"Fine. Just embarrassed," I admitted.

Dad smiled. "You get dressed. I'll make pancakes for breakfast."

"Oh, super!" I exclaimed.

My dad used to be this incredibly strict, stiff person. He had all sorts of rules for me, like I had to wear my hair in plaits, and he had to approve of the outfits I chose for school, and I couldn't ride my bike downtown with friends. But then we started the Babysitters Club, and I found out some important things about myself. Mostly, I found out that I was much more grown-up and responsible than Dad thought I was. When I proved that to him, he started to change. He relaxed his rules, he relaxed around me, he relaxed in general. Things are *so* different than they were a year ago.

Don't get me wrong. I'm not blaming Dad for the way he used to be. Remember, he's raising me alone. He has to be both mother and father, and I think that before, he was just trying too hard.

We are both much happier.

Dad left to start breakfast. He closed my door behind him.

"Tigger, Tigger," I called. I got down on my hands and knees and peered under the desk. "Come on out, Tigger, you 'fraidy cat," I said. "It's safe. There's nothing to be scared of."

Tigger began to creep out. I could see his yellow eyes moving toward me.

"Good boy," I said. But as I straightened up, I banged into the chair.

CRASH.

Tigger dived back under the desk.

"I'm sorry, I'm sorry," I told him. Too late. I knew he'd stay there until he was so hungry he would have to come out for his breakfast.

I opened my wardrobe and managed to get dressed without killing myself. Except for my shoes. I couldn't find them. I looked everywhere. They were the same shoes I'd worn yesterday. Since I hadn't come home from school barefoot, I knew they were around somewhere. Oh, well. I could search for them later.

I made my bed, washed my face, called to Tigger again and ran downstairs. Dad had breakfast waiting. He's an early riser, and he actually *likes* to rush around and get things done before seven-thirty in the morning.

"Mmmm," I said, as I slid into my chair. "Pancakes *and* bacon!"

I reached for my orange juice and knocked over the glass. Juice ran across the table. Dad was standing by the fridge, so he was safe, but the juice cascaded into my lap.

I was wearing a white dress.

"Oh, *no!*" I cried, leaping to my feet. "Dad, I'm sorry! Really I am. I know you said a white dress wasn't practical for school, but I've worn it five times and nothing happened to it be—"

"Mary Anne, it's *all right,*" Dad told me. He handed me some paper towels. "Here, Mop up. Then fill a basin with cold water and soak your dress in it. Just leave it there. I'll keep your breakfast warm in the oven while you change your clothes . . . and find your shoes."

Boy, some morning I was having.

I changed my clothes and ate my breakfast. Then I looked for my shoes. I found them on top of the TV set. I had no idea why they were there. I didn't stop to wonder, though. If I didn't leave right then, I'd miss walking to school with Claudia.

So I put my shoes on and ran out the door. Claudia was standing around on the pavement in front of the house.

"Hi," she greeted me. "What were you doing?"

"Looking for my shoes, changing my clothes and comforting Tigger," I replied. I told her about the morning I was having.

I made a big deal out of it, hoping that, magically, this would put an end to things. You know how when you have a complaint about something—like a teacher who's being mean to you, or the rubber bands on your braces that keep snapping—and you finally tell someone about it, then that's the end of the problem? Well, I was sort of hoping that would happen with my bad day. That if I complained to Claudia, not a single other thing would go wrong.

It didn't work.

We reached school okay, but when I got there, I couldn't open my locker. Finally, I had to find Mr Halprin, the caretaker, and ask him to do it for me.

In maths class I realized I'd left my homework right where I'd done it: at home.

In the dining room I spilled a plate of macaroni and cheese. Not on me, on the floor. Mr Halprin had to come again. We were getting to know each other.

One of the worst things about that day happened right after Mr Halprin left. Logan turned to me and said, "So, is Mr Halprin a close, personal friend of yours?"

Since I'd just been thinking that Mr Halprin and I were sort of getting to know each other, I'm not sure why that remark drove me crazy, but it did. Logan had meant it to be funny. I snapped at him. "Ha. Ha."

"Hey, lighten up," said Logan.

"Easy for you to say," I grumbled.

"Mary *A*-anne." That was Kristy. Our usual group was crowded around our usual table.

"*Wha*-at?"

"Geez," said Logan, under his breath. "Touchy, touchy."

"Well, how would you feel if you dropped a plate of macaroni and cheese in front of the whole dining room?"

"Not that many people saw," Logan told me quietly.

"Oh, no. Only about three hundred, that's all." And having said that, I got up and stalked off to the school library, where I went looking for *Little Women*. It's one of my favourite books, and I thought that reading some familiar passages might be comforting.

The book was not on the shelf.

I walked home from school by myself that afternoon. I didn't bother to look for any of my friends, but I was sure they wouldn't have wanted to walk with me.

At home, I breathed a sigh of relief. I felt safer somehow, even though home was where I had fallen out of bed, scared Tigger and knocked over my orange juice. At least I hadn't done those things in front of three hundred kids.

"Oh, Tigger," I said, as I settled myself on my bed with my own copy of *Little Women*. "You stay here with me."

Tigger cuddled up against me, purring

like an outboard motor. I opened the book to the scene where Beth dies. Maybe I would feel cheered up if I read about someone who was having a worse time than I was.

That was when the phone rang.

I had to disturb Tigger in order to answer it.

"Hello?" I said.

"Hello, Mary Anne? This is Mrs Newton." Jamie's mother. Jamie and his sister Lucy are two of my favourite babysitting charges.

"Hi!" I said.

"Is everything okay?" asked Mrs Newton.

"Sure," I replied. "Why?"

"Well, it's just that you're never late," she began.

I clapped my hand to my forehead. I'd completely forgotten. I was supposed to sit for Jamie that day. The appointment was written in the record book and everything. How could I have been so stupid?

"I'm sorry!" I cried. "I'll come right over!" And I did.

What a day. It was a good thing I didn't believe in superstition. If I did, I might have blamed the day on the chain letter. And then I would *really* have worried—wondering what sort of bad luck was going to be visited upon my friends and loved ones. . .

(By the way, if you're wondering, I called

165

Logan that night and we made up. Also, the orange juice came out of the dress and didn't leave a stain.)

4th CHAPTER

Wednesday

Don't laugh, everybody. Looking back on it, I can see that it wasn't a very bright idea.

I baby-sat for Jackie Rodowsky and he and I tried to make his Halloween costume. Dumb idea, huh? You got it.

It was one of those days when I was sitting for just Jackie because his brothers were off taking lessons (piano for Shea, and tumbling for Archie, I think). Anyway, as you know, Jackie alone is about as much trouble as all three boys together. But for some reason, I wasn't remembering that, so when Jackie asked to make his Halloween costume, I agreed to it. And the rest goes down in baby-sitting history...

Jackie didn't even wait until his mother and brothers were in the car before he suggested to poor Dawn that they make his costume. The door to the garage was just closing as he said, "Dawn? I want to be a robot."

Dawn didn't catch on right away. "You want to play robots?" she asked.

"No, I want to *be* a robot. For Halloween. Can we make my costume this afternoon? We've got everything we need."

"Well," said Dawn, who hadn't brought her Kid-Kit and didn't really have anything planned. "I don't see why not."

"Goody!"

"What are you going to make your costume out of?"

"Boxes and jar lids and springs and buttons and googly eyes. Then we'll paint it."

Dawn felt a bit overwhelmed, but she said, "Okay, do you know where everything is?"

"All over the place," he replied.

"Well, let's start rounding it up. And if we're going to paint, we better work in the basement."

"Aw," said Jackie, "it's too cold down there. Let's make the robot here in the sitting room. When he's ready to be painted, then we'll move him to the basement."

"All right," said Dawn.

"Let's get the boxes first," said Jackie, "since they're the most important. They're out in the garage."

168

Dawn and Jackie went into the garage, and that was where Jackie had his first accident of the day.

I should stop here to tell you a little about Jackie Rodowsky. He and his brothers are some of the club's newest charges. They're look-alikes, with red hair and faces full of freckles. We like them a lot—even Jackie, who is completely accident-prone. Accidents just seem to follow him around and happen to him. I mean, sometimes things occur that he doesn't even have anything to do with. Like he'll be sitting in the living room, and an ashtray will fall off a table in the study. Well, maybe I'm exaggerating. Most of the time, Jackie is a happy-go-lucky bumbler. He gets his hands caught in things, he trips, he falls, he gets locked into places. And sometimes he just plain makes mischief. For instance, there was the time he and his brothers wanted to see what would happen to their socks if the vacuum cleaner sucked them up. (Luckily, not much.)

Jackie is seven, Shea is nine and little Archie is four. Shea and Archie are not accident-prone, which is why they take lessons and Jackie doesn't. Not that Jackie hasn't tried, but, well, for example, he hadn't been taking piano lessons for very long when he managed to break his teacher's metronome *and* her doorbell. (Don't ask me how.) He may have broken a few other things, too.

Anyway, that's Jackie's story, so now you can see why agreeing to make a robot costume was sort of dangerous. But Dawn had said she'd do it.

Out in the garage, Jackie showed Dawn a huge stack of cardboard boxes. "We can use any of these," he told her.

"Are you sure?" replied Dawn. "What are they here for?"

"Oh, anything. Storing stuff, taking rubbish to the dump, recycling newspapers."

Jackie reached for the biggest box he saw. It was on the bottom of the pile.

THUD, THUD, THUD, KER-RASH!

The mountain of boxes toppled over.

Dawn sighed. Her afternoon was just beginning.

When all but three of the boxes (the big one, a medium-sized one and a small one) had been stacked again, Dawn and Jackie brought their boxes inside. They set them on the floor.

"Okay," said Dawn. "What else do we need?"

"Paint," replied Jackie.

"I better get that," Dawn said nervously. Jackie showed her where it was, and Dawn put several jars of ready-mixed poster paints, plus some brushes, with the boxes.

"Now," Jackie went on, "we just need *stuff*." He found several jar lids, a coil of wire and an old Slinky toy on shelves in the basement. In a box marked SCRAPS he found some pieces of felt, five wooden cotton reels and the googly eyes he'd been talking about.

"See?" he said, holding up the plastic eyes with the moving black pupils. "We got a whole package of these once. They're googly."

Dawn had to agree.

"Last thing," Jackie continued. "Buttons. They're upstairs in Mum's sewing chest."

Dawn made the mistake of letting Jackie go upstairs alone. How much trouble, she thought, could he get into with buttons? They weren't messy or dangerous or—

KER-RASH.

Dawn closed her eyes for a moment to collect her thoughts before she headed upstairs. When she reached Mr and Mrs Rodowsky's bedroom, she found Jackie kneeling by the overturned sewing chest. Needles and pins and reels of thread and packets of zips and piles of buttons were scattered across the rug.

"Oops," said Jackie.

It took more than fifteen minutes for Dawn and Jackie to put each item back into its little compartment. Then Dawn insisted on vacuuming the rug, in case they'd missed a stray pin or needle. Jackie wanted to start on his robot while Dawn vacuumed, but by then, she knew better.

"You sit right there," she told him, pointing to his parents' bed, "until I've finished. Then we'll go downstairs together."

At long last, they began work on the robot. Dawn had sensibly spread newspapers over the floor before Jackie opened the bottle of Elmer's glue.

"See, what we do," Jackie said, "is glue these two boxes together to make the body. Then we put dials and stuff all over it—those are the jar lids and buttons and things. And then we make a robot head—well, a hat really—out of the little box. I want to put the Slinky on top of the hat."

"We better paint the boxes before you glue things on them," Dawn pointed out.

"Oh, right," said Jackie. "But first, I have to make the body." He got busy with the boxes and glue. He cut a neckhole. He cut two armholes. Then he cut himself.

"Ow!"

Dawn fixed up his bleeding thumb with antiseptic cream and a plaster.

Then Jackie glued the boxes together. "Now for the paint," he announced.

Dawn helped him carry the boxes to the basement—ever so carefully, since the glue wasn't dry. After Jackie had knocked over a jar of blue paint and he and Dawn had mopped it up, he painted his robot a wild array of colours. The poster paints dried quickly.

172

They carried the robot back upstairs.

"Okay, this is the fun part," said Jackie. And he proceeded to turn the painted cartons into a really splendid robot.

Even though every other word out of his mouth was, "Whoops," he managed to glue the jar lids and reels and buttons all over the body of the robot. Using a fat felt-tip, he drew a gauge and a needle (measuring . . . what?) on the robot's belly. He attached wires, coiled to look like springs. To the head, he glued two googly eyes and the Slinky. He couldn't find a use for the felt scraps, but it was almost time for Mrs Rodowsky and Shea and Archie to come home, anyway.

"Hey!" he cried. "I know! I'll put my costume on so I can surprise them when they walk through the door."

Dawn smiled. "Good idea." She was relieved that the rest of the project had gone so peacefully and safely.

Jackie slipped the boxes over his head. His put on his hat and grinned at Dawn. He was the perfect homemade robot.

For three seconds.

Then his hat fell off. The top of the body came apart from the bottom part of the body, and the bottom dropped to the floor, like the stages of a rocket separating. The reels and jar lids and wires and googly eyes came off and rolled under the couch.

"Oh, no!" cried Dawn.

But Jackie just said calmly, "Oops. I guess the glue wasn't dry. Poor old robot. I'll put him back together tomorrow."

What bad luck, Dawn thought, as she rode her bike home that afternoon. Briefly, she remembered my chain letter and wondered if maybe I shouldn't have broken the chain. Maybe bad luck was being visited upon her, since she's one of my friends. Then, no, she realized. Jackie always has bad luck. He's a walking disaster.

Dawn forgot about the chain letter.

5th
CHAPTER

Another Friday, another club meeting. After babysitting for two little girls, Nina and Eleanor Marshall (I remembered my appointment that day), I checked our mailbox before going to the Kishis'. And in among the bills and magazines I found a small package!

I closed my hands over it, hoping it was for me. But it was probably for Dad. My birthday was over, Christmas was two months away and I hadn't ordered anything from the back of a magazine lately. Maybe it was a free sample. That could be interesting, especially if it was hand lotion or make-up or shampoo.

I opened my hands. The package *was* for me! And it wasn't just a sample. But right away, I felt those chills again. My name and address were made out of letters cut from magazines and newspapers. It was the kind of thing you only see on TV or in the movies when somebody has been kidnapped and the bad guys mail a ransom note. I know it sounds crazy, but my first thought was that Tigger had been kittennapped. I ran inside to check him.

"Tigger! Tigger!" I called.

I found him curled up in a ball of rumbly purrs on the living room sofa.

"Oh, thank goodness!" I exclaimed, letting out a lungful of air. "You're here and you're alive."

I raced over to Claudia's, the box clutched in my hand.

Kristy and Claudia were the only club members there, and Kristy was the one who noticed immediately that the box was addressed not just to me but to:

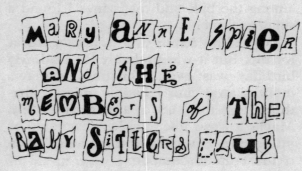

There was no return address.

The three of us looked at each other. I could see fear in my friends' eyes and I'm sure they could see it in mine. We were dying to open the box (and at the same time afraid to), but we waited until Dawn, Jessi and Mal arrived before we did.

Kristy was so nervous about what might be inside that she didn't even conduct an official meeting. In fact, she forgot to put on her visor, and she crowded onto the bed with Dawn and Claudia and me.

"We'll just take phone calls today," she informed us. "We can take care of business on Monday."

We all looked at the box.

"Well," I said, "who's going to open it?"

"You, of course," said Kristy. "It was in your mailbox, and it's addressed mostly to you."

"You're afraid!" I cried. I was relieved to find I had company.

"You're right."

I scowled. "Okay." I began to peel back the paper as slowly and as carefully as if a bomb might be inside. (And these days, who knew?)

I unwound one layer of paper, then another, then a third. Inside lay a harmless white jewellery box.

I gave my friends a look that said, "We are all such idiots. We've been afraid of jewellery."

But Jessi didn't look a bit relieved. "Anything could be inside," she pointed out. "And there are a lot of anythings I wouldn't want to be within a mile of."

My fear returned.

With shaking hands I lifted the lid of the box.

All I could see was tissue paper.

"Claudia? Do you have any tweezers?" I asked. "I'm not touching this."

"Oh, for heaven's sake." Claudia took the box from me and pulled the tissue paper up. She crumpled it into a ball, which she dropped on the bed.

"Ew!" shrieked Dawn, jumping away from the paper, and the rest of us screamed, too.

When we calmed down, we dared—all six of us—to peer into the box.

"What is it?" asked Mallory.

"It looks like a necklace," I replied.

Lying in the box was a tiny glass ball on a delicate gold chain. The ball was hollow, and inside was what looked like a seed—a small, yellowish-brown thing.

I lifted the necklace out, afraid that at any moment it might go up in a puff of smoke, or that *we* might go up in a puff of smoke.

"It's kind of pretty." Claudia interrupted my thoughts. "Really. It's weird-looking and it's unusual. I like it because it's different. It's my kind of jewellery."

I was about to tell her she could have it, when I realized what it had been resting on in the box. It wasn't your usual little piece of cotton.

"Hey, here's a note!" I exclaimed.

"Oh, brother. Which one of us is going to read it?" asked Dawn.

"I—I guess I better," I said. "I mean, Kristy's right. The box was mostly addressed to me."

I dropped the necklace on the bed (everyone scrambled away from it) and opened up the note.

"Handwriting?" asked Kristy.

I shook my head. "Nope. More cut-out letters from the newspaper."

"So what does it say?" asked Claudia.

"It—it says," I replied shakily, "well, see for yourselves."

I spread open the note on Claudia's bed. The members of the Babysitters Club leaned over to look at it, although I noticed that nobody got too close. The note said:

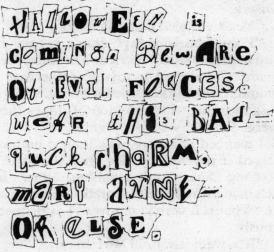

HALLOWEEN is coming. BewAre OF EVIL FOrCES. wear tHis BAD—luck chaRM, mARy ANNE—OR ELSE.

"Augh!" I shrieked.

"Bad-luck charm?" cried Mallory with a gasp. "Oh, I knew it. I just knew it."

I looked at the necklace, which was lying on the bed near the note. "Oh, my gosh, I've already touched it," I said.

"Touched it," Dawn repeated. "You've got to *wear* it."

"Are you crazy? No way!" I exclaimed.

"I think you better," said Jessi. "Are you going to ignore this warning . . . like you ignored the chain letter?"

I looked at the older girls. After all, Mal and Jessi are two years younger than the rest of us. Of course they believed in warnings and charms.

But my friends were no help.

"May-maybe you ought to wear it," said Dawn.

"Yeah. . ." said Claudia slowly.

"I thought you guys didn't believe in superstitious stuff!" I cried. The thing was, I sort of believed it myself. Otherwise I would have put the necklace on right away, just to prove what a bunch of dopes they were.

I glanced at Kristy. She looked embarrassed. I realized that for once she wasn't scoffing. She wasn't laughing, either. In fact, she looked pretty scared.

"What is it with you guys?" I asked nervously.

"It's, well, it's. . ." Dawn began. "See, I

180

had some pretty bad luck with Jackie Rodowsky yesterday." She told us about his unfortunate robot and all the accidents.

"But Jackie is bad luck, just like you said," I told her.

"This was worse than usual," Dawn replied. "It was a pretty bad babysitting experience."

"I failed a spelling test," added Claudia.

"You always fail spelling tests," I said.

"Not lately." Claudia looked haughty.

"I fell in ballet class," said Jessi. "That never happens."

"I lost my watch," said Kristy.

"I got in trouble for talking during maths," said Mal.

"You know what?" Claud added. "Stacey called a while ago. She broke her dad's paper-weight. That one he loves. She can't even figure out how to confess to him."

"Well, I might as well tell you," I went on. "I had the worst day of my life the day after I threw away the chain letter." I described the day, from falling out of bed to forgetting my babysitting job. When I was done, we all just stared at each other. At long last, I picked up the charm and slipped it over my head.

"This thing scares me to death," I admitted. "It's *bad luck*. But what would happen if I *didn't* wear it? Things might be worse than bad."

"Evil," said Mal in a whisper.

"But who sent the charm?" I wondered.
None of us had any ideas.

"And why did they send it to me? Why
do *I* have to wear the thing?"

"Maybe," answered Jessi, "because you
were the one who threw the chain letter
away. This is your bad luck. And all the
other stuff is the bad luck that's being
visited upon your friends."

"What about the rest of the note?" I
asked.

"'Halloween is coming. Beware of evil
forces.' What's that supposed to mean?"

"Well," said Claudia, "Halloween is the
spookiest, eeriest time of year."

"But the evil forces—" I began.

"I think," said Mal, "that we will have
to ward them off."

We all knew that wouldn't be easy. I had
broken a good-luck chain and was wearing
a bad-luck charm. I couldn't change either
situation.

Still, we did have to ward off the evil
forces. The question was—how?

6th
CHAPTER

I was terrified.

Who wouldn't be?

On Saturday, the day after I got the bad-luck charm, I was wearing it while I sat for Jamie Newton. Jamie spilled everything in sight, dropped everything in sight and then fell and skinned his knee. And he didn't just trip and fall. He fell down half a flight of steps. Of course, he cried. A lot. But a plaster helped. Jamie likes plasters!

On Monday, the first day I wore the charm to school, there was a fire in a rubbish bin (which the fire brigade had to come and put out), an explosion in the science lab (no one was hurt, but a bunsen burner was completely destroyed) and an accident in a gym class. (Miranda Shillaber twisted her ankle. She had to go to the nurse and she needed a bandage and everything.)

183

"Maybe," said Kristy at lunch that day, "this is just a big coincidence."

I looked around at Kristy, Claudia, Dawn and Logan. They were all picking at their food. So was I. The hot vegetable that day was mixed beans, and therefore looked incredibly disgusting, but Kristy hadn't made a single comment about it. So I knew she didn't believe what she'd just said. She was too worried and preoccupied even to try to make me sick.

I glanced down at the charm. The little seed was resting on the bottom of its glass globe. I decided that it looked like something that was carefully, calmly planning horrible deeds.

"One accident on the first day I wear the charm," I said, "might be a coincidence. One little spill at the Newtons'. But not spills and broken stuff and Jamie's knee. I could even accept one little fire at school that Mr Halprin puts out by himself with a bucket of water. That could still be a coincidence. But not a fire-brigade fire—"

"And an explosion," continued Logan.

"*Plus* a gym injury," finished Dawn.

"Right," I agreed. And then I went on in a whisper, "You know what else? There have been other signs of bad luck today."

"There *have*?" Kristy replied. "Like what?"

"My father opened an umbrella in the house this morning."

Kristy rolled her eyes.

"But wait, there's more," I said. "On the way to school, a black cat crossed our path."* I glanced at Claudia, who nodded nervously.

"That's right, one did," she said.

"And just before I came into the dining room?" I went on.

"Yeah?" said Logan. He reached over and held onto my hand. I wasn't sure if he wanted to comfort me, or if he was afraid himself.

"I saw a penny on the floor, so I bent down and picked it up. I just did it without thinking. It was already in my hand before I realized it was a *tail-up* penny. I dropped it, but by then it was too late."

Our table was silent. On another day, any one of those bad-luck signs would have made us laugh. But today—the first day I wore the charm to school—three signs, three accidents, the charm and the chain letter were just too much.

"You know what?" I said after a moment. "This charm is a curse. And we have to do something about it."

"That's what Mallory said on Friday," Kristy pointed out. "Remember? She said we had to ward off the evil forces."

"How?" Claudia demanded to know.

Not one of us had an answer. Especially

---

* This is bad luck in America.

185

not Logan, who was looking at us as if we were all crazy. Who could blame him? I was willing to bet that over at Grace and Cokie's table, they weren't talking about charms and curses and evil forces. They were probably talking about the Halloween Hop.

I glanced at them. Five people were at Grace's table—Grace, Cokie and three of the girls in their group of friends. They were staring at our table. I felt my face grow hot.

"Shh, you guys," I hissed. "I think we're talking too loudly. People are listening."

"It's no wonder," whispered Dawn. "This is probably the most fascinating conversation they've heard in weeks."

Kristy, Claudia, Dawn and I began to giggle. Cokie and her friends couldn't stop staring at us, though, and Logan began to get that I've-had-enough-of-girls look. He escaped to a tableful of boys.

"Let's continue this discussion," said Dawn, "but keep our voices down."

"All right," the rest of us agreed.

"We've got a little problem," Dawn went on. "Okay. Mary Anne has a charm. The note that came with it said it's a bad-luck charm."

"Right."

"And we didn't really know whether to believe that until today," Kristy added. "Now, Mary Anne has worn the charm to

186

the Newtons' and had bad luck there and worn the charm to school and found bad luck at school."

"There seems to be bad luck wherever I wear the charm. In fact, there's bad luck wherever *I* am," I said.

My friends all edged away from me, sliding their lunches down the table.

"Thanks a lot!" I exclaimed.

The others looked embarrassed, but they didn't apologize or move back.

"Does anybody know anything about charms and curses?" asked Claudia.

We all shook our heads.

"I read a Nancy Drew book once called *The Mystery of the Ivory Charm*," Claudia, our mystery-lover, went on, "but I don't think it would help us." She paused thoughtfully. "Well," she said at last, "how can we find out about charms and curses and evil forces? We've got to do something."

"We better go to the library," I replied.

"Oh, I *hate* the library!" cried Claudia.

"Even when you're not there for a school assignment?" I asked her. "Even when you're just there on your own?"

Claudia made a face.

"Well, I think we should go anyway," I pronounced. "And I think we should ask Jessi and Mal to come with us. Claudia can go or not go. It's up to her."

"No, it isn't," spoke up Kristy. "It's

not up to her. She's going."

"I am?" said Claudia. "How come?"

"Because this club sticks together," was Kristy's reply. "We'll meet at the front doors to the school as soon as the last bell has rung."

End of discussion.

And that was exactly what we did. Even Jessi, who has her steady sitting job on Mondays and Wednesdays, was able to go to the library, since the Braddock kids were sick with the flu. I invited Logan to join us, but he said he wouldn't be able to go. I guess the thought of being with six girls who were doing research on witchcraft was too much for him.

Even though I was wearing the bad-luck charm and it was really frightening me, I daydreamed contentedly all the way to the library. I kept thinking about books I'd read in which kids go to the library on just this sort of mission, and when they ask the librarian (who is always a white-haired woman about ninety years old) for books on witchcraft, she takes them to some musty old corner of the library (maybe even to the basement) and shows them these big, scary, dusty books that are older than she is. The books are weird, a little *too* helpful, and no one seems to know where they came from.

Well, our visit to the Stoneybrook Public

Library wasn't like that at all.

"What do we do first?" Claudia whispered, as soon as we were inside.

I looked around for a white-haired, ninety-year-old woman. "Ask the librarian," I replied.

"No, we don't have to do that," said Mal and Jessi at the same time. (Since they both like to read, they probably go to the library a lot.)

"We can just go to the card catalogue," Jessi added.

"Children's room or adults'?" asked Kristy.

"Adults'," our experts replied immediately. "We'll find much better stuff in the adult section."

"More informative," Mal added importantly. "But we really have to behave and act grown-up. Librarians are always suspicious of kids in the adult section."

Mal and Jessi led the way to the adult card catalogue. Under the heading "Witchcraft", we found cards for tons of books.

"Do we have to copy down *all* of these numbers and look up *each* of these books?" asked Claudia. "I think I'm getting a headache. I better go home."

"*No way*," said Kristy flatly.

"Besides," I added, "we don't have to look for each book separately. They're in the same section. See? The numbers all start out the same way. If we find this area, we'll have found the right section. That's all we need."

Mal and Jessi looked at me admiringly. Their admiration was nice, but I felt like saying, "I know how to use the library, too, you know."

Considering that the Stoneybrook Public Library is a modern building that was put up just eight years ago, after the town outgrew the old library, I don't know why I thought the witchcraft books would be in a lost, dusty, spooky corner. The new library doesn't have any lost, dusty, spooky corners. The witchcraft books are just in a row of other books on metal shelves under a buzzing fluorescent light.

One piece of good luck was that they were on the bottom shelf, so we could sit on the floor. We began pulling the books out and looking through their tables of contents.

"Here's one called *On Witchcraft,*" I said.

"Here's one called *Witches Through the Ages,*" Dawn said a moment later.

"Here's one called *Strange Phenomena,*" Jessi spoke up.

"And here's one called *Charms and Spells,*" said Kristy.

"Why do we need all this witch and spell stuff?" I wondered out loud.

"How else are we going to ward off the

evil forces of the charm?" asked Mal.

I shook my head. "I don't know. I thought none of us knew. That's why we're here."

"Well, it has to be some sort of spell, doesn't it?" Mal replied. "I figured we just didn't know which one."

I shivered. "Okay. A spell."

We turned back to the books. I began to imagine midnight and a full moon, the six of us mixing up herbs and weird, hard-to-find things, and chanting a spooky rhyme.

"Maybe we ought to ask Karen for advice," I said, smiling.

"*Oh, no!*" cried Kristy. Her little step-sister is totally into ghosts and witches. She even thinks that Mrs Porter, the old woman who lives next door to Kristy, is actually a witch named Morbidda Destiny. "She'd never leave us alone if she knew what we were up to."

I wished I knew what we were up to. But I didn't. Not really. So I turned back to the books. At five o'clock we each chose one to check out. Then we made a dash for Claudia's house and our club meeting.

7th
CHAPTER

Thursday

Halloween is supposed to be scary, but I never realized just how scary it can be for some little kids. I was sitting for Jamie Newton today, and it turns out that he's totally freaked-out by Halloween. Everything scares him. Don't ask me why, but he's afraid of trick-or-treaters. He's even afraid of the costume parade that's going to be held at his nursery school. (Or at least he was when I first got to his house. He didn't have a costume, either, because he said he was afraid to dress up.)

Jessi was right. Jamie was spooked. (So were all us babysitters—but for a different reason.)

As Mrs Newton was leaving that afternoon, she said to Jessi in a low voice, "I hope everything will be okay. This is the first year Halloween has meant much to Jamie" (Jamie is four) "and he's terrified. Mr Newton and I have tried to make it sound like fun, but Jamie has only picked up on the scary stuff."

Jessi nodded. "Okay. Thanks for telling me."

(We sitters appreciate parents who warn us about problems that might come up while we're in charge.)

Then Mrs Newton left with Lucy, Jamie's baby sister, who was getting over an ear infection and had an appointment with the doctor.

"Well, Jamie," said Jessi, as Mrs Newton's car was backing into the street, "what do you want to do today?"

Sometimes it's not a good idea to ask an open-ended question like that. I mean, what if the kid's reply is that he wants to skate around the kitchen floor on bars of soap—or do something even worse? But when you're familiar with the kid you're sitting for, you also know when it's okay to ask such a question. And Jessi had sat for Jamie a few times and knew that he wouldn't suggest anything weird.

"I want to. . . I want to. . . I don't know. . ." said Jamie vaguely.

Jessi began to wish that she'd brought her Kid-Kit along. A sort of unspoken rule among us babysitters is that you always spend time with the kids you're sitting for, unless you're being paid extra to be a parents' helper and are supposed to be washing dishes or folding clothes or something. This might seem sort of obvious, but you'd be surprised at how many sitters just wait until the parents leave and then park themselves in front of the TV until they return, never paying a bit of attention to the kids.

Jessi had no intention of doing that. (None of us would.) "You want to play outside?" she asked Jamie.

Jamie shook his head, his eyes growing big and frightened.

"What's wrong?" asked Jessi.

"Trick-or-treaters might come by."

"Oh, not today, Jamie," Jessi assured him. "It isn't Halloween yet. There won't be any trick-or-treaters until Halloween."

"I hope it's never Halloween," said Jamie.

Jessi led Jamie to the sofa in the living room and sat him down.

"What are you so afraid of?" she asked.

"Halloween," Jamie replied simply.

"But Halloween is fun," said Jessi. "Honest. Everyone gets sweets, and you

194

dress up. You could be a ghost, or a witch—"

Jamie covered his eyes with his hands. "No!"

"Or Superman," Jessi went on.

"No ghosts! No witches!" Jamie cried.

"But they aren't real," Jessi told him. "They're just people dressed up."

"Ghosts and witches scare me. Especially ghosts."

"Why?"

"They just scare me."

"Not all ghosts are mean," said Jessi. And that was when she had her brainstorm. "Hey," she said excitedly, "did you ever hear of Georgie?"

"Georgie?" Jamie repeated.

"Yeah," said Jessi. "He was a ghost—a little ghost—and he was very shy. As shy as a mouse. He didn't like loud noises or too much confusion. He lived in the attic of Mr and Mrs Whittaker's house, and all he wanted was peace and quiet. And to be with his friends, Herman and Miss Oliver."

"Who are the Whittakers?" Jamie asked. "And who are Herman and Miss Oliver?"

"If you really want to know," said Jessi, "we could go over to my house and I could show you some of the books about Georgie."

"Well. . ." said Jamie, who looked pretty interested in spite of himself, "okay."

So Jessi buttoned Jamie into his jacket (a button came off in her hand), and retied his trainers (one of the laces broke as she did so) and nearly had a heart attack.

It's the bad luck! she thought wildly. It's Mary Anne's bad luck being visited upon her friends again. In the moments that followed, Jessi panicked—but only in her mind. The Braddock kids have the flu, she thought, and Lucy Newton has had an earache—that's a lot of sickness—and Jamie is overreacting to Halloween. And now the button and the shoelace. (Not to mention everything else that had happened.)

Jessi took two deep breaths and tried to calm down.

Jamie was looking at her oddly.

"Okay," said Jessi briskly. "If you'll show me where the sewing box is, and if you know where the extra shoelaces are, I'll fix you up and then we'll go over to my house and find the Georgie books."

Which is exactly what they did.

When Jamie was ready, Jessi left a note for Mrs Newton, saying where they were going (in case Mrs Newton came home early), and then she and Jamie left the house. Jessi carefully locked the door behind her.

On the way to the Ramseys', Jamie asked, "Is there anybody my age where you live?"

Jessi shook her head. "Sorry, Jamie. My

sister Becca is eight, and then I have a baby brother, Squirt."

"A baby?" said Jamie. "Like Lucy?"

"Yes, but a little older. Squirt's almost walking."

Jamie nodded. "Whose are the Georgie books?"

"Well," replied Jessi, "they used to be mine, and now they're Becca's, but they're waiting to be Squirt's. They're perfect for someone who's four years old, though. Just like you. That's why I think you'll like them."

"Hello?" called a voice when Jessi opened the front door to her house.

"Hi, Mama. It's me," Jessi replied. "I brought Jamie Newton over for a few minutes. We're going to look at some books."

Mrs Ramsey appeared in the front hall. "Hi, Jamie," she said.

"Hi," Jamie answered shyly.

"I'll explain later," Jessi whispered to her mother as she and Jamie scooted by her on their way to the stairs. Then, "Be careful," she warned Jamie as he started up the staircase. These days, she thought, you really can't be too careful.

"Where are the books?" Jamie asked when he was safely upstairs.

"In Becca's room," Jessi replied.

The door to Becca's room was open, so Jessi went in, scanned her sister's bookcase, and found a skinny picture book. She handed it to Jamie, and the two of them went into Jessi's room to read.

"This book," said Jessi, "is called *Georgie's Halloween*."

"Uh-oh," moaned Jamie.

"No, it's okay. Really," Jessi told him. "We'll just look at the pictures first. Here. See these old people?"

"Are they Mr and Mrs Whittaker?" asked Jamie.

"That's right," Jessi replied. "And here are Herman and Miss Oliver."

"Herman's a cat and Miss Oliver's an owl!" Jamie exclaimed.

"Yup. And here's Georgie."

"*That* little thing?" said Jamie, pointing to one of the pictures. "But he doesn't look mean at all. He's smiling."

"He isn't mean," said Jessi. "Remember? He's even shy." And then Jessi read Jamie the story about the little ghost who was *so* shy that he wouldn't enter the town's contest for best Halloween costume, even though he would have won, hands down.

"Well, that's silly," said Jamie when the story was over. "*I* would have entered the contest."

"You can be in your costume parade at school," Jessi pointed out.

Jamie looked thoughtful. "Maybe," he said at last. "I wonder. . ."

"You wonder what?"

"If Mummy could make me a Georgie costume."

"You want to be a ghost?"

"No. Georgie. Only Georgie. Then if there are any prizes, maybe I'll win. I mean, *Georgie* could win. He could win his prize after all."

"Now that," said Jessi, "is a great idea." She and Jamie smiled at each other.

"Any more Georgie books?" asked Jamie.

"Yup."

"Well . . . let's read them!"

8th
CHAPTER

Saturday

Oh my lord that was my werst siting experyence ever.

Claudia, it wasn't that bad.

yes it was Mal. Just count up all the things that whent wronge.

Okay. Well, there was the dinner.

And the bird

Right, the bird. And Vanessa's tooth.

I think the tooth was the werst. Because of the bloode.

The blood was bad, but the bird thing took so long to solve. And it made the triplets crazy.

Well lets not arg How on erth do you spell

Argue?

Right.

It was another one of those long two-person entries. They turn up in the notebook every now and then—when we're taking care of the Pike brood (they usually need two sitters), or if Jessi and Mal are sitting together, which happens sometimes, since they're younger.

This entry was from a Saturday—two days after Jessi convinced Jamie that not all ghosts are scary. Claudia and Mallory sat for Mallory's brothers and sisters.

It was quite an ordeal. Really, as much as I like Mallory and her levelheadedness, I have to take Claudia's side here. It *was* her worst babysitting experience ever. I'm even willing to go out on a limb and say that it was the worst experience any of us has ever had. Maybe it wasn't as frightening as the time Dawn thought Buddy Barrett had been kidnapped, or the time I had to get Jenny Prezzioso to the hospital in an ambulance, but, well, so *many* things went wrong. And so many things went so *very* wrong.

I might as well get it all out in the open here. Us sitters agreed that this was more bad luck being visited upon my friends. The spate of bad luck was hard to ignore. It wasn't just a little accident here, a piece of unwelcome news there; it was one bad thing after another. Even bad things with Stacey in New York.

Mr and Mrs Pike hadn't been gone for

five minutes when the first bad thing happened. The Pikes were out for a long, late evening, so Claudia and Mal had a big night ahead of them, starting with giving the Pike kids their dinner. Mr Pike had cooked up a batch of some sort of casserole with sausage pieces in it. Claudia thought it looked revolting, so she, personally, wasn't too upset about what happened a few minutes later, but the Pikes—even Mallory—*were*. Apparently this dish is special to them. They call it Daddy Stew. And they were really looking forward to it, especially Byron, who loves to eat. He's sort of a human vacuum cleaner.

Before I get any further, I suppose I should remind you about Mallory's brothers and sisters, since the Pikes are not your average family.

Mallory is the oldest, of course, and she's eleven. The triplets she wrote about in the notebook are her ten-year-old brothers,— Byron, Jordan and Adam. They're identical, and they can be a handful. They like to tease, especially their younger brother Nicky, but they're basically good kids. Vanessa is nine. She's a budding poet and sometimes talks in rhyme, which could drive you crazy. Nicky is eight. He's also a good kid but has trouble fitting in with his family. His brothers think he's a baby, and Nicky hates girls, which is a problem. Margo Pike is seven and going through a bossy stage. Last but not least is Claire, who's five and sometimes really plays up her baby-of-the-family role. What a family.

Okay, back to the Daddy Stew. Mr and Mrs Pike had just left. The last thing Mrs Pike said before the door closed behind her was, "Let the Daddy Stew heat up until six-thirty. Leave the burner where it is."

"Six-thirty!" Byron exclaimed. "I can't wait that long!"

"That's less than half an hour from now," Mallory pointed out.

"But I'm *starving*. I'll die of starvation before then!"

"No, you won't. Come on. Help us get ready in the play room. We're not going to eat in the kitchen tonight. We're going to have an indoor picnic."

"An indoor picnic!" cried the other Pikes. "Goody!" They got busy carrying things down to the play room, then spreading a tablecloth on the floor and laying out the plates and forks and spoons and napkins.

Byron never joined them. No one paid any attention to that. Not until they noticed an awful acrid smell—like smoking rubber.

Claudia sniffed the air. "Is something burning?" she asked worriedly.

Mallory sniffed, too. "Uh-oh," she said.

Claudia, Mallory, Adam, Jordan, Vanessa, Nicky, Margo and Claire raced upstairs to the kitchen. On the stove was a smoking pot of Daddy Stew. Byron was standing next to it. He looked from the pot to his babysitters.

"Oops," he said.

Mallory dashed to the stove and turned the burner off. Then she grabbed a pot-holder and lifted the lid. The Daddy Stew was a horrid, burned, black mess.

"Ew! Ew! Pee-yew!" cried the Pike kids. They held their noses and backed out of the kitchen.

"The Daddy Stew is *ruined*, Mallory. Byron *ruined* it," cried Claire.

"I'm sorry," said Byron. "Honest. I was hungry. And I just thought that if I turned the fire up—"

"Aughh! Aughh!"

Shrieks were coming from the living room, where the Pikes (except for Mal and Byron) had fled to escape the smell of the ruined Daddy Stew.

"Now what?" exclaimed Claudia.

"I don't know," Mallory replied, shaking her head, "but that sounded like more than just a stop-teasing-me-or-I'll-kill-you scream. I think something happened."

The girls left the kitchen (Claudia calling over her shoulder, "You're in charge of cleaning up that mess, Byron!") and hurried into the living room. They found the Pikes running back and forth, stooped over, as if the ceiling were closing in on them.

Above them flew a bird.

"Oh, my lord!" cried Claudia. "Where did that come from?"

"It flew down the chimney!" Vanessa shrieked. "Aughh! Oh, help!"

"Now, wait a sec, guys. That bird is scared to death and you're scaring it even more," said Mallory sensibly. "So either calm down and help Claudia and me, or go and watch TV."

Vanessa made a dash for the TV. Everyone else stayed. They huddled around Claud and Mal in the entryway to the living room.

The poor bird, which was only a little sparrow, kept letting out terrified sparrowsquawks and swooping from one side of the living room to the other.

"How are we going to catch him?" asked Nicky.

"Maybe it's a 'her'," said Adam, just to torture Nicky.

"Never mind that," Mallory told Adam. "We have to keep the bird from flying into something, like the window. It could knock itself out."

"Hey!" said Jordan. "Maybe if we open the windows and doors, the bird will just fly outside."

"I could get my butterfly net," said Nicky. "Maybe I could scoop it up. Then we could take it outdoors and let it loose."

"Yeah, right," said Jordan sarcastically.

"Maybe it'll calm down and land some where," suggested Margo. "We could throw a pillowcase over it."

"I wonder if the bird knows Santa Claus," Claire said dreamily.

Everyone forgot about the sparrow for a moment.

"Huh?" said Adam.

"The bird came down the chimney, just like Santa," Claire explained. "I wonder. . ."

Adam, Jordan and Nicky snickered behind their hands.

Then, "Aughh!" Margo shrieked again as the bird made another arc across the living room, just inches above her head.

"Okay, we're wasting time," said Mallory. "Let's open the windows and doors. That seems like the best idea so far."

Claudia and the Pikes rushed around, opening every window and door on that level of the house.

"Go ahead, little birdie," Margo coaxed the sparrow. Then suddenly, feeling brave (or maybe bossy), she raised her hands in the air and ran toward a window, waving and screaming. "Get out of here, bird!"

The sparrow flew ahead of her—and went right out the window.

"Good job!" Mallory exclaimed. "Thanks, Margo."

"Whew," said Claudia. "All right. Let's close everything up."

Claudia turned around to go back to the kitchen and was met by the sight of Vanessa holding blood-smeared hands to her mouth.

"Oh, my lord!" cried Claudia, who was getting a lot of mileage out of that phrase that evening. "Vanessa, what happened?"

As Vanessa let Claudia guide her toward the sink in the kitchen, she held out her hand. In it was a small, bloody tooth.

"I didn't know you had a loose tooth, Vanessa," said Mallory.

"I didn't know I did, either," Vanessa replied tearfully. Claudia helped her to rinse out her mouth with warm, salty water. When the bleeding had stopped, Vanessa said sheepishly, "I was eating a piece of candy. It was really sticky. I bit down on it, and when I opened my mouth again, the candy pulled the tooth out."

Well, as you can imagine, it was a while before Claudia and the Pikes sat down to their indoor picnic. The kids, especially the triplets, were wild over the bird and Vanessa's mouth. Furthermore, it took a while to make eighteen tunafish sandwiches (two apiece), which was the only thing everyone would agree to eat, given the disappointment over the Daddy Stew.

The rest of the evening was uneventful— until Mr and Mrs Pike were an hour late getting home. Claudia was exhausted, and Mallory was nearly hysterical, wondering why her parents hadn't called. It turned out that they'd been caught in a traffic jam on the motorway and *couldn't* call.

If any of us club members had any doubts left about the power of the chain letter, the doubts were gone after Claudia and Mal's sitting experience. We were in big trouble, all of us. And it was my fault.

I had brought bad luck to myself, my friends and everyone I knew.

9th CHAPTER

"This," said Kristy sombrely, "is an emergency meeting of the Babysitters Club. You all know why you've been called here."

It was Sunday afternoon. The six main members of the club were in Claudia's room in our usual places. And, yes, we all knew why we had been called there.

Because of me. Because I had tempted fate, thrown away a chain letter, and then been sent a bad-luck charm, which I was forced to wear or else. Not knowing what that "or else" meant was the only thing that kept me wearing the charm. Or else death? Death and destruction? Death, destruction and the end of civilization as we know it? Claudia was afraid it could mean the end of junk food. Who knew? We weren't taking chances. We'd done enough of that already.

"So," said Kristy, "something must be

done about Mary Anne's, um, problem."

(If you'll remember, the chain letter had been met by a lot of scepticism at first. Kristy had been the biggest sceptic of all. She'd had no use for charms or spells or bad-luck wishes. She'd scoffed at it all. Now she was as big a believer in such things as Jessi and Mal were. So were the rest of us.)

"Well," said Mallory, "we've got the books. We'd better start going through them. I think a spell to—to, oh, what's the word?"

"Get rid of the bad stuff?" suggested Claudia.

"No, to counteract—that's it, counteract—the bad-luck charm is our only hope."

"Okay, then let's hit the books," said Kristy. The books had all been left in Claudia's room, much to her dismay. We each took the one we'd checked out of the library and began thumbing through it.

"Hey, Claud," I said, "have you noticed these books doing anything weird? Like flying around the room at night, or glowing in the dark?"

Claudia started to laugh, but Kristy glared at both of us. "You cannot," she told us, "afford to take this lightly. Mary Anne, you got us into this mess, so you sure better help us get out of it."

I felt the way I did when I'd forgotten my maths homework and the teacher scolded me in front of the whole class.

"Sorry," I said.

"Sorry," Claudia said.

Embarrassed silence followed. The five of us went back to our books. Occasionally, somebody would turn a page. There was no other sound in the room.

"This is making me crazy!" Claudia cried after a few minutes. She jumped off the bed, opened one of the desk drawers, and pulled out a packet of Rolos. She made a lot of racket rummaging around in the drawer and even more noise crinkling paper as she opened the bag.

"Rolo anyone?" said our junk-food lover.

Claudia has stuff—candy, crisps, gum, you name it—hidden throughout her room. Her parents don't like her to eat junk food, but Claudia doesn't know what she'd do without it. So she hides it. She's got stuff in drawers, behind cushions, under her mattress, in shoe boxes. She's crazy. But we love her anyway.

We each took a Rolo, except for Dawn, who said it would rot her teeth.

"The rest of you will be wearing dentures when you're ninety," she told us. "But I'll still have all my own teeth."

"If I live to be ninety," said Claudia, "I'll just be glad to be alive, teeth or no teeth. You know—"

Claudia broke off when she realized that Kristy was glaring again.

"Okay, okay, okay," said Claudia.

We stuffed the Rolos in our mouths and got back to work.

"Well," said Jessi after a long time, "here's a spell for turning bad luck to good luck. Maybe that would work."

"Sure!" we cried. We all leaned over to look at Jessi's book. Except for Kristy, who was in the director's chair.

"What does it say?" Kristy asked. "I can't see it from over here. Read it aloud."

"Okay," replied Jessi. " 'To reverse the course of luck, press a white rose between the pages of a book of sorcery. After waiting two months—' "

"White rose!" cried Kristy. "Book of sorcery! Two months! This is not rose season, we don't have a book of sorcery—not a real one—and we can't wait two months."

"Well, ex*cuse me*," said Jessi. "I can't help what the book says.

"Hey!" I exclaimed a moment later. "Here's a love spell!"

"A love spell?" repeated Dawn.

"Yeah, you know, to get a guy you like to fall for you. All you need is a lock of his hair, a fingernail clipping, one of his eyelashes—"

"MARY ANNE!" shouted Kristy, and we all jumped.

"Girls?" called a voice. "Everything all right up there?" It was Mrs Kishi.

"No problem, Mum!" Claudia called

back. Then she looked at Kristy. "Would you calm down? You're being ridiculous. I know this is serious, but just—calm down, all right?"

"All *right*."

Once again, we turned back to our books. I began to have trouble reading mine. "Claud, can we put the light on?" I asked. "It's getting awfully dark in here."

"Sure," replied Claudia. She flicked on a lamp and the overhead light, then glanced out the window. "Gosh," she said. "There's a storm coming. Look at the sky."

Mallory, Jessi, Dawn and I joined Claudia at the window. (Kristy remained planted in her chair.) We gazed out at the gathering clouds. A few seconds later we heard the low rumble of thunder.

"Ooh, creepy," said Mallory.

We returned to the books before Kristy had to waste any more energy on her glares.

"Here's something," said Dawn. "Well, it *might* be something." (A clap of thunder sounded.) "I hope that wasn't a warning," she added, looking toward the sky. "Anyway, this spell doesn't exactly counteract bad luck, but it's supposed to get rid of it."

"Let's hear it," said Kristy.

"Okay. 'On a piece of paper, write your name, your birth date, your zodiac sign, and your lucky number.'"

"So far, so good," said Kristy.

"'Place the paper in an airtight glass

container by an elm tree on the night of a full moon.'"

"We could do that!" said Kristy excitedly.

"'The next morning, open the jar, add two hairs from an ox's tail, scrapings from the underside of a sea snake—'"

"Are you making this up?" I demanded to know.

"Unfortunately not," Dawn answered. She sighed and turned the page.

A streak of lightening cut through the sky outside Claudia's window. Inside, the lights flickered. I could tell we were all getting spooked. But we were more afraid of Kristy, so we kept on reading.

Half an hour went by. Nobody found a single spell—a single spell we could use, that is. Even Kristy was beginning to look bored and frustrated.

"Maybe we're going at this all wrong," I said, closing my book.

"What do you mean?" asked Jessi.

"Well, for one thing, we haven't figured out who sent the bad-luck charm. If we knew who did, maybe we could look up a spell to put on that person. A spell to visit bad luck upon the person. Something like that."

"Who says someone *sent* the charm?" asked Claudia. "It just appeared. That was part of your bad luck for throwing out the chain letter."

"But someone *had* to send it. I mean, it came with the note and everything. The question is—who sent it and why?"

"Hmm," said Kristy. "I see what you mean. Like, is it someone we know? Or is it someone evil and unknown—an evil powermaster, or maybe just an evil force?"

Jessi shivered. "Evil powermaster. You're scaring me, Kristy."

"Sorry."

"It *could* be something like that, though," said Claudia.

"Right," agreed Dawn. "I've read enough ghost stories to know."

CRASH! A huge clap of thunder sounded. Jessi and Mal screamed.

"Mary Anne, did you save the box the charm came in? Or the note that was with it?" asked Kristy.

I shook my head. "No way. I didn't want those things hanging around. Why?"

"They might have contained clues. I mean, clues to who sent the charm."

"Sorry," I said. "They're long gone. I threw them out the day I got the charm."

For a couple of minutes, no one spoke. We watched the storm and the flickering lights. Finally, Claudia said, "This reminds me of last Halloween."

"What does?" I asked.

"Almost everything. Remember all those thunderstorms we had last October? We don't usually have a lot of them in the fall,

215

especially at the end of October. Plus, we were solving another mystery then. The Phantom Phone Caller.

"Oh, yeah!" I said. "That's right. This is kind of weird."

"Who was the Phantom Phone Caller?" Jessi wanted to know.

"Well, it turned out to be Trevor Sandbourne, who had an immense crush on Claudia," I told her. Only we didn't know that at first."

"Trevor and I ended up going to the Halloween Hop," Claudia added. "Hey, did I tell you guys I'm going with Austin Bentley this year?"

"No!" we cried.

"Well, I am. But it's no big deal. I like him okay, but that's all." (Claudia used to have a crush on Austin. Bigger than the one Trevor had had on her.) "Who else is going?" she asked.

"Not me," said Jessi and Mal at the same time. (Their parents wouldn't let them.)

"Not me," said Kristy. "I'm tired of going places with Alan Gray. He's too much of a jerk."

"I'm going, even though no one's asked me," said Dawn. "I'll go alone. Who cares?"

"I guess you're going with Logan, aren't you?" Claudia asked me.

"Yup," I replied.

"Gosh, you are so lucky to have a steady

boyfriend," said Dawn. "Someone you can count on."

"Even better that it's Logan," added Claudia. "Half the girls in our grade would kill to go out with him."

"Really?" I hadn't realized that. "Like who?"

"Like Grace Blume. Talk about immense crushes. I bet she hates you, Mary Anne. She probably hates our whole club for taking up so much of Logan's time."

Ordinarily I might have gloated about that, but what with the storm and the rest of our problems, I couldn't even work up a good gloat. The news about Grace just seemed like more bad luck.

10th CHAPTER

Friday, October 30th.

Halloween Hop night! I couldn't believe it had finally arrived. It seemed like just a day or two ago that Logan and I were having trouble deciding whether to dress nicely for the dance or to dress in costume. But that was actually several weeks ago. Now the decision was long made, and I was in my bedroom putting on my costume and getting nervous.

Logan and I were going to the dance as cats. We had both seen the musical *Cats* and had been very impressed with the wild, furry cat costumes. We'd decided to make our own—a rough, tough tomcat costume for Logan, and a delicate kitten costume for me. They weren't nearly as good as the costumes in *Cats*, but they weren't bad either. Tigger crouched on my bed and watched me solemnly. I had modelled my costume on Tigger. I'd taken a black leotard and a pair of black tights and painted some grey tiger stripes on them, like Tigger's. I was wearing grey-striped gloves on my hands and (plain) black ballet slippers on my feet. I have to admit that Logan and I had cheated a little on one part of our costumes: we'd rented fur headdresses from a costume place in town. But we planned to make up our faces ourselves.

Now, seated before the mirror in my bedroom, wearing the leotard, the slippers, and of course the bad-luck charm, I painted black and grey stripes across my face. Then I put on the gloves and the wild fur headdress. I turned around.

"How do I look, Tigger?" I asked. "Just like you, huh?"

Tigger's eyes grew as wide as plates. He got to his feet and backed away, puffing up his tail. The fur over his spine bristled. He was a Halloween kitty.

I burst out laughing. "It's just me, Tigger, you old 'fraidy-cat."

I reached over to pat Tigger, but he sprang into the air and tumbled off the bed. Even though I felt a little sorry for him, I couldn't help laughing. I ran downstairs to show Dad the costume.

When I appeared in the living room, Dad glanced up from a book he was reading and jumped about five feet.

"Gracious, Mary Anne," he said. "That

is some costume. Especially that fur thing."

I smiled. "Thanks. Sorry I scared you, though. I scared Tigger, too."

"Why are you wearing that necklace?" asked Dad.

"This?" I replied, pointing to the charm. (I didn't touch it. I touched it as little as possible.)

"Yes. It takes away from the costume a little."

"Does it? I don't know. I—I just like it."

"Well, anyway, you are one amazing cat."

Ding-dong!

"That's Logan!" I cried. "He and his mum are here!"

"Have fun, Mary Anne," Dad called as I grabbed my coat from the cupboard. "Be home by ten o'clock—at the latest."

"Okay. Mr Bruno will drive us home. See you later."

I flung open the door and said hello to Logan, and we ran down the front walk to his car. We must have been a pretty funny sight, with our headdresses and all.

I tried to get a look at Logan in the moonlight, which was bright. The next night would be a full moon.

"Logan!" I exclaimed. "Your costume is fantastic!"

Logan had refused to wear tights and a leotard like me (I couldn't blame him), so he had bought a few yards of this cheap furry fabric at a sewing store (he had also refused to go into a sewing store by himself—I had to go with him), and he and his mother had made a fur suit for him. He was wearing a fur top, fur pants and even fur-covered shoes. His hands and face were painted in tiger stripes like mine. And then, of course, he had put on the fur headpiece.

Mrs Bruno started laughing as we got into the car.

"What's so funny?" asked Logan. "The costumes?" He was a little sensitive about them.

"No," his mother replied. "You two look wonderful. It's just that I've never driven anywhere with cat-people in the backseat." (With her southern accent, what she actually said was, "No. You two look wunduhful. It's just that Ah've nevah driven anywhere with cat-people in the backseat.")

Logan and I laughed.

I was feeling fairly relaxed. Normally, dances make me incredibly nervous. They are not the perfect event for a shy person who isn't sure of herself. If you're happy with your hair, your clothes, your face, your body and your personality, then you'll love a dance. But I'm never sure of anything about myself. The first time Logan and I went to a dance was a disaster. Now we've been to several together. Each one gets easier, but I still feel self-conscious. I always think everyone's looking at me. And considering I'm with Logan, maybe they are.

At least I didn't have to walk into that big roomful of people by myself. I hung onto Logan's arm as if it were a life preserver, the dance were a sinking ship, and I didn't know how to swim.

Nothing happened.

We just walked in. Everyone kept doing what they were doing, which was mostly eating. It always takes awhile for the dancing to start, even though that's what you're there for.

I looked around for Dawn and Claudia and Austin. I saw Dawn talking to a group of kids I didn't know very well. She wasn't wearing a costume, but she had smeared green make-up on her face and stuck a plastic wart on her nose. She looked like a young, blonde witch. I told you Dawn is an individual.

"Hi, Mary Anne! Hi, Logan!"

Logan and I turned around. There were Claudia and Austin. They were not in costume either, unless you'd consider Claudia's wild floral outfit, gigantic hair clip, and armload of silver bangle bracelets a costume. Most people would. Claudia didn't.

Austin, who was wearing a suit and tie, looked more like her father than her date.

222

"Hi, you guys!" said Logan.

I just smiled, suddenly feeling shy.

"Great costumes," Claudia said. "Who made up your faces?"

"We did them ourselves," Logan told her.

"Wow!"

Logan and Austin started talking about the JV football team, so Claudia took the opportunity to point out Grace and Cokie to me. They were dressed as punk rockers—really impressive costumes. Unfortunately, they caught us looking at them. Immediately they began whispering behind their hands.

"Those two make me so uncomfortable," I said to Claud.

"Oh, they just think they're better than everyone else."

"Really?" I replied. "That's funny. I always thought *they* thought *we* thought we were better than everyone else."

Claudia grinned. "Well, we are."

I grinned, too.

The band was really picking up by then, and more kids had started to dance. Claudia and Austin joined them. Logan knew it would be a *long* time before I would want to dance, so we wandered over to the refreshment table and loaded up on cakes and stuff.

"You know," I said to Logan, "this is better than dancing, but I do have to admit that it's a *little* embarrassing to know your

English teacher is watching you stand around eating Mr Happy Face cookies."

"While you're wearing a fur head-thing," added Logan.

We finished eating. The band played two fast numbers, a slow number and three more fast ones. When another slow one came on, Logan asked me if I wanted to dance. I could tell he was getting bored, so I said yes. Besides, a slow dance isn't really dancing. It's more like leaning in time to the music. I relaxed against Logan.

We danced and danced. It was an odd experience—dancing next to chickens and gorillas, space creatures and storybook characters, not to mention the usual hoboes and witches and goblins. Someone was even dressed as a stick of gum.

Except for one incident, I felt better about that dance than any other I'd been to. The one incident involved Cokie. She and the boy she was dancing with made their way over to Logan and me, and Cokie suggested switching partners. As we did (to my complete dismay), Cokie leaned over to me and said, "Cute costume. And nice bad-luck charm. It really completes the outfit."

Okay, so Dad was right. The charm took away from the cat costume. I couldn't help that. And I couldn't explain to Cokie why I had to wear it. Only my closest friends knew the reason.

A year ago, a comment like that might have made me burst into tears and run home. But that night, I survived, simply waiting until Logan was my partner again. I didn't even tell him about Cokie's rude comment.

Then Logan and I danced the night away.

An hour and a half later, he and his father were dropping me off at my house. As their car backed down the driveway, horn honking, I ran to the porch, turned around, and waved.

I was just reaching for the doorknob, when I saw it: A note was taped to the door. My name was on the envelope—in those horrid, scary, cut-out letters.

My heart leaped into my mouth, but on the street, the Brunos were waiting to see that I got into the house okay, and in the living room, Dad was probably waiting to see if I'd got home in one piece. So I stuck the envelope in my jacket pocket, let myself inside, flicked the porch lights for Logan and even had a talk with Dad.

I don't know how I managed to wait so long before I read the note, but I did. When I was at last alone (with Tigger) in my bedroom, I opened the envelope. The note was made of cut-out letters. This is what it said:

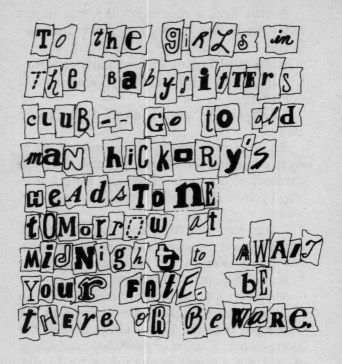

TO THE GIRLS in THE BABYSITTERS CLUB -- GO TO OLD MAN HICKORY'S HEADSTONE TOMORROW AT MIDNIGHT to AWAIT YOUR FATE. BE THERE OR BEWARE.

I shuddered and held Tigger tight. Old Man Hickory's headstone was in Stoneybrook Cemetery. The next day was Halloween. And that night, Halloween night, the moon would be full.

11th CHAPTER

I spent an awful lot of time on the phone the next morning. My father may have relaxed most rules, but one still holds fast—no phone conversation can last longer than ten minutes. Well, that was a tough one. I had to call Kristy, Dawn, Claudia, Jessi and Mallory to tell each of them about the note, and they had *millions* of questions. Each time I'd been on the phone for ten minutes, we'd have to hang up, and then my friend would have to call back.

I really don't know why Dad put up with that (except that he could see that *technically* I was following the phone rule), but I was glad he did. I'd hardly slept a wink the night before. I'd just lain in bed worrying. I jumped at so many harmless sounds and shadows that Tiger finally got fed up with me and mewed to be let out of the room.

Then I was on my own for the rest of the long, spooky night.

I might have been relieved to see morning arrive—especially a Saturday morning—if it hadn't been *Halloween*. Since I was still a nervous wreck, I began calling my friends as early as I dared. That started all the phone calls back and forth. The thirteenth call was from Kristy.

"Hi," she said.

"Oops," I replied. "You know, you're the *thirteenth* call of the morning. That can't be good for you."

"Well, I'm not going to worry about it," Kristy told me. "And I'll put an end to the phone conversations. I am calling an emergency club meeting."

"*Another* one?" I replied. Emergency meetings are supposed to be rare.

"Yes. That note was for *all* the girls in our club, not just you. Well, anyway I think it was for all the regular members. Probably not Shannon. She doesn't come to meetings, anyway. But this is a group matter— a club matter—and it's serious. We're in this mess together, and we'll do something about it together. One-thirty this afternoon in Claudia's room."

"Aye, aye, sir," I said.

I wasn't sure whether Kristy would have thought it was funny that I saluted her.

*   *   *

One-thirty came around awfully slowly. After Kristy called the emergency meeting, the phone stopped ringing. The morning crawled by. Dad didn't know what was wrong. He just thought I was bored and kept suggesting things to do. After I had filled a bowl with sweets for the trick-or-treaters, clipped Tigger's nails, changed the sheets on my bed, and polished some silver, it was lunchtime, thank goodness. Dad and I ate, and then . . . finally . . . I headed over to Claudia's.

I brought the note with me, envelope and all, in case it contained any clues.

Brother, if you thought Kristy was all business at any of the other meetings I've told you about, you should have seen her at Saturday's emergency meeting. I was surprised she wasn't wearing an army outfit or cracking a whip or something. If the graveyard business hadn't been so serious, I might (*might*) have laughed at her.

She was sitting ramrod straight in the director's chair. Her visor was pulled down over her eyes, and two pencils were stuck over her right ear. The club notebook was open in her lap. She was not talking to Claudia. She wasn't doing anything, not even chewing gum. As soon as I came in, she held one hand out for the letter, and gave me the notebook and one of the pencils with her other hand. In case I wanted to take notes, I guess.

229

Claudia and I glanced at each other, then nervously watched Kristy read the note. Kristy let out a low whistle.

"Can I see it?" asked Claud.

Kristy handed it over.

Claudia turned pale as she read it.

Jessi was the next to arrive, and before she even read the note, I thought she was going to pass out from the mere sight of it.

Last to arrive were Dawn and Mallory (who live near each other). They took a look at the note, too, of course, and managed to remain calm, but I could tell they were scared.

All us club members could sense Kristy's nervous, businesslike mood, so when Dawn and Mallory had read the note and returned it to Kristy, we just sat in silence, waiting for Kristy to make the first move.

Kristy got right to the heart of the matter. "We've got to do this, you know," she said. "The six of us have to gather in the graveyard at Old Hickory's at midnight tonight, just like the note says."

"No way!" cried Dawn.

"Um, can I ask a question?" Jessi spoke up. "Who's Old Hickory?"

"Oh, he was this mean old man, James Hickman (his nickname was Old Hickory), who used to live in Stoneybrook," Dawn told her. "He was the richest man in town. Also the stingiest. Also a recluse."

"And what happened to him?"

"They just found him dead in his mansion one day. Some people say he died of old age. Others say he died of meanness. Anyway, he didn't want a big funeral or a gravestone or anything, but this long-lost nephew of his turned up, inherited Old Hickory's fortune, felt guilty and had a gigantic headstone——"

"More like a statue," Claudia interrupted.

"——put up in the graveyard," Dawn continued. "Now it's supposed to be haunted by the ghost of Old Hickory, who's angry about the way he was buried. You know, that his nephew went against his wishes."

Silence.

Finally Jessi said, "And we're supposed to go to a haunted gravestone in a cemetery at midnight on Halloween——when there's a full moon?" She looked incredulous and scared to death.

"I think we better," said Kristy. "We all know what happens when we ignore warnings." She looked meaningfully at me. "Besides, I have a feeling something important is going to take place in the graveyard."

"Yeah, we're all going to die," said Claudia.

Kristy shot Claudia one of her glares. "That is *not* what I mean. I mean, I think there's going to be some sort of, um, confrontation. Everything will get cleared up. So we have to go. But we have to be together on this. We have to be a club, a team. If anyone *isn't* behind me, well, who knows what might happen. So—if you're willing to work with me, to work together, then raise your hand. But you've got to mean it."

Kristy raised her own hand to start things off. Dawn was next. Then Claudia. Slowly, I raised my hand. And at last, Mal and Jessi exchanged sidelong glances and raised their hands.

"Great," said Kristy brusquely. "Thank you. Now, how are we all going sneak out of our houses tonight? I figure we should leave around eleven-thirty."

"Sneak out! Oh, my gosh!" I cried. "I wasn't thinking. I'll never be able to get out of my house at eleven-thirty at night."

"Yes, you will," Kristy told me. "We all will. Think. How could you do it?"

"I don't know. My father's the lightest sleeper in the world. Everything wakes him up. Look up 'Lightest Sleeper' in the *Guinness Book of World Records*. You'll find a picture of Dad."

My friends giggled.

"Well, I won't have a problem," said Dawn. "Mum could sleep through World War Three. All I have to do is walk downstairs and out the front door. She'll never know."

"I share a room!" wailed Mallory. "I'll *never* get out!"

232

"Don't you ever have to get up to go to the bathroom?" asked Kristy.

"Well, yes," replied Mal.

"So if Vanessa asks what you're doing, tell her you're going to the bathroom. She'll probably go right back to sleep."

"Okay. . ."

"I think *I'll* sneak out in stages," said Claudia thoughtfully. "I'll tiptoe to the bathroom, stay there for a while, tiptoe downstairs, stay in the kitchen for a while, then finally just leave."

"That might work," said Kristy. "What about you, Jessi?"

Jessi shook her head. "I don't know, but I'll have to be *real* careful. Mum and Dad had an alarm system put in the house. I'll have to find out how to turn it on and off. And how much time I have to get in and out of the house before I set it off."

Kristy began to look worried.

I knew how to shake her up a little more. "Hey!" I exclaimed. "I think I figured out a way to get out of my house. I just open the window, jump over to that tree branch, and climb down."

"Oh, no!" cried Mallory. "Didn't you ever see that movie *Pollyanna*? The one with Hayley Mills? She falls trying to sneak back into her house and nearly kills herself."

"Whoa," said Kristy. "Forget this idea. Just forget it. Alarm systems, climbing out of second-story windows. You guys were right. This won't work."

Really! I thought. Oh, good!

"I've got another idea," said Kristy.

Darn.

"I know how you can leave your houses pretty late—and *tell* your parents about it."

"How?" asked Claudia, Mal, Jessi, Dawn, and I. We were utterly mystified.

"Say that I'm having a late-night Halloween pyjama party, and that . . . that Charlie will be picking each of you up around ten-thirty and driving you to my house. Then he'll take us to the graveyard instead. Afterward, we really will spend the night at my house. We'll have a pyjama party there, to celebrate, after we've been to the graveyard."

"Celebrate what?" I asked.

"Not being dead," replied Claudia.

"Well, this sounds like a reasonable plan," said Dawn. "Except for one thing. What are we going to do between ten-thirty and midnight?"

Kristy frowned. "Oh, we'll ask Charlie to take us to Seven-Eleven for a snack or something. I'll tell my mum that's part of our party."

Darn. Why does Kristy always have to have such good ideas?

"And," Kristy went on, "Charlie will wait for us while we're in the graveyard. It can't hurt to have a getaway car . . . just in

234

case. Later, he can drive us to my house. And believe me, Charlie can be trusted. He'll help us, and he'll keep the secret. Now do you guys think you can stick to this plan?"

I don't know why, but every last one of us nodded yes. It would have been so easy to say no and not go through with it. But now we were committed.

"Great. Then it's settled," said Kristy. "Charlie and I will pick you up starting around ten-thirty. Be sure to mention the party before then or your parents will never believe you. Then we'll go try to have some fun, and at five to twelve, Charlie will drop us off at the cemetery and wait in the car while we go to Old Hickory's."

"Lucky thing," muttered Claudia.

Kristy's last words before she adjourned the emergency meeting of the Babysitters Club were, *Tell no one about tonight.*"

12th CHAPTER

Saturday - Halloween

There are some things you just never get tired of. Trick - or - treating is one of them. So when Mum and Watson asked me if I'd take Karen, Andrew, and David Michael around the neighborhood, of course I said yes. I hadn't gone trick - or treating since I was eleven, and I kind of missed it.

Anyway, I'd forgotten that trick-or-treating can be a nerve-wracking experience for little kids. It's fun but... it's dark outside, people intend to scare you, and your mind is all cluttered up with thoughts of bats and cobwebs and goblins and who knows what else. So it shouldn't have come as any surprise that my little brother, stepbrother, and stepsister were pretty spooked....

Our emergency club meeting ended in the middle of Halloween afternoon. Kristy had agreed to take David Michael, Karen and Andrew trick-or-treating at five o'clock. She knew they couldn't possibly stay out longer than an hour or two, so she'd have plenty of time to get ready for her spur-of-the-moment pyjama party before she and Charlie had to leave to pick us up.

What Kristy didn't mention in her note-book entry was that she was pretty spooked herself. Her mind was as cluttered as the kids'—only hers was cluttered with thoughts of midnight, full moons, haunted grave-stones, cemeteries and a town meanie nicknamed Old Hickory. While Karen and Andrew worried about rounding a corner and coming face-to-face with a gigantic Raggedy Anne doll or Snoopy dog, Kristy worried about mysterious spells, my weird bad-luck-charm, and who (or what) could possibly have summoned us to the Stoneybrook Cemetery at midnight.

She put her thoughts aside, though, as she helped her charges with their costumes.

"Andrew, are you sure you don't want to wear the mask?" she asked her stepbrother for the third time.

"No! No masks. I don't like them," Andrew said impatiently.

"But Andrew, it *makes* your costume."

"I don't care."

Andrew was going trick-or-treating as

Marvin, this cartoon moose he likes. Without his mask, he just looked like a kid in a brown animal suit. He didn't even have antlers. But Kristy could not convince him to put the mask on.

Karen was dressed as—what else?—a witch.

"Hey, Karen," said David Michael with a wicked grin, "aren't *you* going to put *your* mask on?"

"It *is* on," Karen said witheringly from behind her warty, grayish, pointy-nosed mask.

"Oh, I couldn't tell," said David Michael. He doubled over laughing. "Ha-ha-ha-ha-ha-ha."

"Come *on*, you guys," said Kristy.

"Come on? Where are we going?" asked David Michael innocently.

"*Nowhere*," said Kristy meaningfully, "if you don't settle down."

David Michael closed his mouth. He put his helmet on. He was dressed as a warrior from some Saturday morning adventure show.

"Ready?" Kristy asked the three trick-or-treaters.

Karen began jumping up and down with excitement. "Ready, ready, ready!"

"Buckets?" said Kristy.

Karen, Andrew and David Michael held out their jack-o'-lantern sweet buckets.

"And I've got the torch," Kristy went on.

"Andrew, are you *sure* you don't want to

wear your mask? You'd look a lot more like Marvin with it."

"Very sure," said Andrew, as the four of them started down the stairs to the first floor.

"Should I bring it with me anyway?"

"Nope." Andrew shook his head.

"Okay," said Kristy. Then she yelled toward the kitchen. "Mum! Watson! We're leaving now!"

She and the kids walked out the front door.

"Aughhh!" screamed Karen.

She had run into a ghost.

"Excuse me," the ghost apologized.

"That's okay," Kristy told him. "Don't worry about it. Karen, are you going to scream at every trick-or-treater you see?"

"No," replied Karen, sounding wounded. "Only the ones that surprise me. That ghost surprised me."

Kristy and her brothers and sister made it all the way to the end of the driveway before Andrew tripped over David Michael's homemade sword and fell to the ground.

"Aughhh!" he shrieked.

"Andrew, you're okay," said Kristy. She helped him to his feet, brushing him off.

"No, I'm not," wailed Andrew. "An invisible goblin tripped me."

"My *sword* tripped you," David Michael told him. "And you bent it."

"Oh. Sorry," Andrew replied. He stopped crying.

The kids walked across the street to the home of our associate club member Shannon Kilbourne. Darkness had fallen, and Kristy's little torch and the dim streetlight didn't shine away many of the shadows.

"This is so, so creepy," whispered Karen. She rang the Kilbournes' doorbell. She and her brothers held their buckets out and waited.

The door opened with a creak. A ghoulish face appeared.

"Aughhh!" screamed all three kids. Even Kristy (who'd been thinking about Old Hickory) was startled.

"Oh, I'm *sorry*," said Mrs Kilbourne's gentle voice. "I really didn't mean to frighten you." She lifted her mask.

Andrew glanced over his shoulder at Kristy as if to say, "See what trouble masks can cause?" Then he turned around again.

Mrs Kilbourne dropped a Mars bar into each bucket.

"Thank you," said the witch, the warrior and Marvin.

The kids walked from house to house on the Kilbournes' side of the street. At every door, someone would drop something in their buckets. It was a sugar-feast that would have made Claudia proud.

At one house, a horrible-looking monster was handing out nickels. Andrew was too afraid to take one.

At another house, a princess was handing out peanuts.

"Bor-ring," sang David Michael as they walked away.

They crossed the street. An hour later, their buckets were almost full, and they were standing in front of their own house again.

"There's just one house we've missed," said David Michael.

"Ours?" Karen replied. "You know what Daddy said. We don't get sweets at our own house."

"Not our house—Morbidda Destiny's."

"The *witch's*?" cried Karen. "No way. I'm not going to her house on Halloween."

"Yeah, no way," said Andrew.

"Hey, we've been over there before," David Michael pointed out. "For lemonade. Remember? And nobody died. Anyway, I'm not going to miss a single house on this street. If you're too afraid, then go on home."

Karen and Andrew looked pleadingly at Kristy.

"It's up to you guys," she told them. "If you want to go home, then run next door. I'll be along as soon as David Michael is finished at Mrs Porter's."

"'Fraidy-cats," David Michael whispered.

"Okay, we're coming," said Karen.

She and Andrew each gripped one of

Kristy's hands. David Michael walked boldly in front of them. He marched up the front steps and rang Mrs Porter's bell.

Silence.

"Her house is kind of dark," Kristy said quietly. "Maybe she's isn't at home."

But just then, the door opened a crack.

Kristy gasped. She couldn't see anybody. But a low, eerie voice said, "Hold your buckets out."

Ever so slowly, David Michael, Karen, and Andrew edged their buckets toward the front door. Karen and Andrew never let go of Kristy's hands.

Plop, plop, plop. Something heavy was dropped into each bucket.

"Happy Halloween. Heh-heh-heh," cackled the voice. Then the door closed again.

Kristy shone her torch into the buckets as they hurried down Mrs Porter's steps. "What'd you get?" she asked.

"Apples!" cried the kids in dismay.

"Double bor-ring!" added David Michael.

Well, what do you know? thought Kristy. The witch hands out health food. She smiled to herself. Then her happy thoughts faded. She looked at her watch. Six-fifteen.

Six hours from then we would all be in the cemetery at Old Hickory's grave.

Kristy wasn't sure whether we'd be dead or alive.

13th CHAPTER

I'm not very good at hiding my feelings, or at covering up when something is wrong. This can be quite embarrassing. For instance, I blush a lot when I'm with Logan. And in school, if a teacher criticizes me or my work, I just might start to cry—in front of everybody.

So imagine how difficult it was for me on Halloween evening, trying to pretend that everything was fine—that there was no bad-luck spell and no bad-luck charm, and that in a few hours I wouldn't be hanging around a graveyard like a fool, with five other fools, all of whom could have been in their nice, cosy beds instead of waiting for the angry ghost of Old Hickory to appear.

It was next to impossible.

I was as nervous as Tigger. Every little sound made me jump. Any movement that I caught out of the corner of my eye made me gasp. At dinner, I would have to tell Dad about Kristy's party—but I was sure there wouldn't really be a party that night. I was sure because I knew that my friends and I wouldn't leave the graveyard. Not alive, anyway.

I almost called Logan six different times. I wanted to tell him what was going on, but Kristy's last words at the emergency meeting had been, "*Tell no one about tonight.*" She had spoken as our chairman, and us club members always obey our chairman, at least where really important matters are concerned.

Even so, I knew what we were planning was risky, with or without Charlie and his getaway car. I've read enough Stephen King books to know that you don't go fooling around with the supernatural. And it was just a couple of weeks ago that Dawn had rented this movie called *Night of the Living Dead*, and we'd scared ourselves silly watching it on the Schafers' video. I certainly didn't want to meet any of those living dead in the Stoneybrook Cemetery. Not Old Hickory. Not anyone else.

Then there were all these awful horror movies that had been on TV the past week, and in honour of the actual Halloween, I'd seen *Halloween* and *Halloween II*.

I wouldn't have been a bit surprised if, when the six of us ventured into the graveyard and were looking around for Old

Hickory's tombstone, a clammy hand had reached out from the beyond and—

"Eeeeeiiii!" I screamed, sending Tigger flying. I was sitting in our living room, and a hand really *had* touched me on the shoulder.

"Mary Anne!" exclaimed my father. "What's got into you?"

"Oh. . . Oh, it's you, Dad."

Dad looked like he wanted to say, "Who did you expect?" Instead he said, "Dinnertime." Then he added, "It's just sandwiches. We'll be up and down during the meal, because of the trick-or-treaters."

I nodded. The reason I was sitting in the living room in the first place was because I was on trick-or-treat duty, answering the doorbell and dropping Milky Ways into waiting buckets and bags. It was only six-thirty, and already we'd given away 27 bars.

I followed Dad into the kitchen, trying to figure out how to tell him about Kristy's party. At last, I just blurted it out. As soon as we were sitting down, our sandwiches before us, I said in a rush, "Dad, Kristy's having a pyjama party tonight for the Babysitters Club. It's a late one so that we can, um, all help with the trick-or-treaters first. It was a last-minute idea, which is why I'm telling you now. Oh, by the way, you won't even have to drive me there. Charlie's coming over here to pick us all up. Around ten-thirty. Isn't that nice?"

"Splendid," Dad replied.

"Can I go?"

"*May* I go?" Dad corrected me.

"May I?"

"Of course."

"Oh. Thank you!"

The doorbell rang and I jumped a mile.

After that had happened four more times, Dad finally said, "Mary Anne, please. Tell me what's wrong. Is it Halloweeen jitters?"

"Um . . . yeah. Yeah, it is." That was a good excuse.

"Aren't you a little old for that? You know there aren't any ghoulies or ghosties, long-leggedy beasties, or things that go bump in the night, don't you?"

Well, I really wasn't too sure. So I didn't answer my father. Instead, I pulled the bad-luck charm out from under my sweater. I had made a decision. If my friends and I were done in by Old Hickory . . . or whatever . . . at the graveyard that night, I wanted Dad to have *some* idea of what had happened. I hadn't told Dad anything about my bad-luck mystery, but I wanted him to know, at least, that I had the charm.

"Dad?" I said. "Do you believe in bad luck?"

"Well, I—"

"Because a couple of weeks ago I was at that junk store downtown and I saw this

246

necklace and thought it was really pretty. So I bought it. It only cost, um, a dollar-fifty," I lied. "Anyway, I've been wearing it ever since. But then this girl at school told me it's a bad-luck charm. So I'm really nervous. I've been wearing a bad-luck charm for days and days now."

"Why are you still wearing it?" Dad wanted to know.

Good question.

"I don't know. I guess now I'm afraid to take it off," I said lamely.

"Well, let me see it."

I stood up and walked around the table to Dad. He hadn't really taken a close look at the charm before then. I'd been wearing it under my clothes a lot. The Halloween costume was an exception. If I'd worn it under my leotard, it would have made a lump.

I leaned over, and the charm swung toward Dad.

He fingered it for a moment. Then a smile spread slowly across his face. "Well, I'll be," he said, looking rather fond. (Of the *charm*?)

"What?" I asked curiously.

"My grandmother used to have one of these. This isn't a bad-luck charm, Mary Anne. You know what's inside the glass? It's a mustard seed, which is a symbol of faith."

"*Really*? I—I guess my friend didn't know what she was talking about."

Dad and I cleaned up the kitchen then and continued to hand out Milky Ways. While Dad listened to a jazz station on the radio, I did some thinking. Boy, did I do some thinking. First I thought of Cokie at the dance, and how she was just as big an idiot as the rest of us for believing that my mustard seed was a bad-luck charm. Then I realized that, since none of my friends ever speaks to Cokie, we hadn't *told* her it was a bad-luck charm. For that matter, we hadn't told anyone except Logan, who keeps secrets better than the Pentagon does. So why did Cokie call my necklace a bad-luck charm? How would she know . . . unless she had something to do with it? Suddenly, answers to the mystery began to fall into place as easily as the pieces to a jigsaw puzzle when only five empty spaces are left.

I remembered Grace's enormous crush on Logan, and that Cokie and Grace are best friends. All of a sudden, I was sure I knew who was behind the mystery of the charm, and maybe even why, although I still didn't know why my friends and I had been summoned to the graveyard.

"Dad, may I make a phone call?" I said. "I won't be long."

My father dried his hands on a dish towel. "Sure," he replied. "I'll answer the doorbell."

In the interest of privacy, I used the phone upstairs.

248

I dialled a familiar number. Karen Brewer answered the phone. "Hi, Karen," I said. "It's Mary Anne. Is Kristy there? This is important."

Kristy was on the phone in a flash. "Don't tell me you can't come tonight," she said.

"Oh, I can come all right. Now it's more important than ever that we get to the graveyard. Listen to what I found out: I showed the charm to my father, and it isn't a bad-luck charm at all."

"You mean it's a good-luck charm?" Kristy said incredulously.

"No. It isn't even a charm. And it doesn't have anything to do with luck." I told her what it was. "But you know what?" I went on. "Last night at the dance, Cokie saw the necklace and she called it a bad-luck charm. Now if it isn't really some symbol of bad luck that everyone knows about, and if we never told anybody that we thought it was a bad-luck charm, then why did Cokie call it one?"

"Unless. . ." said Kristy, catching on quickly.

"Right," I replied.

Kristy and I talked much longer than I had intended. That was because Kristy was in the middle of bad-mouthing Cokie and Grace, when suddenly she cried, "Oh! Oh! I'm not sure exactly what's going to go on in the graveyard tonight, but I do have an idea. We've got to talk to the others and tell them what you found out. More important, we have to get to Old Hickory's long before midnight. Charlie can take us there right after he's picked everyone up. Listen, we'll need some things. Bring a mask with you. And a torch. Oh, and some string and a couple of white sheets and. . ."

Kristy was off and running with another of her famous ideas.

14th CHAPTER

Just as planned, Charlie arrived at our house a little after ten-thirty. Kristy was with him, of course, and they had already picked up Jessi and Claudia. As soon as I got in the car, Kristy began making sure I'd brought along the things we'd need.

"Got everything?" she asked.

"I think so."

"Torch?"

"Check," I replied.

"Sheet?"

"Check."

"Mask?"

"Check."

"Great. And I've the tape player."

"I've got two torches, a mask, a sheet and the string," added Claudia.

"Perfect," said Kristy. "We're really going to *get* 'em! . . . Are you scared?"

"Terrified," I admitted. "You?"

"Terrified, too. But there's nothing like a little revenge. . ." Kristy grinned wickedly. Charlie was keeping quiet. He must have thought we were all loony.

"Hey, you didn't tell Logan about this, did you?" Kristy asked suddenly.

"Not on your life. I don't think he'd have let us go to the cemetery without him. He'd want to come along and protect us. Worse, he might have tried to stop us. He might have phoned in an anonymous tip to our parents or something. Even so, not telling him wasn't easy. I tell him almost everything."

"Yeah," said Claudia wistfully. Then she snapped out of it. "Good for you," she said briskly. "I just hope the rest of us can keep this secret. Some of us have pretty big mouths."

We all knew Claudia meant Kristy. Even in the dark, I could see Kristy stick her tongue out at Claudia. But I didn't think Kristy would blow *this*. It was her idea. Too much was at stake. Could Charlie be trusted, though? I sort of wished we hadn't let an outsider in on our plan. Even an outsider with a car.

We stopped at the Schafers' and the Pikes' and picked up Dawn and Mallory. Then we headed for . . . the graveyard.

"Um, excuse me," Mal spoke up at one point, "but I have a problem."

Inwardly, I groaned. We didn't need

any problems. "What is it?" I whispered.

"Well, my brothers and sisters and I always hold our breaths when we go by graveyards. I'm not positive about this, but I think it's so that we won't breathe in any souls of dead people and get possessed. Once when we were out with our father, he parked the car in front of a graveyard while he mailed a letter. We all nearly turned blue. But now we're going to be *in* a graveyard for at least an hour. And I can't hold my breath for more than a couple of minutes."

Everyone tried not to laugh, although Charlie wasn't very successful.

"Mal, I understand that you're worried," I told her, "but I have gone by graveyards a million times and never held my breath. I've walked around *in* graveyards and never held my breath. And to my knowledge, no soul has ever possessed me."

"I've never held my breath, either," said Dawn and Claudia.

"I used to," Jessi admitted. "But when I stopped, nothing happened. Nothing happened when I stopped saying 'Rabbit, rabbit,' on the first day of a new month, either. I don't think you need to worry, Mal."

"Right. Worry about this," said Dawn. "We've just reached the graveyard."

"Pull up over there," Kristy commanded Charlie, "and wait for us.

Remember everything I told you. Be prepared to go for help, okay?"

"You girls are crazy," was Charlie's only reply.

"Now, said Kristy, facing the rest of us like our gym teacher. "On to Old Hickory's."

Kristy wanted us to march to the tombstone in a line, but nobody wanted to be either first or last, so we went in a huddle. We tiptoed through the silent, moonlit cemetery, passing stark white tombs and every now and then a bunch of flowers or a wreath of greenery.

"Here it is," I said after we'd walked halfway across the cemetery.

"Here?" squeaked Jessi. "In all these trees? It's pitch black! Why are there trees here?"

"Old Hickory's nephew planted them. More stuff his uncle didn't want, but he went ahead and put them in anyway," Claudia said.

"Okay. Enough talk. Get to work, you guys," ordered Kristy. "We better rig up the ghosts first."

It was surprisingly easy. We stretched a length of twine from the top of Old Hickory's tomb to a tree branch not far away. Claudia and I had each sewn a curtain ring to the middle of the sheets we'd brought along. We attached the ring of one sheet to the tree-end of the twine and left the "ghost" up in the tree. We hung the other "ghost" from a branch of a second tree in the clearing.

Altogether, the six of us had six rubber masks, seven torches and Kristy's tape player, not to mention the ghosts. Kristy played us a sample of her Haunted House sound-effects tape. My hair nearly stood on end.

Kristy was just rewinding the tape when Dawn said, "SHH! I heard something."

We stood stock-still, listening.

Not a sound.

Kristy checked her watch. "It's eleven twenty-five," she whispered. "Even if that sound wasn't them, we should probably get to our posts. I bet they'll be along any minute now."

"Our posts?" Mal repeated.

"Yeah. This is very important. Listen." Kristy gave out a bunch of orders. When she had finished, we scattered. I put on my mask, grabbed my torch and hid behind Old Hickory's tombstone with the tape player.

I was squashed up against the grave— on Halloween, near midnight, under a full moon. I had just proved something. Charlie was right. We really were crazy.

Kristy, also wearing a mask, climbed the tree to the ghost that was attached to the twine. Claudia handed a torch to her.

Dawn hid with the other ghost, holding

her torch and wearing a mask.

Claudia, in charge of lighting, hid behind another tree. She was holding two torches and wearing a mask.

Jessi and Mal crouched beside other tombstones, each wearing a mask, each carrying a light.

Then we waited.

We waited and waited and waited. It seemed like forever. When I dared to flick on my light long enough to read my watch, I saw that it was only 11.32.

That was when we heard the voices.

None of us said a word. We didn't have to. We knew what we were supposed to do.

The voices came closer. They grew louder. Just as I had suspected, they belonged to Cokie, Grace and maybe three or four of their friends.

We didn't wait much longer. Up in the tree, Kristy let out a low whistle. It sounded like a bird call. That was our signal. (The other girls never even noticed it.)

I turned on the tape player—full blast.

Claudia began shining her torches around in weird patterns.

Kristy shone *her* light on the ghost in the tree and let him loose. He glided right down to Old Hickory's tombstone, where I caught him.

"Aughh! Aughh!" shrieked Grace.

"Help!" Cokie screamed.

But we weren't finished.

Dawn turned her light onto the second ghost, the one hanging from the other tree, and Jessi and Mal stepped from behind the graves, each holding her mask in front of her face with the torch lighting it up from behind. It was a pretty horrible spectacle— even for me, and I knew about the "special effects."

One of Cokie's friends was standing as still as a corpse and crying softly, "Oh help, oh help, oh help," over and over again. The others looked like they were getting ready to run away.

"Now!" ordered Kristy.

She jumped out of the tree, and the six of us surrounded Cokie and Grace and the others. We were all holding flashlit masks before our faces. Really—I'm surprised nobody had a heart attack.

The next few moments were pure panic and confusion. The other girls tried to run away, but we wouldn't let them. At last we put down our masks. The girls got a look at us.

"*You!*" exclaimed Cokie, taking everything in. "You little sneaks!"

"Us? Sneaks?" said Kristy innocently. "Look at you guys."

For the first time I noticed that Cokie's crowd wasn't empty-handed. They were also carrying sheets and masks and stuff.

"Is this what was supposed to happen?" spoke up a new voice. It was a male voice.

"Charlie!" Kristy shouted angrily. "I told you to stay in the car!"

But it wasn't Charlie who stepped into the clearing. It was Logan.

I was thoroughly confused.

"Logan?" I asked incredulously.

"Mary Anne?" he replied, just as incredulously.

"Somebody better explain what's going on here," said Dawn.

"Well, it won't be me," said Cokie, smirking.

"Or me," said Grace and the others.

"Then I'll talk," Logan cut in. (Cokie groaned.) "I was eating this nice, pleasant dinner tonight," he began, "when the phone rang. This voice told me to go to some grave in the cemetery at midnight tonight if I wanted to see something really amazing. Well, I'm curious and I like a little adventure, so I decided to go. Only I left early because I had no idea where the grave—Ol' Hiccup's or something—was. But when I got to the cemetery, who did I see, but Charlie Thomas, and he directed me to the grave and I found my good friends" (Logan sauntered over to me and put his arm across my shoulder) "scaring the pants off *these* guys. Boy, are you cowards," he said to Cokie and Grace.

Grace looked absolutely crestfallen.

But not Cokie. "Talk about cowards," she said, "your girlfriend here was scared to death of the necklace we sent her, just because we said it was a bad-luck charm."

"So you *did* send it!" I exclaimed. "The chain letter, too?"

"What chain letter?" Cokie replied. She looked blank. I knew that the girls really *hadn't* sent it.

"But why?" asked Claudia. "Why did you send Mary Anne the charm and ask us to come here tonight?"

"Why do you think?" snapped Cokie.

"Believe me, if we had the vaguest idea," said Kristy, "not only wouldn't we be asking you, but we wouldn't be standing around in this graveyard in the middle of the night."

Cokie crossed her arms. Everything about her said, "I'm not talking."

But Grace spoke up. "Oh, we might as well tell them." (She said *them* as if she were referring to a swarm of flies.) "We just wanted to make you—all of you, but especially Mary Anne—look like, well, like jerks. We kind of wanted Logan to get fed up with you. . ." Grace's voice was fading away. It was hard to tell in the darkness, but I think she was blushing.

"Fed up?" Logan repeated, only he really said, "Fayud up?"

"Yeah." Grace kicked at a stone with the toe of her trainer. "You spend most of your time with Mary Anne and the girls in the Babysitters Club. There are other girls at

Stoneybrook Middle School, you know."

"Of course I know," replied Logan. "I'm not blind. And when I see anyone I like as much as Mary Anne and her friends, maybe I'll do something. But right now Mary Anne is—is my. . ."

Now Logan and I were blushing. I think he wanted to say *girlfriend*.

"Plus, I *like* babysitting," Logan finished up.

"So there," Kristy said to Cokie. She turned to the rest of us. "Come on. Let's go. Charlie's waiting." She turned back to Cokie and the others. "We'd offer you a ride," she said sweetly, "but the car's full. See you in school on Monday."

"Oh. Oh, you're not, um, going to tell anyone about this . . . are you?" asked one of Cokie's friends nervously.

"Who? *Us?*" I replied.

And Logan just said, "Maybe, maybe not," and smiled smugly.

Then my friends and I gathered up our equipment and walked off.

15th CHAPTER

At Kristy's house later we laughed so hard that her mother had to come into her bedroom twice to ask us to quiet down. She wasn't mean about it or anything, but she did point out that there were seven other people plus a cat and a dog in the house who were trying to sleep.

However, in Kristy's room were six people who were so relieved they were nearly hysterical.

"It's over! My bad-luck mystery is over!" I said, after Mrs Brewer left for the second time. I tried to keep my voice down.

Kristy's room is gigantic. (Well, it *is* in a mansion. I hope I get to live in a mansion someday. Or at least in New York City.) Kristy's bed is gigantic, too. It's so big that four of us—Kristy, Jessi, Mal and I—were sitting on it with room to spare. (That room was taken up by a large bowl of popcorn, an unsteady tray of drinks and our masks.) On the floor, Claudia and Dawn were lying on top of some sleeping bags. (We hadn't even needed to bring our sleeping bags to Kristy's, since the Thomases and Brewers have eight altogether.)

Ever since we got back from the grave-yard we'd been giggling, eating, trying our masks on again (turning out the lamps, shining the torches behind the masks, and screaming), reliving the adventure in the graveyard and talking about my mystery.

"I was so surprised when Logan showed up," said Dawn. "I know this is really awful, Mary Anne, and I'm sorry, but when I first saw him, I thought—just for a split second—that he was in on whatever Cokie and Grace were up to."

"Don't apologize," I told her. "That crossed my mind, too."

"Boy, we really got them!" cried Kristy, gloating. "We really scared them."

It was one-thirty, and not one of us was sleepy. We could only talk about the night and the mystery.

I took a handful of popcorn from the bowl. "You know," I said, "now that the mystery is over, I think I'll keep wearing the ch—I mean, the necklace. It really isn't a charm. And knowing that it's a symbol of faith, well, I don't know. I just like it. It reminds me of Logan and me. We're faithful. Especially Logan. He's been very faithful to me."

Jessi was frowning.

"What is it?" I asked her.

"Something's bothering me," she said slowly.

"What?"

"Something Cokie said in the cemetery. Only . . . I can't quite remember."

Jessi looked so serious that we all stopped to think.

"Do you remember what she was talking about?" Mal asked Jessi.

Jessi shook her head. "No, I just remember thinking that the mystery wasn't solved after all."

"Well, let's see," I said. "We know that Cokie and Grace sent the necklace. And they were going to try and scare us at Old Hickory's tonight, so they left the letter on my front door, too."

"Weren't Cokie and Grace both at the dance last night?" asked Dawn. "How could they have left the letter?"

"Well, then one of their friends must have done it. Anyway, they were behind it. And it was probably Cokie who phoned Logan tonight. What else is there?" I asked. "The mystery's solved. We don't even have to worry about spells and bad luck anymore."

"*That's* it!" exclaimed Jessi. "I knew something was wrong. It's the bad luck.

The chain letter. Cokie said she didn't send it."

"I think she meant it, too. She looked confused," I added.

"And," Jessi continued, "the chain letter started the mystery. If Cokie and her friends didn't send it, who did?"

A hush fell over Kristy's room.

"A better question," I went on, "is— would Cokie and Grace have done what they did if I hadn't broken the chain?"

"Huh?" said Claudia.

"I mean," I said slowly, trying to think of how to explain my new fear, "maybe there *is* good and bad luck after all. Maybe Cokie and Grace were my bad luck. If I hadn't broken the chain, maybe they'd never have sent the necklace to me or tried to trick us or anything."

"Whoa," said Kristy under her breath.

"Remember?" said Dawn. "Our bad luck started as soon as Mary Anne threw away the chain letter—which was before Cokie and Grace sent the necklace."

Dawn and Claudia exchanged a frightened look. In an instant, they had moved the popcorn, masks, and soda to the floor, and squeezed onto Kristy's bed with the rest of us club members.

"I wonder how long bad luck lasts," said Mallory.

"Maybe we need a spell after all," I added. "Where are our library books?"

"I had to return them," Claudia replied. "They were overdue."

"Well, let's try to remember some of the spells," I said.

"Oh, please," said Kristy. "No. Not that again."

"We have to . . . don't we?" I asked.

"We do not," Kristy replied sharply. "Well, hey—we could make up our own spell."

"We could?" asked the rest of us.

"Sure, why not?"

"Because we don't know magic, that's why," said Mal.

"Oh, who cares? All we need is, like . . . Mary Anne, pull out one of your eyelashes for me—"

"No way!"

"Better yet," Kristy went on, "go get Boo-Boo. We'll take a sample of his fur."

Get *Boo-Boo*? I thought. Boo-Boo was crazy. I'd be taking my life in my hands. "Why don't I just go get scrapings from the underside of a sea-snake?"

My friends began to laugh. I put the popcorn back on the bed. The pyjama party felt more like a pyjama party again.

"You know," I said, "when you think about it, even if bad luck really was visited upon us when I threw out the letter, I think it's over now. I mean, those of us who went to the dance had fun. And we pulled a good trick on Grace and Cokie. Our luck is changing."

"I got an eighty-five on a maths test," said Claudia. "And Stacey straightened everything out with her father." Claudia pulled a make-up kit out of her overnight bag, and I began playing with her compact.

"I found my lost watch!" said Kristy with a grin.

"I don't have to get braces for six more months," Mal told us.

"My brother's getting A's in his new school in California," said Dawn.

"My ballet teacher told my parents I'm one of her best students ever," added Jessi.

"Then it's over," I told my friends. "No matter where the chain letter came from, just like I said before—the bad-luck mystery is over."

"We can stop being witches and go back to being babysitters," said Kristy.

I opened Claudia's compact. I closed it. It had a nice clasp.

Claudia handed me a jar of eye shadow. "Here. Try putting this on," she said.

I opened the compact again. And then—I dropped the jar of eye make-up. It landed on the compact.

It broke the mirror.

"Uh-oh," I said.

And Jessi, wide-eyed, added, "Oh, no, Mary Anne. You know what that means, don't you? Seven years of bad luck!"

"No! Really?" I cried, but I was laughing. "Well, I can take it. I've decided that since my mustard seed is a symbol of faith, we're protected . . . Because I have *faith* that we're protected. So, go ahead, you guys. Break all the mirrors you want!"

STACEY'S MISTAKE

This book is in honour of
the birth of my new godson,
Andrew Cleveland Gordon.

1st CHAPTER

Dear Stacey,

Hi! Iám so, so exited! I cannot wait to see you. I realy didn't belive that the frist time we got to see each other again woud be in new york. Just five more days and we'll be their. Iám bringing lots of speding money. Can we go to ~~that~~ ~~store~~ that big huge depratment store. And lets go to some art musims or at least one. I can't wait!

Luv ya!
Claudia

It could only happen in New York. Only in New York could you be sitting in the middle of your absolutely gorgeous blue-and-white bedroom reading a postcard, and see a gigantic cockroach sneak out from behind the dressing table and have the nerve to run right across the rug and disappear under the cupboard door. In any other place, a cockroach would have the good sense to stick to yucky places like laundry rooms or greasy kitchens. But in New York, they get really bold and start invading bedrooms.

My first thought, after he disappeared into the cupboard was, Oh, how disgusting. Now do I have to go and *look* for him? My second thought was, I hope my friends don't see him (or any of his buddies) when they visit this weekend. My friends live in Connecticut, and the worst insect they've ever seen is a bee. A cockroach would freak them out. (I left the cockroach alone in the cupboard. There was no way I was going after him!)

If I'd known what was going to happen when my friends came, I might have taken the cockroach as a bad sign, a sign that the weekend was going to be a mistake. (Do you have *any* idea what I'm talking about? You must be pretty confused by now, so I'd better give you the background to this story.)

For starters, I'm Stacey McGill. I'm thirteen years old and I live in New York City. I've lived here all my life, except for last year. Last year, my parents and I moved to Stoneybrook, Connecticut, which was where I met these friends I've been talking about. My friends are Claudia Kishi (she's the one who wrote the postcard), Kristy Thomas, Mary Anne Spier and Dawn Schafer. The five of us had a great business called the Babysitters Club. But after only a year (well, a year and a couple of months) in Stoneybrook, my mum and dad and I moved back to New York. (These moves have to do with Dad's job, and the explanations for them aren't too interesting.)

I have to admit that I wasn't very upset at the idea of moving back to New York. I've always loved the city, and I missed it when we were in Connecticut. Believe me, *I really* minded the idea of leaving my new friends, but I was thrilled to be getting back to such a bustling, busy place. I love people and shops and shopping and museums and restaurants and theatres. I don't love cockroaches, but I'll take one or two of them any day over the quiet of Stoneybrook. Stoneybrook is a very pretty little place with nice people, but if you want excitement, you have to drive all the way to Washington Mall, outside Stamford, which just does not live up to Fifth Avenue.

Anyway, I had moved back to New York, and my friends and I hadn't seen each other for a while. Claudia and I had just been starting to talk about my visiting Stoneybrook for a weekend, when something happened.

That something was Judy.

I don't know Judy's last name. She's the homeless woman who lives on our street. (Some people call her a tramp.) Now I bet you're wondering about something. You've heard me mention a cockroach in my bedroom and a tramp on my street. Just where in New York do I live? You're probably asking yourself. Well, I live in a very nice neighbourhood on the Upper West Side. As I said before, New York cockroaches live *everywhere*—and lately, so do homeless people. Homelessness is a serious problem in New York. There are thousands and thousands of people like Judy. Some of them live in shelters or welfare hotels, some live in underground stations or railway stations and some actually live on the street. Judy is one of the ones who actually live on the street. She sleeps in doorways or on top of grates where warm air blows up from the underground. She gets her food from rubbish bins or begs for handouts.

It is not a nice life.

I see Judy at least twice a day (when I go back and forth between my nice, comfortable block of flats, complete with doorman, and my nice, comfortable private school),

274

and I have an idea of what her life is like. Although I'm sure you can't completely understand homelessness until you've experienced it.

What I see when I see Judy is a woman who looks a lot older than she really is. (She looks about a hundred, but Dad says she's only forty-two. I don't know how he knows this.) I see a woman who owns so few things that she won't part with any of them. And I mean, she hangs onto empty tin cans, bottle caps, newspapers and used plastic cups. She carries her stuff around in old, wrinkled, falling-apart shopping bags. She's a walking rubbish dump—but that stuff we'd call rubbish is her life. I see a woman who is almost always hungry, who has huge sores on her legs, whose hair is matted, and whose face and hands are permanently red from being exposed to the sun, wind, heat and cold.

Judy and I couldn't be more different. Yet we're friends. Well, sort of. When Judy is in a good mood, we smile and say hello to each other. Judy calls me Missy. When she's not in a good mood, which is often— watch out! Judy will stand on the pavement and just shout for hours. She screams and yells, then finally she quietens down and mumbles crossly. When she's in those moods, she doesn't call me Missy. She doesn't call me anything. I don't think she even recognizes me.

So what does Judy have to do with my friends' visit to New York? Well, it's like this: The people in our street who see and hear Judy every day began to get worried about her. They decided that it was time for them, plain old ordinary citizens, to see what they could do to help Judy and other homeless people in the neighbourhood. So they organized a big meeting that was to be held for an entire Saturday afternoon. Most of the adults in my block of flats (including Mum and Dad) were eager to go. Which meant that a lot of kids were going to need babysitters. Remember the Babysitters Club I belonged to in Stoneybrook? Well, I tried to carry the club back to New York with me, except that I'm the only member of the city branch. For some reason, most of my friends here don't seem interested in sitting. On the one hand, this is nice, because there are plenty of little kids in my block of flats, so I get lots of jobs. On the other hand, I have to turn down lots of jobs, too, and I always feel bad about that. Besides, I miss the meetings our club used to hold.

Well, anyway, a total of five sets of parents rang me a whole month in advance to ask me to babysit on the afternoon of the big meeting. I felt bad about turning four of the families down, especially when the parents were all going to be in the same place at the same time. If only—

And that was when I got my brilliant idea.

"Mum! Mum!" I called.

I ran into our kitchen. As New York flats go, ours is fairly large. The clue that you have a large flat is if you can actually eat in your kitchen. If you've got room for a table and chairs in there, it's a big flat. And our kitchen had room for a table and chairs.

That was where I found my mum—sitting at the table. She was paying bills. I wasn't sure if bill-paying time was the right moment to approach her with my idea, but I decided to risk it.

"What is it, honey?" Mum replied.

I sat down opposite her. I explained the babysitting situation. Then I said carefully, "Um, remember when Kristy's mother got remarried?"

"Yes?" Mum looked a little confused.

"Remember how the Babysitters Club took care of those fourteen children all week before the wedding?"

"Yes?"

"Well, I was thinking. All in all, there are ten kids in the five families that asked me to sit. If my friends were here, we could easily take care of the kids for just one afternoon. And I'm dying to have Claudia and everyone to stay. They could come for the weekend. What do you think?"

"Four guests?" said Mum thoughtfully. "That seems like a lot of people. It would be fine if it were just Claudia, but—"

"Please? In a way it will help Judy."

"Do you think you're up to it?" asked Mum.

"Of course! I haven't been sick for ages." (I have diabetes, and Mum and Dad worry about me a lot, but recently, as long as I've stuck to my diet and given myself the insulin injections, I've been fine.)

"Well," said Mum, "it's okay with me, but you'll need your father's permission, too."

"Thanks, Mum!" I cried. I gave her a kiss. Then I waited for Dad to come home from work. I pounced on him the second he stepped through the door.

"Please, please, please?" I said, after I'd explained everything.

Dad adjusted his glasses. At long last he said, "All right."

My parents didn't seem too excited then, but you should have seen them a few days later. They told me I could take that Friday off school. This was because it turned out that my friends had that Friday off since there was a teachers' meeting in Connecticut, so they had a three-day weekend. Mum and Dad said that as long as they were coming into the city—their first trip to New York without their parents (and Dawn's first trip ever)—they might as well get the most out of it.

Then my parents even suggested that I give a party on Friday night so that my Connecticut friends could meet my New

York friends. I couldn't believe my good luck. What a weekend the five of us would have—three days in the city, a party and a babysitting adventure.

Claudia and I phoned each other and wrote constantly as the weekend approached.

"What should I wear in New York?" Claud asked once.

"What you wear in Connecticut," I told her.

"*Exactly*?"

"Believe me, you see *everything* in the city. Once I saw someone dressed as Batman."

"Maybe it *was* Batman," said Claudia, giggling. "But really. What will your friends wear to the party?"

We weren't getting anywhere. "Wear your black outfit. That really cool one," I told her. Claudia has incredible clothes. And I wanted her to wear an outfit that was sleek and black and covered with silver stars and sparkles.

"Oh, okay," said Claud. "Boy, I am so excited! I don't think I can wait two more weeks. How can I wait two weeks?"

I didn't know. I was dying of excitement myself.

But the two weeks passed—somehow— and finally it was Friday morning, and time for me to get in a taxi and meet my friends at Grand Central Station.

2nd CHAPTER

Dear Stacey,
  I can't wait! I can't wait!
I can't wait! New York, here I
come! I've been reading everything
I can find about New York.
Please can we eat at Serendipity,
or maybe at the Hard Rock Cafe,
if we can get in there? Do you
think we'll see anyone famous?
Does anyone famous live in
your block of flats?
Is your block on the route of
the Macys Thanksgiving Day
parade? Just curious.
                   See you soon!
                   Love,
                     MaryAnne

Obviously, Claudia and I weren't the only ones excited about my friends' trip to New York. Mary Anne was nearly frantic. The thing about Mary Anne and New York is that, if this is possible, she has a crush on the city. I'm serious. She's starstruck. She feels the same way about New York that most kids feel about their favourite film star or rock group. And coming to New York at thirteen without her dad (she'd been here before, but it's different when your father's dragging you around) was for Mary Anne like getting the opportunity to *meet* her idol.

I thought about that as I put my coat on and left our flat that Friday morning.

"'Bye, Mum!" I called.

"'Bye, Honey! Say hi to everyone for me."

And have fun and be careful, I thought.

"And have fun and be careful!" she added.

It never fails. Mum *always* says that as I leave the flat. Sometimes I try to escape before the words leave her lips, but so far, I haven't been able to.

In the hallway, I pressed the "down" button and waited for the lift to arrive. Then came the stomach-tossing ride to the lobby. Our lift doesn't just rise and fall, it zooms.

The doors opened and I crossed the lobby, calling hello to Lloyd and Isaac, who were on duty at the desk, and thanking

James, who held the door open for me. Some people think I'm spoiled, living in a building with a doorman, but I'll tell you something, I just feel safe. I like doormen for security. (But it *is* nice to have someone to hold the door open for you when your hands are full.)

I left our block of flats and walked up the street to Central Park West, where I hailed a taxi. Mum gives me the money for a taxi every time I'm going more than ten feet away from the flat, unless I'm going to be with a group of people. She doesn't like me walking around the city alone, or even taking the bus or underground alone. I can't tell if she's being overprotective or just sensible. In a big city like New York, you really can't be too careful.

I closed the door of the taxi. "Grand Central Station, please," I told the driver.

He didn't say anything. (Cabbies hardly ever do.) He just pulled the taxi into the traffic.

I settled back in the seat and thought about the friends I would see soon. In a way, it's surprising that the five of us are friends, because we're so different. Or maybe that's *why* we're friends. Isn't there some old saying about variety being the spice of life? And opposites attracting? If we were alike, we'd probably be really boring and not at all interested in each other. Well, there isn't any danger of that. Let me tell you a little about the friends I was going to meet. I'll start with Kristy Thomas, since she's the chairman of the club.

If I thought the last year of my life (moving from New York to Connecticut and back again) had been crazy, wait till you hear about Kristy's. Kristy, Claudia and Mary Anne used to live in the same neighbourhood. Kristy's house was next door to Mary Anne's (the two of them are best friends), and across the street from Claudia's. At the beginning of seventh grade (last year), Kristy had this idea for starting a babysitting service in her neighbourhood. She saw how long it sometimes took her mother to find a sitter for David Michael, Kristy's little brother. If Kristy and her big brothers weren't available, her mum sometimes had to make four or five phone calls before she found someone who was free. So Kristy teamed up with Claudia, Mary Anne and me, and we formed the Babysitters Club. (Dawn joined us later.) We'd meet three times a week, and parents would ring us while we were meeting. The great thing about this arrangement was that parents could reach four sitters with just one phone call, so they were practically guaranteed a sitter. No more phoning the whole world.

This was Kristy's idea, and it was brilliant. That's one thing Kristy is known for— her brilliant ideas. She has them all the time. The other thing she's known for is her mouth. She can't keep it closed and sometimes it gets her in trouble. I really hoped Kristy would behave herself in New York and not do or say anything embarrassing. But I couldn't count on that. Kristy is a little immature. She even *looks* immature. She's small for her age, and she doesn't pay much attention to her clothes. In fact, she almost always wears the same kind of outfit: jeans, sweater and running shoes.

What about Kristy's crazy year? Well, ever since she was little, Kristy had lived with her two older brothers, Sam and Charlie, David Michael, who's seven now, and her mum, who was divorced. But when Mrs Thomas decided to marry Watson Brewer, a millionaire she'd been dating, Watson moved Mrs Thomas and her family across town to his mansion. Kristy not only lives in the lap of luxury, but she inherited a stepsister and stepbrother whom she adores, and of course, Watson, her stepfather. What a change for her! (I'm making it sound better than it is. Kristy is still getting used to having been uprooted, and to her new home and neighbours and neighbourhood.)

Claudia Kishi is the club's vice-chairman. She's also my best friend. Well, she's my Connecticut best friend. I have a New York best friend, too—Laine Cummings. She'll be at the party tonight, and she and Claudia will meet for the first time. Claudia is the vice-chairman because the girls always hold their meetings in her bedroom. They chose her room because she has a private phone and a private phone number. During meetings, when lots of calls for jobs come in, the girls don't keep any line but Claudia's busy. This is important.

I know I said that all the girls in the club are different, but there *are* some similarities between Claudia and me. The two main ones are our taste and the fact that we are (face it) sort of sophisticated. At least, we're more sophisticated than Kristy, Mary Anne and Dawn are. We both love clothes and wear trendy outfits like short skirts and baggy sweaters. And we both like to do things with our hair. I used to get mine permed, but I don't do that anymore. I let it grow out, and now it's just thick and fluffy and blonde. You should see Claud's hair, though. She's Japanese-American and has long, silky black hair. And boy, does she go out of her way to do special things to it. For instance, she'll part it down the middle, fix one side in three or four plaits and let the other side fall loosely over her shoulder. Also, she's always experimenting with hair clips and bows and headbands. Jewellery, too. To cap it all, Claudia is just plain gorgeous, with dark, almond-shaped eyes and a creamlike complexion. She has never once had a spot, and probably never will. Claud's hobbies are art (she's really talented), and reading mysteries. Unfortunately, she's a terrible pupil, as you could probably tell from her postcard.

The secretary of the Babysitters Club is Mary Anne Spier, and she has a big job. She's the one who has to keep the club record book up to date. Kristy insists that the club members, in order to run the business professionally, write a summary of every job they go on. The summaries are recorded in the club notebook. Mary Anne also has to keep up the record book. The most important pages in the record book make up the appointment calendar. There, Mary Anne arranges the sitting jobs. She is careful and neat and rarely makes a mistake.

Although they're best friends, Mary Anne and Kristy are very different. They may both be fairly small for their age (and they even look alike with their brown hair and brown eyes), but the similarities end there. Kristy is loud and a bit cynical; Mary Anne is quiet and shy, dreamy and sensitive (she cries easily). She may even be a little romantic. She's the only one of us to have a steady boyfriend. (His name is Logan Bruno.) And her family is certainly different from Kristy's. While Kristy's was big even before Mrs Thomas married Watson

Brewer, Mary Anne has just her dad and her kitten, Tigger. Mrs Spier died when Mary Anne was really young. Mr Spier used to be incredibly strict with Mary Anne, but over the past year, he's loosened up a lot. Now Mary Anne has stopped wearing the jumpers and kilts and loafers her father used to choose for her, and has started wearing more trendy clothes. She's branched out in terms of friends, too. She and Dawn are very close, and then there's Logan. Mary Anne would *never* have had a boyfriend last year. . .

The other person coming to New York was Dawn Schafer. Dawn is now the treasurer, which used to be my job. Dawn had been a sort of substitute officer (we called her an alternate officer) before I moved, so she easily filled my position. (In case you're wondering, when I left the club, the girls replaced me with two sixth-graders, junior officers named Mallory Pike and Jessi Ramsey. They weren't coming to visit because I didn't know Mal that well and I didn't know Jessi at all. Also, their parents wouldn't have let them come.) The treasurer's job is to keep track of the money the club members earn, and to collect weekly subs, which are spent on club supplies and other things we need.

Dawn was not an original member of the club. She moved to Connecticut from California about four months after Kristy started the club. She moved because her parents got divorced, so this past year has been a crazy one for Dawn, too. Besides having to adjust to life without her father, she had to get used to the East Coast, especially to cold weather. She had to start at a new school in the middle of a year, and make new friends, and her mum had to find a job.

She's fitting in pretty well now, but her brother, Jeff, is finding it tough. He keeps getting into trouble at school, which is difficult for Dawn's mum. But Dawn seems happy enough. She's very close to her mother. Besides—she's got the Babysitters Club!

Dawn is an individual. She's a health-food freak. She does things her own way and doesn't care what people think of her. I suppose that means she has a lot of self-confidence. And she really stands out in a crowd. Her hair falls all the way to her waist and is so blonde it's almost white. Her eyes are a clear, pale blue. I remember feeling practically speechless the first time I saw her.

The more I thought about my friends, the more eager I became to see them. But the taxi was just crawling along. We seemed to be approaching a traffic jam at Columbus Circle. There was nothing to do but settle back and wait.

So I did. When we *finally* reached Grand

Central, I paid the cabbie and scrambled out of the taxi.

In a few minutes, the members of the Babysitters Club would be reunited!

3rd
CHAPTER

Dear Karen and Andrew,

Hi, you guys! How was your weekend? Did you have fun with your mum? I'm on the train to New York with my friends. What a time we're having. There's a buffet car on the train where you can get snacks and lemonade and stuff. We've been there twice already. Our seats are great. We feel like we're on a plane. There are lights overhead that you can turn on and off, and the seats move back and forth. When we get to Grand Central Station in New York City, we'll meet Stacey!

I love you!
— Kristy

290

Meet Stacey? Ha. Kristy showed me that postcard and I'm sure my friends *meant* to meet me as planned—but it didn't quite work out that way.

I practically killed myself getting inside the station and rushing to the information desk, which was where we were supposed to meet. I made a point of getting there five minutes ahead of time, just in *case* their train was early. (An early train is a real miracle.) Their train was due at 11:25. I reached the desk at 11:20.

You can't miss the information desk. It's in the middle of the entrance hall at Grand Central, and says INFORMATION as plain as day. You can't miss the entrance hall either. All these constellations and things are painted on the ceiling. It's beautiful and unusual.

I stood by the desk, alternately watching the people and watching the clock.

Eleven twenty-five, 11:30, 11:40.

Where were my friends? I began to feel nervous. Maybe something had happened to them. Maybe their train was late. Or maybe they hadn't come after all. I considered ringing Mum and asking her if they had tried to reach me at home. Straight away, I decided not to do that. If they *hadn't* phoned, Mum would probably alert the police.

I waited five more minutes, then turned around and asked a woman at the information desk if there were any reports of delayed trains.

The woman shook her head. Then she asked, "Which train are you waiting for?"

I told her.

"Nope," she said, frowning. "That was right on time."

"Uh-oh."

"Were you supposed to meet someone?"

I nodded. "My friends. We were supposed to meet here. They've never been to New York alone before."

"This is a big station. I'm sure they're around somewhere," said the woman kindly. "They probably just got mixed up. Or maybe they've discovered all the shops here."

As I've said, it would be hard *not* to find the entrance hall and the information desk, but it was possible. For all I knew, my friends were wandering around in the underground or something.

(If they were shopping, I would kill them.)

I tried to work out what to do next. I thanked the woman and stepped away from the desk. I looked out at the hall. It was crowded, but not too crowded. My friends definitely were not there. I was just about to ask the woman if she could put out an announcement for them, when I heard, "Stacey!"

It was Claudia's voice, but I couldn't see her.

"Stacey!" she called again.

I turned around. My friends were struggling down the steps that lead from one of the outside entrances to the station. Where on earth had they been?

"Where on earth have you been?" I cried as I dashed to them. Since I already sounded like my mother, I went ahead and added, "I was worried sick!"

"We're sorry, we're sorry," Claudia replied breathlessly. She had a suitcase the size of a goods wagon with her.

For a moment, I forgot about the botched-up plans. I just looked at those four familiar faces rushing toward me. There was Mary Anne, grinning and looking excited beyond belief; Kristy with a smile a mile wide; Dawn, who seemed to be trying to cover up sheer terror with a tight-lipped smile; and Claudia, who managed to appear both happy to see me and ready to strangle her suitcase.

We met at the bottom of the marble stairs and all tried to hug each other at once.

"Stacey, your hair! It looks fantastic!" exclaimed Claud.

"We've been wandering around, oh, *everywhere*!" said Dawn.

"Mary Anne, I love your shirt!" I told her.

"I can't believe I'm here!" she replied.

"What's to eat?" asked Kristy.

"Where have you been?" I asked again.

I led my friends away from the stairs and they put their things down. Kristy and Dawn were each carrying a rucksack. Mary Anne was carrying a small duffel bag. But Claudia had that goods wagon.

"What's *in* that?" I wanted to know.

"What should I answer first?" Claud replied. "'Where have you been?' or 'What's *in* that?'"

"'What's *in* that?'"

We were all giggling. This was like old times. But I have to admit that I felt sort of . . . conspicuous. My friends were making a lot of noise, there was Claudia's suitcase, Kristy was wearing a baseball cap with a picture of a collie on it, Dawn was looking around as if she expected someone to murder us any second, and Mary Anne had just pulled a giant map and guidebook to the city out of her handbag.

"Put that away!" I whispered loudly to her. "You look like a tourist."

"Well, I am one."

"But I'm not. Come on. Put it away. We don't want people to think we don't know where we're going. That makes us easy targets."

"For what?" asked Dawn nervously.

"For—never mind," I said, feeling exasperated. What was the matter with Dawn anyway? She's usually so cool.

"I thought you wanted to know what was

in my suitcase," said Claudia.

"I do," I told her.

"My clothes," she replied.

"For how long? The next two years?"

"*No*," she said testily. "The next two days."

I should have known. Once, my friends and I went on a trip to the Bahamas and Disney World. Claudia brought almost her whole wardrobe with her.

"And where were you guys?" I asked.

Kristy took over. "I'm not sure," she replied honestly. "When we got off the train, we just kept following people, and then we went up an escalator, we walked through a building and found ourselves outside."

I didn't say anything, but to get to the escalators they had to have been in the entrance hall—which meant they walked right past the information desk. And what possessed them to go on an escalator anyway? I hadn't said anything about going on an escalator. Oh, well. It was over now. And we were together.

I drew in a deep breath, let it out slowly, smiled, and said, "So what do you want to do first?"

"Well," Mary Anne spoke instantly, "I'd love to see Central Park. It's eight hundred and forty-three acres of fun. Or maybe we could go to South Street Seaport, located in the Wall Street area of lower Manhattan and featuring nineteenth-century build-ings, three piers and a maritime museum." Mary Anne grinned smugly. She looked quite proud of herself.

How did she do that? I wondered. She was a walking guidebook.

Kristy noticed the look on my face and said, "I don't get it, either. She talked like that during the entire train trip, and I never even saw the guidebook."

Mary Anne made a face at Kristy. "Maybe we should just go and have lunch," she suggested. "How about the Hard Rock Cafe? It features all kinds of—"

"The Hard Rock Cafe?" repeated Dawn. "Is that in a safe neighbourhood?"

I looked at Dawn curiously. Where was all that self-confidence? "Dawn? Are you okay?" I asked her.

"I'm fine. It's just that I've never been to New York before," she reminded me. "And it's not as if I lived in a city when we were in California. We lived *outside* Ana-heim—in a teeny little suburb. It just hap-pened to be near Disneyland and some other fun places. But last night? I was listening to the news and I heard about these two murders in New York, and then this building collapsed and crushed someone."

"And *then*," added Kristy, "someone fell down an open manhole and was attacked and eaten by alligators and sewer rats."

"*Really?*" said Dawn, her eyes widening.

"I'm making it up!" cried Kristy.

"You are? But I've heard that there *are* alligators in the sewers. And pick-pockets—"

"In the sewers?" asked Kristy.

"*No.* On the streets. And tramps and muggers and purse snatchers and rats and cockroaches."

Uh-oh.

"How about lunch?" I said. "You guys must be starving. I think the Hard Rock Cafe is a good suggestion. We can hop on a bus—"

"With *this*?" asked Claudia, pointing to her suitcase.

I groaned. The suitcase probably wouldn't fit on a bus, or through the front door of the Hard Rock Cafe for that matter. "I suppose we'll have to go back to my flat first and drop that off," I said. "Of course, it's entirely out of the way."

Claudia looked all huffy. "Couldn't we leave it somewhere?" she asked. "In a locker or something?"

"Not if you want to get it back," I told her. "We'll have to hail a taxi, get the driver to put that thing in the boot, which by the way means we'll have to give him a huge tip, take it to my block of flats, and then take a bus back to the restaurant."

"I'll pay for the taxi," said Claudia contritely. She reached out for a handle on the end of her suitcase and began pulling it towards the stairs. The suitcase was on little wheels. I wanted to die. How embarrassing. Why hadn't I noticed the wheels before? Only grandmothers pull around suitcases on wheels.

Somehow we managed to get up the stairs and out of the building. No sooner had we walked out of the door than Dawn screamed.

"What? What is it?" I asked.

"Th-*that*!" Dawn was pointing to a pile of rubbish—and a pink tail.

The tail moved. It was attached to a tiny mouse.

Kristy started to laugh and Mary Anne poked her.

I ignored all of them and hailed a taxi.

The cabbie (who was very nice) loaded Claudia's suitcase into the boot, and then my friends and I piled into the cab. They squashed into the back seat and I sat in the front with Philippe (the driver). When we got to my block of flats, the doormen were kind enough to let us leave the suitcase behind the front desk, so at least we didn't have to go upstairs. Then Kristy, Mary Anne and Dawn decided to leave their rucksacks and the duffel bag behind, too, which made sense.

At last we were on our way to the Hard Rock Cafe.

4th CHAPTER

Dear Jeff,

Is New York ever scary. I'm not sure you'd like it here. It's all cramped and crowded. That's what happens when you try to cram eight million people into such a small area. To make up for it, New Yorkers just keep building taller skyscrapers. Fifty years from now, people will probably have apartments on the three-hundredth floor. Today I saw a gigantic rat, and a person without a home who picked through a rubbish bin until she found half a hamburger. She ate it without even washing it off.

Your terrified sister,
Dawn

"Oh, my lord!" cried Claudia. "Look at that! Look at *that*!"

We had reached the Hard Rock Cafe and were standing outside. I have to admit that the front of the restaurant is pretty spectacular. There's an amazing Cadillac (just half of it) suspended over the entrance, and the number plate reads "God is my co-pilot."

It is extremely cool.

But I wished my friends weren't quite so loud in their admiration of the Cadillac. They were making a lot of noise again and sounded like tourists.

"Did you make a reservation?" asked Mary Anne.

I shook my head. "You can't. They don't take reservations."

"Oh, I hope we can get in," said Kristy, still gazing at the Cadillac.

"We'll get in," I told her. "But we might have a little wait. If this were the weekend, though, we'd probably have to wait in a forty-minute queue outside. Come on."

"Forty minutes," I heard Dawn mutter in amazement as my friends followed me inside.

I approached the man who was behind a desk near the doorway and said, "Five for lunch, please."

"Oh, you sound so grown-*up*!" squealed Mary Anne.

(I wanted to kill her.)

300

"That'll be about five minutes," said the man. "Why don't you just step aside, and someone will seat you shortly."

"Okay," I said. "Thanks."

The five of us stood around and gazed at the restaurant. There's an awful lot to see.

"It's everything I dreamed it would be," said Mary Anne with a sigh.

Claudia and I glanced at each other and smiled.

The restaurant *is* fun to look around. First of all, it's huge. Second, it's a sort of shrine to rock music. There's a lot of memorabilia hanging on the walls. Things like the Talking Heads' guitars and a poster of David Byrne. Mostly there are a lot of guitars. And signs. Signs everywhere. We were standing right underneath one that said THIS IS NOT HERE. (Kristy started giggling.) Another said WHO DO YOU LOVE? Another said LOVE ALL SERVE ALL. And everywhere—on the menus, the walls—were the words SAVE THE PLANET.

"It's a bit nineteen-sixties, isn't it?" commented Dawn.

"Actually," began Mary Anne, "the Hard Rock Cafe—and I might add that there are Hard Rock Cafes located in Dallas, London, Tokyo, Stockholm—"

I don't know what point Mary Anne was about to make, but luckily she was interrupted by a man who showed us to a table.

He seated us right under a glass case which held a weird pair of black-and-white checked platform boots. Under the boots was a brass plaque that read CHUBBY CHECKER.

"Chubby Checker?" Dawn said as we sat down.

Every last one of us shrugged, even Mary Anne, although I'd been certain she was going to open her mouth and say something like, "Chubby Checker. Didn't you know? That was a group that used to backup Elvis Presley in nineteen fifty-six," or something.

But she didn't. Instead, a young woman whose nametag said Meddows came over and handed us our menus.

"Oh, this is so exciting!" exclaimed Mary Anne.

It was only 1:20, and already Mary Anne had said that at least six thousand times. I hoped she would stop.

We studied the menus and then Meddows returned to take our orders.

"I'll have the Poppied Fruit and Avocado Salad, please," said Dawn, and added, "it sounds so Californian."

"I'll have the 'Pig' Sandwich, please," said Claudia.

"Me too," said Mary Anne.

"I'd like the Chef's Salad," I said.

"And I," Kristy began, "will have the fill-it-mig-nun."

302

"The *what*?" I said with a gasp.

Meddows smiled. "I know what she means," she said. She scribbled something on her pad. Then we all ordered lemonades and she left.

"*Kristy*," I whispered loudly, leaning across the table, "that is pronounced 'fillay meenyon,' *not* 'fill-it mig-nun.'"

"*Sorry*," said Kristy crossly.

I was mortified. There we were in one of the coolest restaurants in all of New York City, a cool waitress to go with it, and Kristy had just ordered fill-it mig-nun.

I wanted to die. I wanted to crawl under the table and *die*.

Somehow we got through lunch and paid for our meal. But we didn't leave straight away. There was a little stand near the exit to the restaurant selling Hard Rock Cafe T-shirts and sweat shirts.

"Ooh, look!" said Mary Anne breathily. "A souvenir shop! I've just got to buy a T-shirt for Logan. That will be the perfect souvenir for him. I promised him a New York souvenir."

So Mary Anne bought a T-shirt for Logan and one for herself, and then Kristy, Claudia and Dawn bought T-shirts for themselves and for Mallory and Jessi. They even talked *me* into buying one.

"These can be our club uniform!" exclaimed Kristy. "We can wear our shirts to meetings."

"Oh, wow, that will be so cool!" said Mary Anne.

I looked around for a place to hide, but there was none.

We stepped outside. We had walked exactly four feet when a shabbily dressed man planted himself in front of us. We tried to go around him. He blocked our way.

"Oh, no," moaned Dawn.

The man held out a paper cup. "Spare a quarter, ladies?" he asked.

Mary Anne looked at me questioningly.

But Kristy immediately opened up her handbag and pulled out her purse.

I shoved her purse back in her handbag, closed the handbag, and steered my friends clear of the man. "*Never* open your handbag in the middle of the street, especially not when someone asks you for money," I snapped.

"But that poor man—" Kristy began, looking over her shoulder at him.

"I know," I said more gently. "I feel sorry for him, too. But opening up your handbag is a great way to get ripped off. He might just have grabbed your purse and run. Or someone else might have. You guys are in New York now, so watch yourselves. You have to be on your toes."

Dawn turned so pale I thought she was going to faint.

Mary Anne changed the subject. "So where are we going now?" she asked. "I

304

thought we could go to Bloomingdale's, and then maybe to the Museum of Modern Art. You wanted to go there, right Claudia? And after that—"

"Whoa," I interrupted her. "Wait a minute. It's much later than I thought it would be by the time we finished lunch." (I didn't add that this was because we'd wasted so much time trying to meet each other and then struggling with Claudia's goods wagon.) "We've only got time to do one more thing, I think. Then we have to go back to my flat and get ready for the party. Oh, and there's something else we have to do, but I'll explain about that later."

"Time for just one more thing?" said Claud in disappointment. "Well, I suppose I'm the only one who wants to go to the museum."

She was right. Everyone else wanted to go shopping, so we ended up heading for Bloomingdale's.

In all honesty, I have to say that although Bloomie's used to be my favourite department store, I had recently realized that it is always crowded and always hot. It could be ten degrees outside, but in Bloomingdale's it would be two hundred and thirty-six.

My friends were completely in awe of the store, though. More in awe than they'd been of the Hard Rock Cafe. This was understandable. Bloomingdale's is huge.

I've actually got lost in it. And there's so much to see, you hardly know where to look. Counter after counter and rack after rack spreads before you. There's jewellery, clothing, fur coats, lingerie, toys, furniture, household goods, electric goods. People come after you, offering samples or telling you about special offers. It can actually be a little overwhelming.

We wandered through the makeup department and let a woman spray us with perfume. Then we sniffed at our violet-scented wrists and felt very adult. That was pretty much the last good moment of the shopping adventure.

The next thing I knew, a store detective had come after Mary Anne. He demanded to look in her handbag. When she opened it, he pulled out a half-used jar of eye shadow.

"I believe this belongs at the Clinique counter," he said.

"I th-thought it was a sample," Mary Anne stammered.

(Everyone was looking at us.)

"You're supposed to try the makeup at the counter, not pocket it," I told her.

The man was very nice and let us go, telling us not to let it happen again. I'm sure he thought we were tourists kids from the sticks. (He was four-fifths right.)

After that embarrassing incident, Dawn tripped trying to get on a down escalator and nearly started an avalanche of people. And everywhere we went, Kristy kept exclaiming things like, "Look how *expensive* this is! In Stoneybrook it would only cost half as much," or "Mary Anne, come here. Look at this—a *hundred* and *sixty* dollars for *one* pair of *shoes*!"

I decided that if we got out of the store alive, we could call the afternoon a success.

5th
CHAPTER

Dear Mum, dad, Mimi and Janine --
Hi! How are you. I'm fine. New
York is so so cool. The peopel are so
so cool too everyone is dressed like
magazin moodles. We whent to a restarant called
the hard rock caffe and we whent to Blomingdels.
I bought a pair of baggy sox and mary
ann allmost got arested but don't tell
her father. We also met the kids we'll
be siting for tomorrow. Tonight stacy
is having a party for us at her
flat.

Love ya.
Claudia

The one other thing my friends and I had to do before we got ready for the party was go around my block of flats and meet the families whose kids we'd be taking care of the next day. I'd promised the parents we'd do that. They were a little concerned, and I could understand why. I mean, they didn't know my friends, and just because I'd said the five of us used to be in a babysitting business together was no real reason to trust Kristy, Mary Anne, Claudia and Dawn. But they trusted me. All they wanted to do was meet my friends.

So after our safe return from Bloomingdale's, the five of us left our things in my bedroom and then headed for the twentieth floor of the building. I thought we could start at the top and work down.

"'Bye, Mum!" I called as I ushered my friends into the hallway.

"'Bye, girls!" my mother replied. "Have fun and be careful!"

"No problem!"

I pressed the lift button and we waited.

"Couldn't we take the stairs?" asked Dawn after a moment.

I shook my head. "If we took the stairs from here to the twentieth floor we'd never be able to walk again."

"But . . . well, have you ever got stuck in the lift?" Dawn wanted to know. "It took a long time for the doors to open when we came up to your flat."

"Never," I told her firmly. "I have never been stuck. You aren't claustrophobic, are you?"

"She's just a born worrier," said Kristy. "For heaven's sake, Dawn, I can think of worse things than getting *stuck* in a lift. What if the cable broke and the lift crashed all the way to the basement?"

"*Kristy!*" exclaimed Claudia, Mary Anne and I. (Dawn was speechless with fear.)

The lift arrived and we convinced Dawn to get in it. We went to the twentieth floor. Uneventfully, I might add.

The twentieth floor is the top floor of my building. Like most older blocks of flats, it's not *just* the top floor, though—it's the penthouse. (It's owned by Mr and Mrs Reames.) Unlike my floor, where there are six flats, the penthouse is *one* flat that takes up the *entire* storey. As you can imagine, it's huge. It's bigger than the whole *house* my parents and I lived in in Connecticut. If you took our second storey and laid it down next to the first, all that space would still be less than the space the Reameses have.

Another thing about the penthouse—the lift lets you off in the Reameses' front hall, which is decorated with paintings and vases and things. Also an umbrella stand. Of course, the door between the hallway and the Reameses' actual flat has about thirty-five locks on it, but getting off in *their* hall is a lot nicer than getting off in *ours*, which is dark and has nothing in it but the doors to the flats and the rubbish chute.

"Okay," I whispered, as the lift doors opened and we stepped into the Reameses' hallway. "This is the penthouse. It's the biggest, most expensive flat in the building. The Reameses are really rich. They're *nice*, but rich. So don't touch anything."

"Should we have fun and be careful?" asked Claudia slyly.

"Just be careful. Now, there's only one kid here. Leslie Reames. She's four. And she's a little like Jenny Prezzioso, so be prepared."

"Another spoiled brat?" wailed Mary Anne.

"A *picky* brat. . . But not a bad kid."

I rang the Reameses' bell. Their maid answered.

"Hi, Martha," I said.

"Hello, Stacey," she replied. "Come on in. Leslie's dying to see you."

We stepped inside and every single one of my friends gasped. Kristy even said, "Will you look at this place? It's like a museum."

I think Martha pretended not to hear her.

The Reameses' apartment *is* like a museum. It's even more opulent than the fancy houses in Kristy's neighbourhood.

My friends were falling all over themselves in a very embarrassing way. You'd think they'd never seen antiques before.

"Stacey! Stacey!"

Little Leslie Reames came tearing through all those antiques and flung herself at me. When I say *little* Leslie, I mean little. Leslie was premature—she weighed less than four pounds when she was born—and she's never caught up with kids her age, size-wise. She's teeny, like a spider, with spindly arms and legs. However, she makes up for her size by having a mouth that rivals Kristy's.

"Hiya, Leslie," I said. I swung her into the air and she squealed.

Mr and Mrs Reames came into the living room then and the introductions began. When we were finished, the Reameses spouted their Leslie list, which I've heard a thousand times already.

"Remember her wheat allergy," said Mrs Reames.

"And she *must* wear a jacket at all times tomorrow," said Mr Reames.

"Even indoors?" I heard Kristy whisper to Mary Anne.

"No prolonged running," added Mrs Reames.

And then Leslie spoke up: "And keep me away from dogs."

My friends must have passed the Reameses' inspection, because when we left, Mr Reames said, "Martha will drop Leslie off at your flat at about a quarter to twelve tomorrow, Anastasia."

(Mr Reames may be nice, but he's the only person in the world who would even *think* of calling me by my full first name.)

I was lucky. My friends kept their mouths shut until we were in the lift, the doors had closed behind us and we'd started to move.

"Whoa!" exclaimed Mary Anne. "Wheat allergies."

"No prolonged *running*?" cried Dawn, momentarily forgetting that she was in a lift.

"Worriers of the world unite!" added Claudia.

And Kristy said, "ANASTASIA!" She laughed until she cried. She slumped to the lift floor. The rest of us had to drag her to her feet as we reached eighteen and the doors opened.

"Now, calm down," I whispered loudly as we approached flat 18E. We were on a normal floor, under a normal buzzing fluorescent light, ringing the bell of a normal apartment.

An attractive black woman answered the door.

"Hi, Mrs Walker," I said. "I brought my friends to meet Henry and Grace."

Mrs Walker smiled and showed us into a flat that was laid out exactly the same way

313

as ours. But boy did it look different. Both Mr and Mrs Walker are artists and they work at home. (They turned their dining room into a studio.) Their flat is filled with modern art—paintings and sculptures and wall hangings. Some of it I like, some I don't like. (Or maybe I just don't understand it.)

"Henry! Grace!" Mrs Walker called as Kristy, Dawn, Claudia, Mary Anne and I gathered in the Walkers' living room.

A few moments later, two little kids peered at us around the kitchen doorway.

"They're shy," I whispered to my friends. Then I spoke up. "Guess what we're going to do tomorrow, you guys," I said. "We're going to go to the museum and see the dinosaurs. And after that, maybe we'll go to the park."

The kids' faces lit up. They stepped out of the kitchen.

"These are my friends," I told Henry and Grace. I introduced everybody. "Henry is five and Grace is three," I added.

Grace nodded and held up three fingers.

"I'm going on six," Henry said softly.

Mr Walker came out of the studio then. He was paint-covered, and I knew we'd interrupted him, but he just smiled and then he and his wife talked to us for a while.

Fifteen minutes later, we were back in the lift, and Mary Anne was looking starstruck. "I can't believe it," she said. "Mrs

Walker illustrates books. I met a celebrity!"

"Did you see that painting over their couch?" exclaimed Claudia. "It was fantastic. I wish I could talk about art with the Walkers sometime. Mr Walker has even had his own show here in New York. Do you know how *major* that is?"

We agreed that a show was major but didn't really have time to talk about it, since our next stop was just two floors down, on sixteen.

"The Upchurches," I told my friends. "Two girls. Natalie is ten and Peggie is eight. Natalie will be the oldest kid in the group tomorrow. Wait till you see the Upchurches' flat. Oh, but don't say anything about it, you guys. And there's no Mrs Upchurch. The parents are divorced and the kids live with their father, okay?"

"Okay," said Kristy, who usually assumes that people mean *her* when they say not to mention something.

I just knew the Upchurch girls would surprise my friends—and they did. They are smart, worldly New York kids. They're not sassy, they're just sophisticated, I suppose. (They're probably a lot like I was when I was younger.)

Natalie answered the bell and we walked speechlessly into the flat. It's decorated entirely in black and white and chrome, and is exceedingly ugly. Having been told not to comment on it, my friends didn't know what *to* say. Luckily, Mr Upchurch sat us down, so we talked about our sitting experiences and what we planned to do the next day.

Then Natalie and Peggie began telling us about the creative theatre group they belong to.

"We express emotions through actions," said Peggie.

"We've learned that the theatre is really a stage for *life*," added Natalie.

Kristy waited until the five of us were in the lift before she said, "I hope Peggie and Natalie can handle something as down-to-earth as dead dinosaurs in a museum."

We giggled. Then it was on to the eighth floor, where we met the Barreras—Carlos, who's nine; Blair, who's seven; and Cissy, who's five, knows Leslie Reames, and can't stand her.

"They had a nice, normal flat," commented Dawn, as we headed for the fifth floor, our last stop.

"Aren't there any other celebrities here, Stacey?" asked Mary Anne.

"Mary Anne, this is a block of flats, not Burbank. We're lucky to have Mr and Mrs Walker. If you're looking for movie stars, forget it."

"*Sorry*," said Mary Anne huffily, not sounding one bit sorry.

Dennis and Sean Deluca, who are nine and six, were the last kids my friends met that afternoon. The Delucas haven't lived in New York long, so Dennis and Sean were like my friends in some ways—everything was new to them . . . and a lot of things frightened them. I made a mental note not to let Dawn spend much time with the Delucas.

At long last we got back in the lift and headed up to my floor.

"You know," said Claudia, "it just occurred to me. The weather is beautiful today, and we found all those kids at home, cooped up in their flats."

"Well, there's no playground nearby," I told her.

"I thought you live near Central Park," said Dawn.

"We do," I replied, "but kids don't go there alone, not even at Natalie's age. It isn't safe. However, that is just what's going to make tomorrow so great. The museum and the park will be a terrific treat for all the kids. Now, come on. Here's my floor. We've got a party to go to!"

6th CHAPTER

Dear Dad and Tigger,

New York is absolutely fabulous. Can we move here? (Just kidding.) We met a true and honest celebrity -- two of them actually. Mr. and Mrs. Walker. They're artists. Mr. Walker has had his own show, and Mrs. Walker illustrates books. Now it's time to get ready for Stacey's party. Don't worry -- Mr. and Mrs. McGill will both be at home. Tomorrow we take the kids to the American Museum of Natural History and Central Park. I know everything there is to know about the museum and the park, and I can't wait to see them again.   Love, Mary Anne

"Okay," I told my friends, "it's five o'clock. I invited people for seven, so we have two hours to get ready. We have to prepare the food, choose tapes to play and get dressed. Oh, Laine is coming over in an hour to help us, so maybe we should get dressed first."

"Laine's coming over early?" asked Claudia.

Laine, if you remember, is my best friend here in New York. Claudia was my best friend in Connecticut. Each girl knew about the other, but they hadn't met. That night would be the first time. I was certain they would get along, since *I* like them both so much, although when I thought about it, I realized that they didn't have much in common. Laine is *super*-bright, and Claudia may be bright, but she doesn't do well in school. Claudia likes arts and crafts, Laine likes foreign films; Claudia reads Nancy Drew mysteries, Laine reads French poetry; Claudia likes junk food, Laine likes gourmet food. (She has even eaten pigeon.) Still, since opposites attract, I just knew Laine and Claudia would hit it off. Besides, they did have one thing in common—me!

"Yes," I answered Claudia. "I wanted you and Laine to get to know each other before the party starts. Also, Laine always comes over to help whenever anything is going on here."

Claudia just nodded.

"Well, let's get dressed," said Mary Anne.

"Does this mean I have to stand up?" asked Dawn. We were sprawled around in the living room and Dawn looked exhausted.

"Yup," Mary Anne told her. "Now Kristy, Claudia and Dawn, you have to wear what Stacey says. So do I."

"What Stacey says?" I repeated as we walked down the hallway to my room. "What do you mean? You guys can wear whatever you want."

"Oh, no," said Mary Anne. "No way. This is New York. I want us to dress New York so we fit in.

"Maybe we should wear our Hard Rock Cafe T-shirts," said Kristy. "They're as New York as you can get."

Mary Anne scowled at her. Then she added, "You especially, Kristy. You wear what Stacey says."

"I hope Stacey says jeans, a sweater and trainers, because that's all I brought. And who made you Fashion Boss of the World, anyway?"

"What if I say to wear an overall, platform shoes and a beret with a paper windmill on top?" I asked.

"Stacey, this is *serious*," wailed Mary Anne. "We've got to look our best. We're going to meet all your friends. Aren't you worried about what we wear?"

320

"No," I replied. "But if it'll make you feel better, Mary Anne, I'll tell *you* what to wear. Let's see what you brought." (I glanced at Claudia's goods wagon. She had just opened it and about twenty outfits had fallen out.) "And if there's anything you need to borrow," I added, "I'm sure Claudia will have it."

"Stacey," Claudia began coldly, "for your in—"

"Hey, hey," said Dawn. "Everyone, *calm down*. We're wasting time. Just concentrate on getting dressed."

Half an hour later we were ready. Well, maybe not ready, but at least we were dressed. Mary Anne looked at all of us (even me) critically.

"Kristy, borrow an outfit from Claudia, okay?" she said.

Kristy was wearing a red sweater, jeans, and trainers.

"Claudia and I are not exactly the same size," said Kristy, who is not only quite short, but completely flat-chested. "Now get off my case."

"Okay, okay. . . Stacey, is it all right if Kristy wears that tonight?"

"Of *course*," I said.

Mary Anne continued her inspection. Claudia had on the black outfit we'd talked about over the phone so long ago. And she was wearing her hair simply, for once— brushed back from her face and held in place by a white beaded headband. Dawn had chosen an over-sized peach-coloured sweater-dress, lacy white stockings and black ballet slippers. I was wearing a short, short yellow dress that flared out just above my hips, white stockings, yellow ankle socks and a pair of new shoes that my parents hate. It was an interesting outfit, one I'd thought up while we were dressing.

And what was Mary Anne, the fashion guru, wearing? Well, here's a clue. She looked like she'd walked right out of the pages of *Little House on the Prairie*. I had chosen a bright big-patterned sweater and a pair of black trousers for her. She'd looked at them, shaken her head, put them back in her duffel bag and put on another outfit—a ruffly white blouse, a long paisley skirt and a pair of little brown boots. It was very mature and attractive but, well, Mary Anne was the only one of my friends who, when dressed up, actually *looked* as though she came from Connecticut. We could tell, though, that the clothes were new and that she really wanted to wear them, so no one said anything to her, despite the grief she'd given us earlier.

"Well," I said brightly. "Everyone passes my inspection. Come on. We'd better get busy in the kitchen. Except for you, Claud. Why don't you stay here and look through my tapes. Choose some to

322

play tonight and put them in the living room by the tape deck, okay?"

"Okay," agreed Claudia. I could tell she was pleased that I'd given her such responsibility.

Mary Anne, Dawn and Kristy followed me into the kitchen. We began opening bags of crisps and pretzels, and packets of cheese biscuits and sweets, and arranging everything in bowls or on plates.

"Mum?" I called. (Mum was home, but she was at her desk in the study, staying clear of things.)

"Yes?" I heard her reply.

"Did you remind Dad about the French bread sandwiches?"

"I rang him this afternoon. He'll bring them when he comes home tonight."

"Oh, okay. Thanks!"

The party wasn't actually a dinner party, but I knew most of my friends wouldn't have eaten and would be hungry—especially the boys.

"Stacey?" said Mary Anne. "What do you do at a New York party?"

I tried not to look exasperated. "Exactly what you do at a Connecticut party," I told her, and was relieved to hear the doorbell. "That must be Laine!" I cried.

Ordinarily the doormen buzz us when someone comes over, and then we go to our intercom and ask who's downstairs. But Laine comes over so often that the doormen know her and let her upstairs without calling us.

I dashed to the hallway. "Laine?" I said, before opening the door.

"It's me!"

I opened the door. "Hi! Oh, I'm glad you're here! Come on in and meet my friends."

The six of us gathered in the living room and I introduced everyone. I saved Claudia for last. "And *this*," I said, "is Claudia Kishi. Laine, Claudia. Claudia, Laine."

Laine was taking off her coat and my friends were watching with interest. I knew they were wondering what she was wearing. . . Well, even I was surprised.

Laine was beyond chic. She had chosen a short black dress, black stockings and simple black flat shoes. On one wrist was a single silver bangle. On her dress was one of those silver squiggle pins. Her fluffy brown hair was newly permed and perfectly cut. She looked wonderful—at least nineteen. My friends were speechless. Claudia looked good, too, but well, maybe only fifteen—at the most. Her hair was long and flowing, and her outfit was great, but not particularly adult.

"So you're the members of the Babysitters Club," said Laine, smiling. "Stacey's told me a lot about you."

"She's told us about you, too," replied Claudia, and added, "You're the one she had the big fight with after she found out she was diabetic, right?"

That was true—Laine and I had had a fight—but what was Claudia doing? I looked at her, aghast.

"And you're the one she had the fight with when your little club almost broke up," Laine countered.

I groaned. This was not a good sign. Not a good sign at all. The party looked like it was going to be a big mistake.

7th CHAPTER

Dear Mum,
   Tonight was Stacey's party.
It was interesting. We met her
friends and they met us. (New
York meets Connecticut.) I
suppose her friends are nice, but
it was hard to tell. Did you and
your friends ever fight when you
were my age? Maybe we can
talk about this when I get home.
You'll probably receive this card
after I get home, anyway.
Don't worry. New York isn't
awful but the party sort
of was.

              I love you!
                   Dawn
P.S. They have to have doormen
   here to keep murderers away.

I have to admit that I felt a little sorry for Dawn and also for Kristy that evening. By now, you've probably guessed that the party didn't go too well. Every one of my close friends was aggravating me. Mary Anne was being a pest. She kept pretending to be an expert on New York, trying to impress everyone and be all adult and sophisticated. And Claudia and Laine wouldn't stop sniping at each other. Maybe I'd been naive to think that they'd get along. Why should they? Each knew the other was my best friend, so they were *jealous*. I should at least have *suspected* that that might happen.

Now to be honest, Dawn and Kristy were driving me crazy, too. Dawn was just so nervous about everything, and Kristy never thought before she spoke. But I did feel sorry for them by the end of the evening, and you'll see why.

Let me go back, though, to Laine's arrival. I could hardly believe what Claudia had said to her. If she was feeling jealous of Laine, why hadn't she let me know beforehand? Oh, well. She hadn't. Instead, she had sniped at Laine and Laine had sniped back. (She's not one to ignore an attack.)

Dawn, Mary Anne, Kristy and I had glanced at each other nervously, and I was about to give Laine a job in the kitchen, when Mary Anne said, "Laine, Stacey says you've just moved to the Dakota Apartments, located at Seventy-second Street and Central Park West, built in eighteen eighty-four. Wasn't the movie *Rosemary's Baby* filmed there?"

Laine looked somewhat bewildered. "I—I don't know. I think the story was sort of supposed to take place there or something. I've never seen the film or read the book, though. I'm not allowed to."

"*Really*?" squealed Mary Anne. "Me neither! I'm not allowed to either! We have something in common, don't we? Hey, I've heard that some famous people live in the Dakota. Is that true? Do you know them?"

Laine looked at me questioningly. I wanted to crawl under the couch or something. Mary Anne was as excited as a puppy at dinner time.

"Well, yes," Laine replied. "John Lennon lived there. And Yoko Ono still does."

Laine mentioned a couple of other stars, and I thought Mary Anne would pass out from the sheer joy of it all.

"Oh! Oh!" she shrieked. "You're kidding, aren't you? No, you're *not* kidding!"

"Lord," Claudia mumbled. Then she spoke up. "Guess who lives in Stoneybrook, Connecticut, Laine," she said.

"Who?" asked Laine.

"Herbert von Knuffelmacher."

"I—I don't think I know who that is," said Laine.

"Exactly," replied Claudia. "Nobody does."

I had no idea what Claudia was leading up to, and I didn't want to find out.

"Whoa! Look at the time," I exclaimed. "People are going to start turning up before we know it. Claud, would you and Dawn clear that table in the living room," I said, pointing, "and arrange the paper plates and things on it. Let's see. Mary Anne, you open a couple of bottles of lemonade and put them by the cups. Oh, and put some ice in the bucket. And Kristy and Laine, come and help me in the kitchen."

Somehow, the next half hour passed uneventfully, although the uneventfulness did turn to silence, which I counteracted with a very loud old tape by some group my parents used to like called the Doors. Then Dad turned up with the French bread sandwiches—gigantic ones—and all five of my friends and I had to get busy slicing them into manageable little sandwich sizes. We stuck a fancy toothpick in each one to hold it together.

We had just finished when the buzzer buzzed.

"Great!" I exclaimed. "The first guest!"

"I thought I was the first guest," said Laine at the same time that Claudia said, "I thought we were your first guests. Remember us? The Babysitters Club?"

I rolled my eyes, thinking, Ooh, touchy,

as I ran into the hallway and pressed the "talk" button on the intercom. "Yes?" I said.

"Jim Fulton is here," Isaac told me.

"Thanks," I replied. "Oh, and Isaac, from now on, you can let everyone come up whose name is on that list I gave you. You don't have to buzz each of them."

"Right," replied Isaac. "Have a nice day." (Isaac says that at any time of day or night.)

"Jim Fulton?" I heard Mary Anne say behind me. "You didn't say there were going to be boys at the party . . . did you?"

"Yes I did. Why?"

"I don't know. . . New York boys. . ."

"What are you worried about? You've got Logan. You know how to act around guys."

"I suppose so. What will we talk a—"

The bell rang. I opened the door and found not only Jim Fulton but Read Marcus there. (Read is a girl. Jim and Read have gone out a couple of times.)

"Hi, you guys!" I said. I let them in, put their coats in my bedroom, and then introduced everybody.

Just as I was finishing, the bell rang again. And kept on ringing. For a while, I was busy letting people in and telling them where to put their coats. Apart from Laine and the club members, I had asked about twenty kids to the party. Thirteen of them

330

were boys. This was to even things up a little, so that there wouldn't be too many girls. I thought this was very nice and thoughtful of me. I wasn't trying to set up any of my friends. I just didn't want them to feel like they were sticking out— unattached hicks from Connecticut or something.

When I had let the guests in, I ventured into the living room. What I found was not your usual party scene. At the beginning of most parties, I've noticed, the boys and girls divide up and stick to separate sides of the room. The girls gossip and the boys do weird things like turn their eyelids inside out. This goes on until people feel comfortable enough to mix.

That night, my friends were divided up, but not boy *versus* girl. Instead, it was New York *versus* Connecticut, with one exception. While Claudia, Kristy and Dawn huddled in a corner, and my other friends stuck together by the food table, Mary Anne stood with Jim and Read. She was talking a mile a minute. I was pleased (at least *some* people were mixing) until I got close enough to them to hear what Mary Anne was saying.

"Imagine—first the Empire State Building, one thousand four hundred and seventy-two feet high, was the world's tallest building. Then the Twin Towers of the World Trade Center were complete and *they* were the tallest, but only until nineteen seventy-five. Now something *else* is taller. The Sears Building, I think, which isn't even in New York."

"Mm-hmm," Jim and Read murmured politely, and Jim threw me a look that plainly said, "Get us out of here."

Before I could, Mary Anne went on, "So have either of you seen the house at Seventy-five-and-a-half Bedford Street? I bet it's really cool."

"Huh?" said Read.

"You know. The house that's only nine feet six inches wide? Edna St Vincent Millay once lived there. The poet?"

"Hey, Mary Anne," I jumped in, "I don't think you've had anything to eat yet. Come over here and get a piece of French bread."

"But I'm not hungry," protested Mary Anne.

As I pulled her away, I heard Jim whisper to Read, "What a weirdo."

I thought about saying something to Mary Anne, but decided not to. At least, not right then. I didn't want to spoil the party for her. I headed over to my wallflower friends instead.

"You guys," I said to Kristy, Claudia and Dawn. "What are you doing here?"

"The same thing everyone else is doing over *there*," Dawn whispered, pointing to the rest of the kids, "only there's more of them. . . And they're having fun."

"Well, don't just stand there. Go and *talk*," I said. "Have you forgotten how to? It's really simple. You just open your mouths and let some words out."

"It is *not* that simple and you know it," Kristy whispered.

"It is, too," I replied. I took Kristy by the elbow and led her over to Coby Reese. Coby and I have been friends (not great friends, but good friends) since we were a year old and our mothers used to take us for walks together. Coby is very cute. More important, he's a nice guy who's easy to talk to.

"Hey, Coby," I said. I nudged him away from another boy, Carl Bahadurian, who was getting ready to prove that if you cross your eyes and someone hits you on your back, your eyes will *not* be permanently crossed. "Coby, this is Kristy Thomas," I said. "She's a big sports fan. Kristy, Coby is the star forward of our basketball team. He holds two school records."

"*Really*?" Kristy's eyes lit up. She was definitely interested—in a boy! She really was changing!

I left the two of them alone.

The party limped along. Eventually, my New York friends and my Connecticut friends began to mix. But as the evening wore on, I saw some strange things. I saw Mary Anne walk right up to a group of kids she hadn't even been introduced to and ask them how often they'd ridden the Staten Island Ferry. The kids gave each other "weirdo" looks. I didn't blame them.

I saw Dawn glance nervously out the windows and then ask Read Marcus where the fire escape was.

"There isn't one," Read replied. "The building's too tall for an outside escape. There are fire stairs at each end of the floor."

"Oh," said Dawn. "Thank goodness."

Later, I saw Mary Anne with a small group of kids who (for once) didn't look bored. At last, I thought, she's given up quoting statistics. What was she talking about instead?

". . . never been to New York before," she was saying. "She saw a mouse and thought it was a rat! And she was afraid we'd get trapped in the lift. She even believes there are alligators in the sewers! Isn't that crazy?"

The kids burst out laughing. Then all eyes turned towards Dawn. Unfortunately, Dawn was nearby, and I know she overheard.

Ooh, wait until I get my hands on Mary Anne, I thought.

However, by this time, everyone had loosened up, and a lot of kids were dancing. Guess who'd been dancing longest of all? Kristy and Coby! I couldn't believe it. At least one of the Connecticut girls was fitting in with my other friends.

A fast song ended and a slow one started. Kristy wrapped her arms around Coby's neck and they smiled at each other. And Claudia chose that moment to tap Coby on the shoulder and say, "May I have this dance?"

Kristy drew back in horror. If looks could kill, Claudia would have been dead and buried. Kristy flounced over to the couch and sulked.

It was eleven o'clock by then and kids were starting to leave. One by one they got their coats and drifted out the door. Even Coby, although he did say a special good-bye to Kristy, and they exchanged phone numbers and addresses.

Finally, only Laine and the members of the Babysitters Club were left.

We were utterly silent.

8th
CHAPTER

Dear mum, Watson, Charlie,
Sam, and David Michael
We are having a great time. Stacy threw
this super-cool party tonight, and
everyone got along great. I met this
terrific guy named Coby. And we all
met Stacey's New York best friend,
whose name is Laine. Laine and
Claudia are like sisters now. It's
amazing. I can't believe how easily
Mary Anne, Dawn, and Claudia and I
fit right into the New York scene.
　　　　　　　　　　Ciao,
　　　　　　　　　　　　Kristy

I don't think I need to tell you what a bunch of lies Kristy's postcard was. Hardly anyone got along. Laine and Claudia were more like wicked stepsisters than real sisters, my New York friends thought Mary Anne was a jerk, and thanks to what she'd said, they thought Dawn was a jerk, too. And Kristy and Coby may have hit it off, but Claudia totally spoiled Kristy's evening by butting in on Coby and flirting with him.

After Laine, Claudia, Mary Anne, Dawn and Kristy and I had looked at each other silently for a few moments, I said brightly. "Wow, what a mess we've got to clean up. Let's get to work."

"Just a sec," Laine interrupted. "You invited me to spend the night with you guys. Do you still want me to?"

"Of course I do," I replied.

"Well, now," Claudia spoke up quickly. "Laine should only have to spend the night here if she wants to. We wouldn't want to force her into anything."

"*I*," said Laine, "am only going to spend the night here if I'm *wanted*."

"You're wanted by me," I said nervously.

"And me," said Kristy.

"And me," said Dawn.

"And me," said Mary Anne.

Claudia said nothing.

"Claudia?" I prompted her.

Still nothing.

"What'd I do to you?" Laine asked Claudia sharply. "I didn't do anything and you act as though you hate me."

"You *did* do something," Claudia replied haughtily.

"What?"

"Don't you know?"

"No."

"Well, I'm not going to *tell* you."

"Oh, that's mature. You're a jerk."

"And you're a stuck-up snob."

"You know something?" Kristy spoke up. "Laine's right. You *are* a jerk, Claudia."

"Excuse me?"

"I said, 'You are a jerk, Claudia'."

"I heard you the first time," Claud snapped.

"Oh. It's just that you said, 'Excuse me,' which usually means you haven't heard properly," Kristy said sweetly.

"Kristy—shut up. Or else tell me why I'm an alleged jerk."

Claudia may not be a great pupil, but she picks up words like "alleged" from reading Nancy Drew stories.

"You," said Kristy, "are not an 'alleged' jerk, you're an actual jerk. You interrupted Coby and me. We were having a great time and you flirted with him and spoiled the whole evening."

"I did *not* flirt with him!" Claudia cried. "He was the only boy here that I—I wasn't

338

afraid of. And I didn't want to be a wall-flower *all* night. No one was asking me to dance."

"It's no wonder," I heard Laine mutter.

What was happening here? I was crushed. I'd wanted so badly for all my good friends to get to know each other and like each other, but they were becoming enemies, even the club members.

"Could—could you guys, um, keep your voices down?" I asked. "If you don't, Mum and Dad are going to come out here and try to help us patch things up."

"We're beyond patching," said Mary Anne.

"Well, let's at least move into the living room," I suggested.

I'd hoped that once we were in the midst of the mess, my friends would start to clear up, and that eventually they'd forget about their problems and we could relax.

I must have been crazy.

No sooner had we set foot in the living room than Dawn—quiet, even-tempered Dawn—said icily, "Claudia and Laine aren't the only jerks around here." She looked directly at Mary Anne, who, I might add, is her best friend.

"*Me*?" asked Mary Anne incredulously. "Are you saying I'm a jerk, too?"

"Allegedly," replied Dawn.

"Why?"

"You don't have *any* idea?"

Mary Anne shook her head. I could see her confidence (what there was of it) oozing away. Her eyes grew bright with tears.

"Then try this," said Dawn. "See if it sounds familiar. 'She saw a mouse and thought it was a rat. And she was afraid we'd get trapped in the lift. She even believes there are alligators in the sewers. Isn't that crazy?' Then imagine a lot of sniggering and laughing."

Mary Anne looked at the rug. The tears slipped down her cheeks. She's a champion crier.

Laine looked at everyone disgustedly. "Can we get back to the original issue here?" she said.

I was so confused and upset that I couldn't remember what the original issue was. "Huh?" I replied.

"You asked me to spend the night," Laine said slowly, as if she were speaking to a really little kid.

"Oh. Oh, yeah. Well, you're still invited."

"Thanks," Laine replied. She looked around the living room. Mary Anne was sniffling and wiping her eyes. Dawn was sprawled in an armchair, her feelings apparently wounded for life. And Claudia and Kristy were glaring at each other, arch enemies. Occasionally, Claudia's glare would switch to Laine. "Thanks," Laine said to me again, "but I think I'd rather not. I'm going to ring my dad and get him to pick me up." Then she added under her breath, "A funeral would be more fun than this."

While Laine waited for her father, she helped clean up. The six of us wandered silently around the living room, tossing paper plates and cups and napkins into binliners. Then we carried the leftover food into the kitchen. We were wrapping up the remaining French bread sandwiches when the buzzer buzzed.

I ran for it. "Yes?" I said.

"Mr Cummings is here."

"Okay. Thanks. Laine'll be right down."

"Have a nice day."

"Good night, Isaac."

Laine gathered her things together. I walked her into the hallway. "It's been great," she called to Kristy, Claudia, Mary Anne and Dawn.

"Yeah, a great pain," Claudia muttered.

"Laine, I'm sorry," I said quietly.

"Don't worry about it," she reassured me. "Everything will get straightened out. I'll phone you tomorrow."

The lift arrived and the doors swallowed her up. She was gone.

I wished I didn't have to go back inside my flat. Imagine—not wanting to go into your own home. Of course, I did anyway. But I was so angry with all my friends—

even Kristy and Dawn, whom I also felt sorry for—that I marched right inside, shut and locked the door behind me, and said firmly, "Kristy and Dawn, you sleep on the sofa bed in the study. Mary Anne and Claudia, you sleep on the sofa bed here in the living room. I'm sleeping in my own bed."

My friends nodded. They got their stuff out of my room. Half an hour later, we were ready for bed. Not one of us had spoken since I'd made the bed announcement. I told my friends to gather in the living room.

"Look, you guys," I said. "It's been a long day. It hasn't been a great evening. We're all tired. But I'm calling a truce. The truce has to last until at least tomorrow night. Because tomorrow, we've got ten kids to sit for, and we can't do that if we're not speaking. So, truce?"

"Truce," mumbled Kristy, Mary Anne, Dawn and Claudia.

As I was walking down the hall to my room, Dawn called after me. "Stacey? Are the doormen on duty all night? And do your locks work? And, oh, by the way, you do have an alarm system, don't you?"

"Yes," I told her, even though the alarm system part wasn't true. Then I went to bed.

9th CHAPTER

Dear Mimi
   Remember when the Babbysiters club took car of forteen children? At Kristy's house. Well today was are day to take car of ten kids what a job that was. We met the kids yetserday, just to say hi to them and today their parnets dropped them of at Stacey's flat. They all know Stacey but some were confused when they saw the big crowd and their were some tears.
   I luv you.
   Claudia

When I woke up the next morning I felt pretty subdued. I wondered how the others were feeling. I had purposely separated Kristy and Claudia, and Dawn and Mary Anne, but I knew that had not solved the real problem.

What *was* the real problem? I lay in bed and thought about it. Maybe there were several problems. I finally decided that was true. In fact, there were three problems:

1. People get out of sync when they're on a trip. Their routine is different and they're spending more time together. Those changes might put them on edge.

2. My Connecticut friends had desperately wanted to impress my New York friends. This was especially important to Mary Anne.

3. Laine and Claudia were jealous of each other, but neither would admit it.

Hey! I thought. We've got a lot of problems here, but none of them are exactly mine. Although I *am* the host of these people, so it would help (a lot) if everybody could get along.

What I did have to worry about was babysitting for ten kids all afternoon. They were going to start turning up around eleven-thirty and it was already nine o'olock. I got out of bed and went to the window, hoping the weather was nice. I peeked outside—a perfect day. The sky (what I could see of it) was a glittering blue, not a cloud in sight. Great. We could take the kids outdoors. Being stuck *in*doors in one apartment with ten children and five squabbling babysitters was not my idea of a wonderful afternoon.

I tiptoed down the hall and into the living room, where I found a note from my parents saying that they'd gone out for breakfast. Mary Anne and Claudia were still asleep.

I peeked into the study. Kristy and Dawn were awake. Not up, but awake.

"Morning," they said sheepishly.

"Morning," I replied. "How are you feeling? Did you sleep okay?"

"Like a log," Dawn replied. "I didn't think I would. I thought, you know. . ."

"Ghoulies and ghosties?" I supplied, smiling.

"More like burglies and ratties."

"You know," I said, "you do have to be careful here. You have to be careful in any big city. But be reasonable, too. You'll make yourself crazy if you worry about everything."

"I know."

"Besides," added Kristy, "I bet there are things to worry about that you haven't even imagined yet."

"*Kristy,*" I said.

"Well, it's true. Like getting food poisoning in a restaurant. Or getting run over by a bus. Or getting bitten by an animal in the children's zoo in Central Park.''

I didn't know whether to strangle Kristy or laugh at her. Shaking my head, I left the study to wake up Claudia and Mary Anne. I was beginning to feel edgy again. Was Kristy going to be a pest for the rest of the weekend? Would Dawn worry herself into a frenzy?

"Hey, you guys," I said, gently shaking Claudia and Mary Anne.

The living room, at least the part of the living room around the sofa bed, was a huge mess. I knew most of the mess was Claudia's. Mary Anne is usually fairly neat. (Actually, Claudia is, too. It's just that she had those two years' worth of clothes with her.)

"Rise and shine!" I said cheerfully.

"Ohhh," groaned Claudia. "Please."

I remembered then how I hate my mother sticking her head in my bedroom and saying that.

"It's nine o'clock," I informed them. "No, it's nine-oh-six. The children are going to start coming in about two and a half hours. So we'd better get up and get going. We've got to make some plans."

"You sound like a cruise leader," mumbled Claudia.

My only reply to that was, "Remember our truce."

★　　★　　★

An hour later Mum and Dad had returned, and my friends and I had dressed, eaten breakfast, folded up the sofa beds, and tidied the living room, study and my bedroom. We were sitting around in my room.

"It's a bit like the old days, isn't it?" I said. "This could be a club meeting. My room could be Claudia's room, and I could be the treasurer again—"

Kristy jumped up from where she'd been sitting on the floor, ousted me from my armchair, reached over to my desk, grabbed a pad of paper and a pen, stuck the pen over her ear, and said, "Even though I don't have my visor on, I call a meeting of the Babysitters Club."

(In Stoneybrook, Kristy conducts meetings from Claudia's director's chair and always wears a visor and sticks a pencil over one ear.)

Claudia made a rude noise, but Kristy said sharply, "*Truce*". Then she went on, "Remember when we were going to sit for the fourteen kids before my mum got married to Watson? We made a list of all the children, in age order. That was pretty helpful. Let's do that again. Mary Anne, you're the secretary. You make the list. Stacey, go over the names and ages of the kids."

"Okay," I replied. And we got to work. When we were finished, Mary Anne's list looked like this:

natalie Upchurch – 10
Dennis Deluca – 9
Carlos Barrera – 9
Peggie Upchurch – 8
Blair Barrera – 7
Sean Deluca – 6
Cissy Barrera – 5
Henry Walker – 5
Leslie Reames – 4
Grace Walker – 3

"It does put things in perspective," Dawn commented.

"Maybe we should make name tags," Kristy suggested. "We did that with the fourteen kids, too. Remember how useful they were?"

I shook my head. "No name tags," I said firmly. "It's not a good idea. It's not safe. We don't want strangers to know the kids' names."

"We don't?" Dawn said in a trembly voice.

"Oh, lord," muttered Claudia, giving Dawn an exasperated look.

"TRUCE!" said Kristy, Mary Anne and I at the same time. If we hadn't all been so edgy, that would have been funny. But none of us laughed. We just shut up.

"So what are we going to do today?" Kristy asked after a little while. "You mentioned the museum and the park,

Stacey, but we should have some sort of schedule in mind. Oh, and what time do we bring the kids back? How long is the meeting their parents are going to?"

"I don't know exactly," I answered. "I mean, no one does. But Mum said she thought it would be three or four hours. I think we should bring the kids back between three-thirty and four."

Kristy nodded. Then we decided on a tentative schedule for the afternoon, which included lunch at the museum. (The parents were going to give us money in advance to cover expenses such as food and the admission to the museum.)

At 11.35 the doorbell rang. I looked at my friends. "Well," I said, "this is the beginning. I hope we're up to this."

I really meant that last part. We had conducted our meeting civilly (the truce was working), but that was about all you could say. There hadn't been any laughing or joking or teasing. Just grim business.

"Come on. Let's see who's at the door."

It was Leslie Reames and Martha.

"Goodbye!" Martha called happily as she left Leslie in our doorway. It was Martha's afternoon off, and she looked as if she planned to enjoy it.

Leslie stepped inside. "Remember my wheat allergy," she said. "And not too much running, and I hate dogs."

We babysitters refrained from rolling our eyes.

Unfortunately, the next kids to arrive were the Barreras. It was unfortunate because Cissy dislikes Leslie so much. I couldn't blame Cissy, really, but we'd have to try to keep the girls apart. Cissy is a sturdy, playful tomboy who has no time for delicate, nervous Leslie. She and her brothers are a bit rough and ready. They're not bullies. They're just lively and full of fun.

Before a fight could break out, though, the Walkers arrived. Peggie and Natalie were right behind them, and a few minutes later the Delucas brought Dennis and Sean.

Our living room was packed. Mr and Mrs Walker and Mr and Mrs Deluca hadn't left yet. Henry, Grace and Sean were in tears, and Leslie was screeching because Carlos Barrera had invited her to come and see the Barreras' new puppy. Carlos was trying to be nice; Leslie thought he was being mean.

"It's time to get rid of the adults," I whispered to Kristy.

Before I could say anything, though, my parents came into the living room and announced, "The meeting will start in ten minutes. We had better get going."

With difficulty, the Walkers left Henry and Grace, and the Delucas left Sean. The three kids were still crying.

"Have fun and be careful," Mum said to me.

The flat door closed behind the adults. I locked it. Then I returned to the living room. I looked into the faces of the ten children and four other babysitters. Every last one of them looked nervous—no, scared.

10th CHAPTER

Hi, Mal!

Guess what we did today. We went to the American Museum of Natural History. It was so, so cool. You would have loved it. So would your brothers and sisters. Especially the triplets, I think. Dinosaur skeletons everywhere. And big cases showing animals (stuffed ones) in their habitats. But we had a scare. Boy, did we have a scare! We lost one of the kids we were sitting for. We almost panicked... until Mary Anne helped us to remember that a good baby-sitter keeps her head at all times. Anyway, everything turned out fine, of course.

See you at the next club meeting!

Dawn

352

"Okay," I said. "First things first."

I had decided to take charge, but being in charge felt funny. Kristy was usually in charge. She was the chairman, the leader, the one with the big ideas. However, I was the only one who knew all these kids, the only one who knew where the museum was and the only one who knew her way around Central Park. I was also the only one with keys to the flat *and* the only one who was a resident of the block of flats. Therefore, I was the only one the doormen would allow to walk outside with the kids.

I called my friends over. "Kristy," I said, "you keep Leslie and the Barreras apart. Dawn, you and Mary Anne and I will each calm down one of the criers. Claud, you keep an eye on the rest of the kids. As soon as things are under control, we'll leave."

My friends followed the orders, but I could tell that Kristy didn't like doing it. Even so, we were ready to leave in just fifteen minutes. As we were letting the kids out the door, I had a great idea.

"I know how to keep the children together while we walk to the museum," I whispered to the other sitters. I raised my voice and addressed the kids. "How many of you have heard the story about Madeline?" I asked.

All but Grace said, "I have!" (I suppose Grace was too young.)

"It's about twelve little girls who do

everything in two straight lines," I told Grace. "They sleep in two rows of beds and eat at two sides of a long table. And when they go for a walk they walk in two straight lines. That's just what we're going to do. I want each of you to choose a partner and hold hands. Then one of us sitters will walk with each pair. We'll have two lines of kids and one line of sitters. Remember to hold hands."

It worked. We looked like an army drill team, but the kids seemed to like it, even the older ones. They assembled in the hallway. Then Dennis Deluca commanded, "March!" and we marched down the hall. We squashed into the lift. We marched in place while the lift zoomed to the lobby. We marched out of the lift and past the doormen.

"Hup, two!" Blair called to Isaac and Lloyd at the desk.

"Have a nice day," Isaac replied.

We marched out of the front door, which James held open for us, turned left and marched up the street toward Central Park West. We passed Judy, the homeless woman.

"Hup, two!" Blair cried cheerfully.

But Judy was in one of her moods. "They'll make you eat rotten vegetables! You have to watch out for those theatre people!" she replied bafflingly. She was shrieking at the top of her voice and Grace began to whimper. But Dawn quietened her down straight away.

We reached Central Park West, turned the corner and marched to the front entrance of the American Museum of Natural History. It was interesting: the babysitters were more in awe of the sight of the museum than the kids were. I expect that was because most of the kids pass the museum at least twice a day, but not my friends. Dawn, Claudia, Mary Anne and Kristy stopped marching and stood at the wide steps to the main entrance of the great stone building. They gawked.

"Wow," said Mary Anne under her breath. "I've been here before, but I'd forgotten what the museum looks like. It's so . . . so, I don't know, impressive."

"It's beautiful," murmured Dawn.

"Remember that," I told her. "New York isn't just burglies and ratties and pickpockets and rubbish. It's culture, too. It's museums and art galleries and theatres and architecture."

The children couldn't have cared less about culture, though. As we stood at the bottom of the steps, they began talking and exclaiming.

"Can we go to the Naturemax Theatre?" asked Carlos. "It's got the biggest cinema screen in New York."

"I want to go to the planetarium," said Natalie.

"Yeah, they've got a laser show," said Dennis.

"There's a *Sesame Street* show," added Cissy.

"I just want to see the stars," said Natalie. "They make me feel at one with the universe."

"Huh?" replied every last one of us.

Then Henry spoke up shyly. "Please can we go inside and see the dinosaurs and animals?" he asked.

In the end, that was what we decided to do. The planetarium and the special shows cost extra money, and we didn't have endless funds. But we could easily afford the general admission to the museum. So we stepped inside, paid our fees and found a map of the museum. I had brought along a copy of the museum guidebook which Dad had bought the last time we were there. It was really helpful, and we could use it to answer questions the kids might have.

"Where do you want to go first?" I asked the kids.

"Wait, I can't get my badge on," said Blair.

We'd each been given a metal badge with a picture of an animal skeleton and a human skeleton on it when we'd paid our fee. I helped Blair fasten his badge to his shirt collar. "Okay, where to?" I said again.

"Dinosaurs!" cried all the kids except for Peggie, who said, "Gift shop. Puh-*lease*?"

"Before we leave," I told her.

Dawn was studying the map of the museum. "Dinosaurs are on the fourth floor," she informed us.

"Let's go!" I said.

We took a lift up to four, and had to make a decision straightaway: Did we want to see the Early Dinosaurs or the Late Dinosaurs?

We started with the early ones and entered a great, high-ceilinged hall. All the kids had been there before, but still they drew in their breaths at the central display in the room. (So did the sitters.) It was really impressive: freestanding, complete skeletons of a stegosaurus, an allosaurus, and best of all, an impressively gigantic brontosaurus.

Henry Walker stood by the brontosaurus and stared and stared. "I wish I could have seen a real bronto," he informed me, sounding as if he were on intimate terms with prehistoric creatures. Grace looked frightened and began to cry, though. I ended up having to carry her around while she hid her eyes in fear of the "monster bones."

After oohing and ahhing and looking up some things in the guidebook, we moved into the hall of the Late Dinosaurs, Grace still in my arms. I like the late dinosaurs better. They're so weird. And they have more interesting names.

"Monoclonius," Peggie sounded out.

"Styracosaurus," said Carlos slowly.

Blair's favourite, which he couldn't pronounce, was the corythosaurus, a duck-billed aquatic dinosaur.

Henry stood gawking in front of another display of giant rebuilt skeletons in the middle of the room—two trachodonts, a tyrannosaurus, and a triceratops.

We could barely pull him away from the skeletons, but after about fifteen minutes, the other kids (especially Grace) were ready to move on.

"Please, please, *please* can we go to the fish place?" begged Cissy.

I knew what she meant and why she wanted to go there, and I wanted to go, too, even though the ocean-life stuff was all the way down on the first floor.

"Let's go," I told the other sitters. "There's a ninety-four-foot replica of a blue whale hanging from the ceiling. It's really amazing. The kids love it."

So we headed down to the first floor. We were no longer in our Madeline lines (we felt funny marching through the museum that way), which may explain how we got all the way to the blue whale before we realized that Henry was missing.

We counted heads three times. We retraced our steps to the lift. We called for Henry.

No answer. I felt my knees and stomach

turn to water. "We've lost a kid!" I cried.

"Oh, my lord!" said Claudia in a horrified voice.

"Now just a sec," said Mary Anne, who usually stays calm in emergencies. "I think each of us should take two kids—well, except for me; I'll just take Natalie since she's the oldest—and search one floor of the museum. Stacey, you go to the lower level. Claud, you stay on this floor. Dawn, you go to two. Kristy, go to three. And Natalie and I will go back to four. Look very carefully and we'll meet at the information desk near the main entrance in fifteen minutes. Got it? If we haven't found Henry by then, we'll tell a guard or an official or someone."

No one argued with Mary Anne. We split up immediately. Sean Deluca and Grace and I searched the restaurants and gift shop on the lower level.

No Henry. When our fifteen minutes were up, we raced to the information desk. I was in a full-fledged panic. I'd never lost a kid before. Why did I have to lose the first one in the middle of New York City?

But my fears dissolved when we stepped out of the lift and walked around the corner. Ahead of us was the information desk. And there were Mary Anne, Natalie, and Henry. I ran to them and hugged Henry. Then Grace hugged her brother— fiercely.

"Thank you, Mary Anne!" I exclaimed. Then I turned to Henry. I was about to scold him when I saw Mary Anne shake her head.

"He went back to find the brontosaurus," she whispered to me, "but he was terrified when he couldn't find *us*. He'll stay with the group now."

The other sitters and kids turned up then, and my friends and I looked at each other. We grinned with relief.

11th CHAPTER

Hi, Nanny!

Here I am in New York! They call it the Big Apple. I don't know why. Have you ever been here? We took ten kids to the American Museum of Natural History. Then we went to Central Park. I didn't know there would be so many things in the park, but there's a zoo, a merry-go-round (the Freidman Memorial Carousel), a boat pond, a statue of Alice in Wonderland, an ice-skating rink, and even more. You can go roller-skating, horseback riding, bike-riding, boating, or— Uh-oh, I ran out of room!

Love,
Kristy

As soon as we'd found Henry, I decided we should leave the museum. We'd been there a while already, and anyway, the weather was so great I thought the kids would enjoy being outdoors.

We'd forgotten one thing, though. No one had eaten lunch! So we went to Food Express, a huge fast-food restaurant on the lower level of the museum, and ordered burgers or sandwiches and lemonade. Leslie and Dawn and I had salad, though. Salad is healthier, and for Leslie it's safe because of her wheat allergy. I thought she'd kick and scream at the idea of a salad, but she gobbled it up.

After lunch I was really ready to get outdoors. Unfortunately, a big gift shop is right next to the restaurant, and I *had* promised Peggie we'd go to it. So we went inside and the kids exclaimed over everything, mostly the dinosaur things—mugs and T-shirts and puzzles and charts and stuffed animals. It was Dinosaur Heaven. We didn't have enough money to buy souvenirs, though, so we looked around for a while, then ushered the kids outside empty-handed.

"*Now*," I announced triumphantly to my friends, "you are going to see the park to end all parks."

"I've been to Central Park before," Mary Anne spoke up.

"Oh, so you've seen the crouching panther statue," I said.

"Huh?"

"And you know where the Dene Shelter is, too, I suppose."

"The Dene Shelter?"

"Oh, please, Stacey, can't we do the fun stuff?" cried Cissy.

"Like what?" I teased her.

"Like the zoo."

"I thought the zoo was closed down so they could rebuild it," said Dawn.

"The main zoo is," I told her, "but not the children's zoo."

"Oh, let's go there first!" said Grace. It was one of the few things she'd said all day. Basically, she had just cried about the monster bones. And when Mary Anne had asked her what she wanted for lunch, she'd replied, "A hangaber."

It was quite a walk to the zoo. I mean, a long one. But walking was the fastest and cheapest way to get there. We formed our Madeline lines again in front of the museum, crossed Central Park West, and entered the park, which spread out before us, at Eighty-first Street. Then, heading south and west, we zigzagged through the park, sticking to paths and roads.

My friends couldn't believe what they saw—and what they didn't see.

"Right now," commented Kristy as we walked through a wooded area, "if I couldn't hear traffic, I'd think we were in some great forest. You can't see the city at all."

363

It was true. We were walking through a thick grove of trees. Leaves crunched under our feet. We could smell earth and evergreen needles, and, well, it's hard to describe, but simply that scent of growing things. I had smelled it in Stoneybrook, oh, and in the Brooklyn Botanical Gardens. But not in too many other places.

We couldn't see any buildings or streets or cars or even people.

At last we emerged from the woods onto a road. Ahead of us was a huge pond. A hotdog seller had set up his stand by the side of the road.

"Thank heavens," I heard Dawn murmur.

"What?" I asked her. "You hate hot dogs."

Dawn looked embarrassed. "Not that," she replied.

"Did you think we were going to get mugged back there or something?" I said.

"Well, you always hear stories about people getting mugged in Central Park," she said with a little shiver. "And not just at night," she was quick to add when she saw me open my mouth. "Also, homeless people live in the park, don't they?"

"So?" I replied. "Just because they're homeless doesn't mean they're going to hurt you."

Dawn looked away from me. I think she was going to say something else but she set her mouth in a firm line, stared straight ahead and marched forward with Natalie and Peggie.

Our lines had deteriorated by then, but that was okay. The lines were more useful on the street and in the flats. We were still holding hands in groups of three, though, and that seemed safe enough.

We crossed a road and followed a path through what seemed like a more normal park, with trees here and there, benches, playgrounds, a baseball diamond. I barely noticed any of it, since I cross the park pretty often.

But my friends, and even the kids (who also come to the park pretty often), kept exclaiming over things.

"Look! Look at that man! He's walking . . . *nine* dogs!" cried Sean, after counting them furiously.

"There's a lady feeding pigeons!" said Grace excitedly.

"Yeah, a whole *flock*!" added Henry.

"Oh, my lord, would you look at *that*?" exclaimed Claudia.

I had to admit that what she saw was strange and unusual—even for New York. An old man with a flowing white beard was riding an adult-sized tricycle. Attached to the back of the tricycle was a kid's red car. And riding placidly in the car were three fluffy white Persian cats. They looked like the man's beard.

"Oh, wow!" I cried.

My friends turned to me with smiles.

"Haven't you seen him before?" asked Kristy.

"No. Well, not for a few years. I'd forgotten about him."

"It's nice to see you get excited about something," said Claudia as we walked along. We'd almost reached the zoo.

"What do you mean?" I asked.

"I mean, you act as though there's nothing new or exciting in this city. Like you've seen it all before and so now nothing really matters any more."

"I do?" I said. That was something to think about.

We were standing in front of the entrance to the children's zoo and were about to pay the admission fee, when Peggie cried, "Oh, the clock! The animals are going to dance!"

The Delacorte Clock. Something else I'd forgotten about. How could I have? Was this what happens when you grow older? Or was I becoming a New York snob? Someone who's lived in the city for so long that she takes everything for granted? And then a jarring thought occurred to me: Maybe my friends were as exasperated with me as I was with them.

I shook myself free of the thought as the fifteen of us ran to the nearby clock tower I used to love when I was a kid. It wasn't just any clock, though. As it struck the hour (I looked at my watch—two o'clock) the circle of statue animals, each holding a musical instrument, began to revolve slowly.

We watched solemnly until the song ended.

Peggie sighed with happiness. (So did I.)

Then we paid the small fee to enter the children's zoo. From the outside, it looks like a really boring building. But when you go through the building and go outdoors again, you find yourself in a storybook land. The animals are housed in brightly painted buildings. There's a castle, a gingerbread house, and even Noah's Ark with a (fake) giraffe's head poking through the roof. And you can pet lots of the animals.

I wished I'd brought my camera along. My friends and I kept pointing at things and giggling.

"Look!" cried Claudia, nudging me.

I glanced up in time to see a goat trying to nibble a piece of paper that was in Blair's back pocket.

We watched Leslie wrinkle her nose up at a bunny rabbit.

We watched Natalie talk to some birds.

"Do you think she's communing with nature?" asked Kristy.

My friends and I burst out laughing. I knew we were feeling more like "our old selves," as my mother would say.

When the kids grew tired of the zoo, I decided it was time for a rest—and maybe dessert. There were lots of stall-holders about, and it was hard to pass by every one we saw.

"Who wants dessert?" I asked the kids as we left the zoo and came across an ice-cream seller, a popcorn seller and a toy seller.

Stupid question. The kids wanted *every*thing. The toys were too expensive, but we bought thirteen tubs of ice-cream (none for me or Dawn) and two giant boxes of pop-corn. Then we sat down on some wide, flat rocks and ate . . . and ate.

"Stacey?" said Lesley when we were finished. "I don't feel too good."

Uh-oh, I thought. I can't *stand* seeing people throw up.

Dawn remembered that. Without my saying a word, she took Leslie aside. She rocked her and talked to her quietly. Ten minutes later, Leslie hopped up and announced, "Okay! I'm all better! Let's go!"

Another crisis had passed.

"Thank you, Dawn," I said gratefully. "You know how I feel about. . ."

"The P-word?" suggested Dawn. We laughed. "I may be nervous about the city," she went on, "but I can handle a little, um, P. Anyway, she didn't get sick."

"But she might have," I said, shuddering.

"Hey, let's get going!" cried Mary Anne.

"There's a whole park to explore, and we've got to take these kids home in an hour or so."

By now we were so relaxed that we let the kids run ahead of us. My friends and I linked arms and followed them. The Babysitters Club was together again.

12th CHAPTER

Dear Janine —

Hi, how are you? Ime fine. We whent to Centrle park today and saw a clock and whent to the childrens zoo. Remerber when you read Stewart little to me we saw the boat pond where he had his scarry adventiure. We saw a staclew of Alice in wonderland. The kids climed all over it. They were. allowed to. I'll be home by the time you get this postcrad. I hop you had a good weekend.

Love,
your sister Claudia

It had been a long time since I'd just wandered through the park. Usually my friends and I go tearing through it to get to the east side of the city. I hardly ever wander around looking, the way I used to do when I was a kid.

But that was how we spent the rest of our time in the park. First we ambled west until we came to—

"The merry-go-round!" Leslie shrieked. "There it is! Please please please please please can we ride it?" She jumped up and down on those little legs of hers that looked like they couldn't support a mosquito.

The merry-go-round costs next to nothing to ride, so I paid for the ten kids. Then, as an afterthought, I gave the man enough money for five more fares.

"Come on, you guys," I said to the members of the Babysitters Club. "We're riding, too."

My friends looked doubtful at first. Then they grinned and scrambled for horses. So there we were, bobbing up and down on a merry-go-round in the middle of a park. I felt as though I was in *Mary Poppins* (which, by the way, is my favourite film ever). It was as if Mary Poppins and Jane and Michael Banks and I had jumped into one of Bert's chalk drawings on a London pavement and were riding the merry-go-round in a make-believe world.

"Stacey?" said Mary Anne, interrupting my daydream.

"Yeah?" (I was afraid she was going to spout some fact, like how old the merry-go-round was, or how much it had cost to create, or how many horses were on it.)

But all she said was, "This is really fun. I'm glad we came to the park today."

"Me too," I replied.

The merry-go-round wound down, and the older kids reluctantly slid off their horses. My friends and I helped the younger ones climb down, and then we set off again.

"I didn't know the park was so big," commented Kristy.

"And you haven't even seen half of it," I told her.

"Here are the checker-people!" called Henry suddenly.

"The checker-people?" I repeated, and then I realized what he meant. We'd come to a group of tables, a bit like picnic tables—with benches attached to the sides. Only these tables aren't as long as picnic tables and the tops are very special. They've got checker-boards built right into them. A lot of old people and some not-so-old people, bring their checkers or chess sets to the tables in nice weather and enjoy games and company.

Blair Barrera tugged at my hand. I looked down at him.

He indicated that he wanted to whisper something to me, so I leaned over.

"They're very serious," he said, nodding toward Henry's checker-people.

He was right. A lot of the players had brought along clocks or stopwatches so they could put time limits on their moves. They sat at those tables in silence, concentrating as hard as if they were taking IQ tests.

So the players were not pleased when Leslie suddenly shrieked, "Cut it out! Stop that, Cissy. *Stop* that! You are an old toad!"

"I am not. You are," Cissy retorted. "Because I'm rubber and you're glue, and whatever you say bounces off me and sticks to you. Nyah, nyah, nyah."

"Unh-unh," sang Leslie, hands on hips. "I'm rubber and *you're* glue."

"No, *I'm* rubber—"

"You guys!" I cried desperately.

Four checkers players and two chess players were glaring at us. I felt as if we had just screamed in a library.

"Come on," I whispered to my friends. "Let's get the kids out of here."

We hurried along a path that wound down a little hill, and found ourselves in a wide-open area. A group of kids were playing softball. Two guys were tossing a Frisbee back and forth.

Claudia burst out laughing.

"What?" I asked.

"There's a *dog* playing Frisbee!" she cried, pointing to a German shepherd just as it leaped into the air, expertly catching a Frisbee thrown by its master. "And it's a better player than I am!"

We walked and walked. By the time we reached the boat pond, the kids were looking tired and we babysitters were feeling tired. We sat down on some benches. There was plenty to watch. For a start, a golden retriever kept diving into the pond for a swim, leaping out, shaking himself off all over whoever was nearby, and diving in again.

Then Carlos spoke up. "I wish I had my boat with me."

"Do you have one of *those* boats?" asked Dennis enviously.

"Those" boats are specially powered sailboats and sloops that can be controlled from the shore. Their owners turn them loose in the pond and then direct them here and there, running back and forth at the edge of the water, making the boats zigzag and loop, using the remote controls to keep them from crashing into each other. They're a bit like bumper cars, except you can't ride in them; you can only watch.

"Of course I've got one," replied Carlos. "Haven't you?"

"No," said Dennis. "I want one, though. Has yours ever been in an accident?"

374

"Only about a million of them. It survived."

"Like Stuart Little," added Peggie Upchurch.

"Who's Stuart Little?" asked Sean.

"*Who's Stuart Little?*" repeated Peggie, looking alarmed.

"Peggie, not everyone reads as much as you do," said her older sister.

"I read a lot!" protested Sean.

"Then you should know who Stuart Little is," said Peggie.

"*I* don't know who he is," spoke up Leslie.

"Me neither," said Grace softly.

"Perfect," I replied. "Then I'll tell you who he is. He's a mouse. A man named E. B. White wrote a book about him."

"Is he real?" asked Leslie, wide-eyed.

"Who? E. B. White?" said Kristy.

"*No!* Stuart Little."

"He's made up," Kristy told her, and pulled Leslie into her lap for the story.

"Stuart," I began, "was something of a surprise. He was a mouse who was born to human parents, Mr and Mrs Little. They were expecting a baby, of course, but they got a mouse. The Little family lived right here in New York City, and one day Stuart took himself over here, to this very pond."

I told the kids about Stuart's adventure in the pond, and the wind that blew up, and his scare. Even the kids, like Peggie, who had heard or read the story several times already, listened dreamily. (Partly because they were tired, I think, but who cares?)

When I finished the story I said, "I think it's time to start for home, kids. We don't have to be back for a while, but we've got to walk all the way through the park again, and that's going to take some time."

"Aw, Stacey, do we *have* to?" whined Cissy.

"Yes, we do," I told her. I wasn't sure if she was whining because she didn't want to leave the park or because she didn't want to walk home. At any rate, I told her to climb up for a piggyback ride. Kristy did the same with Grace, Dawn did the same with Leslie, Mary Anne did the same with Henry and Claudia did the same with Sean. We set off.

Soon we stopped by the Alice in Wonderland statue and let the kids climb on it. Then we walked on. We passed roller skaters and a man who was performing magic tricks. But we never saw the crouching panther. I'd forgotten where it was; I remembered only that it was on a route Laine and I used to take when we would rent skates and go careering around the park.

By the time we were nearing the west side of the park and Eighty-first Street, the piggy-back riders were walking again and the ten kids were ahead of us babysitters. They were huddling together and whispering.

"They're up to something," I said to Claud, nudging her. "I just know it."

"Well, we're lucky," she replied. "Whatever it is, it's quiet."

Famous last words. *Just* as she finished speaking, and *just* as I was about to yell ahead to the kids not to cross Central Park West without us, they turned around and began singing loudly, "For they are jolly good sitters, for they are jolly good sitters, for they are jolly good sit-*ters*, which nobody can deny." (Except for Grace, who sang, "For they are jelly good sitters, which nobody can peny.")

I'm sure my face turned red. Kristy's did. And so did Claudia, Mary Anne's and Dawn's. A group of people were nearby, watching and smiling. At first I wanted to hurry the kids across the street and home, away from our audience. Then I thought, why does everything embarrass me so much? Why does *this* embarrass me? It's cute. The kids are doing this because they like us and they had a good time today.

"Thanks, you guys!" I called, running to catch up with the kids.

"Yeah, thanks!" cried my friends.

And the fifteen of us formed our Madeline lines again and crossed the street, tired and happy. We took a left and hup-two'd down the pavement. We turned onto my street and passed Judy.

Blair decided to try again. "Hup, two!" he said to Judy.

"Hup, two!" she replied. Then she noticed me and added, "Hello, Missy."

Blair grinned.

We marched to our building, past James and Isaac and Lloyd, into the lift, and rose up and up. Our adventure was over.

13th CHAPTER

Dear Logan,

As Claudia would say, "Oh, my lord!" You will not believe what we did last night. We had the most glamorous, exciting Saturday night in the history of the universe. We went to a Broadway play. We sat right in the middle of the theatre, up close. And we ate dinner out -- just the five of us, plus Stacey's friend Laine. And we RODE IN A LIMO. (Limo is short for limousine.) We really did. This is the truth. Uh-oh, I've run out of room, so I'll have to tell you the rest when we get back.

Love,
Mary Anne

After what happened between Laine and Claudia the night before, I would never have believed that we'd spend Saturday evening with Laine. But we did. And what an evening it was. Did we have fun! You know one reason I had so much fun? Because I pretended I was a tourist, not a native New Yorker. I saw everything through new eyes. But before I go any further, let me tell you how the evening came about and how our babysitting adventure ended.

When we reached my flat, we found it full of people. All the parents were there, waiting for their kids. The meeting had ended earlier, and everyone was talking about the homeless problem. They stopped when we came in, though, and for a few moments, there was pandemonium.

Grace literally threw herself at her mother. The Deluca kids chattered away nonstop. Leslie announced, "I almost threw up, but didn't."

Mrs Reames looked horrified. "Did you eat something with wheat in it?" she cried. She was talking to Leslie but looking at me—accusingly.

"No, no," I said hurriedly. "A little too much ice cream, I think. On top of too much excitement."

Henry chose that moment to say to his father, "I got lost! But then I got found."

Mary Anne told Mr Walker what had happened in the museum.

For the most part, the kids were excited and enthusiastic, so their parents were pleased. When everyone left, Mum and Dad and my friends and I collapsed in the living room. My parents seemed as tired as we were.

"The meeting was *very* long," said Mum.

"But productive," added Dad. "We made a lot of headway. We came up with some plans that should start to help Judy and the other homeless people around here. For one thing, we're going to open a soup kitchen."

"One of the churches is going to help us, too," Mum was saying when the phone rang.

I answered it in the kitchen. "Hello?"

"Hi, it's me. Laine."

"Hi!" I replied. I know Laine had said she would phone, but considering how badly the party had gone, I was a little surprised to hear from her.

"How was the babysitting?" she asked.

I told her about our adventure.

Then Laine went on, "Well, guess what. You won't believe this." She paused dramatically. "I'm not sure whether to tell you about this, but, well, Dad got free tickets— house seats, excellent ones—to *Starlight Express*. They're for tonight. He and Mum don't want to go, so he offered them to me. This may be a bad idea, but would you and your friends like to go to the play? He could get six seats, all together. And he'd order us the limo. I don't know about Claudia, but I feel awful about last night and I'd like to start again.''

I should explain a few things here. One, Laine's father is a big-time producer of Broadway plays. That's how the Cummingses got enough money to move into the Dakota, and that's why Laine's father is always being given tickets to things. Two, the tickets he's given are usually for ''house seats'', which are also in really prime locations. Like about six rows back (not up in some balcony that's two miles away from the stage), and smack in the middle of the theatre. Three, the Cummingses are forever hiring a limo to take them places. They don't own a car (owning a car is a real pain in New York), but instead of taking taxis they get a lo-o-o-ong limo. It's called a stretch limo and can seat about a million people and has a bar and a TV inside. When the chauffeur beeps the horn, it plays the first two lines from *Home on the Range*.

I, of course, was completely bowled over by Laine's invitation. Free tickets? Six of them? The *limo*? But I knew I had to check with my parents and my friends. I told Laine I'd call her back. Then, after getting permission from Mum and Dad to go to the play, I gathered my friends in my bedroom.

''So what do you think?'' I asked when

I'd explained the situation. I watched their eyes grow wider and wider, so I knew they were excited. Possibly, Mary Anne was overcome with emotion. She seemed unable to move or speak.

Still, I kept remembering Laine calling Claudia a jerk, and Claudia calling Laine a stuck-up snob and everybody accusing each other of things.

"Laine says she wants to try again," I added.

Claudia cleared her throat. "We-ell," she said slowly. "If Laine wants to try again, then so do I. And I promise I'll really give her a chance."

"Ya-hoo!" Kristy shouted, jumping to her feet.

"Broadway . . . wow," Mary Anne managed to say.

Dawn looked at Claudia. "Oh, my lord," she said, and giggled.

Then I rang Laine back. We agreed to meet for dinner at a little restaurant that's between our flats. After dinner, the limo would take us into town to the play. Later, it would bring us home.

Mary Anne immediately became hysterical about clothing. This time I was able to say, "You guys, wear the fanciest outfits you brought."

In all honesty, people don't necessarily get dressed up for the theatre any more. You see everything from jeans to fur coats there. (Often, you see jeans and a fur coat on *the same person*.) But since my friends and I were going to be arriving and leaving in a limo, I decided it would be fun to get dressed up.

This presented a problem for Kristy, but she borrowed a dress from Mary Anne, some accessories from Dawn and Claudia and a pair of shoes from me. She was all set. When the five of us left the bedroom and entered the living room, my parents made a big fuss over us.

"Let me just take your picture," said Mum. (She took twelve.)

"Have a great evening," my father added. He slipped me some money. "Now if *anything* goes wrong, phone us. Do you have change?" (I nodded.) "I don't even want you taking a taxi by yourselves late at night. So if something happens with the limo, try to find a nice, well-lit coffee shop and ring from there. Don't stand around on the street."

"We could hang around in the theatre," I said hopefully, thinking of the stars we might see there. "I would call from the lobby."

Dad barely heard me. He had a lot more instructions to give out. So did Mum. They were worried about letting us loose for the evening. Mum was so worried, that as we left the apartment she said, "Have fun and be very, VERY careful."

I was worried about other things. Namely, how everyone would get along that night. As we walked to the restaurant, my heart began to pound.

But the thought of the free tickets and the limo must have mellowed my friends. When we reached the restaurant, Laine was already there and she and Claudia just smiled sheepishly at each other.

A waiter seated us at a large round table, and we ordered our food. Nobody did any apologizing. (It didn't seem necessary.) But nobody did any sniping, either.

Laine told us about the play we were going to see. "It's the story of a train race. My father said the set is really amazing. The costumes, too. And every actor and actress is on roller skates."

"You're kidding!" exclaimed Claudia. "Awesome."

Somehow, we started talking about places we'd visited. Laine was going to California over Christmas and had never been there before. So Dawn told her about California. Then Laine told us about a trip to Japan she'd been on. Claudia was fascinated.

I couldn't believe it when I looked at my watch and saw that the time was 7:35. "We'd better get going!" I cried. "The show starts at eight."

"Yeah, the limo must be here," added Laine.

It was. It was right in front of the restaurant. We climbed inside, feeling like celebrities and hoping someone would see us. Then we turned on the TV for a few seconds (just so Kristy would be able to tell people that she'd actually watched TV in a limousine), examined the bar and settled back to watch the streets slip by as we zipped to the Gershwin Theatre.

We were ushered to our seats. The magnificent set spread before us. No curtain was hiding it, so the audience could get a good look at the hills and roads and passages that snaked around the stage for the roller skaters.

At 8:05 the play began. We were in awe. The cast roared through the set at top speed, taking curves practically on the edges of their wheels. Sometimes they looked as if they were going to fly right off the stage and into the audience. The story seemed like an old one (will the underdog beat the mean new guy in the race?), but there was so much action that we were on the edges of our seats from the beginning until the end.

When it was over, Mary Anne sighed with pleasure. "A Broadway play. A limo. I've died and gone to heaven."

We left the theatre and climbed back in the limousine. We were tired, but we just talked and talked all the way home. Claudia and Laine began teasing me.

"Once Stacey left her lunch on the radiator," said Laine, "and it made the whole classroom smell. That was in fourth grade."

"Once she had to babysit for some snobby kids and she used this weird kind of psychology," said Claudia. "She tamed the kids all right, but they thought she was nuts."

We laughed. And since we were getting on so well, I said, "Laine? Do you want to stay the night? You could make up for last night."

Laine looked thoughtful. "I do want to," she answered, "but I think you guys need time to be alone. I mean, without me. We had fun this evening—and Claud, I'm really happy I got to know the *real* you—but now I should probably go home."

She was right. I was glad Laine felt she could be so honest with us. The evening, I decided, had been perfect. Not only had it been fun, but now that the members of the Babysitters Club had relaxed and got used to travelling together and being in New York, they'd been able to feel comfortable with Laine.

The limo cruised up the West Side, dropped my friends and me off in front of my building, and then headed for the Dakota with Laine.

But before Claudia climbed out of the car, she and Laine exchanged phone numbers and addresses.

14th CHAPTER

Dear Shannon,

Hi! How's our associate club member? Have you had any interesting baby-sitting jobs this weekend? Wait till you hear about the one we had. It involved ten children and Central Park, but I'll tell you more the next time I see you. After our sitting job, we went out to dinner, and rode to a Broadway play in a LIMOUSINE. Then we tried to have a (fake) club meeting, for old times' sake. I wish you had known Stacey better. I think the two of you would have been friends.

See you soon!
Kristy

Our club meeting was really fun (a lot more fun than the uncomfortable one we'd held that morning), but it wasn't an actual meeting at all. We were just fooling around. It really was "fake", as Kristy had written to Shannon Kilbourne. (By the way, in case you're wondering, an associate club member is someone who doesn't come to meetings, but whom my friends can call on if they're offered a job they're too busy to take. A sort of backup. They have two associate members. Shannon is one. Guess who the other is? Logan, Mary Anne's boyfriend!)

When Dawn, Claudia, Kristy, Mary Anne and I entered my flat, Mum and Dad were waiting up for us (of course). They looked only a little worried, and as soon as they saw that we were in one piece and heard that we'd had a good time, they went to bed.

My friends and I looked at each other. Great! The night was ours. Remember how tired we'd been after our afternoon of sitting? And how tired we'd been when we climbed into the limo to come home? Well, suddenly we weren't tired any more. We got our second winds.

"Everybody, change into your nightdresses and come to my room," I said.

"Oh, good," said Kristy. "Let's have a meeting of the Babysitters Club."

Fifteen minutes later, Claudia and I were

lying across my bed on our stomachs, Mary Anne and Dawn were sitting cross-legged on the floor and Kristy was settled in my armchair.

"This meeting of the Babysitters Club," said Kristy, "will now come to order." Usually Kristy speaks fairly loudly, but since Mum and Dad were nearby, trying to sleep, she kept her voice down. "Any official business?" she asked.

"No," we replied.

"Any problems with the club notebook or record book?"

"No."

"They're not *here*," Claudia added.

"Just play along," I whispered, nudging her.

"Anybody had any sitting jobs she needs to talk about?"

Well, now this was getting out of hand. It was silly. No one was really paying attention to Kristy. Dawn and Mary Anne were trying on my sparkly silver nail polish. Claudia was looking longingly at a film magazine on my desk.

Kristy sensed that she did not have control of the "meeting".

I spoke up. "This doesn't have much to do with babysitting, Kristy, but how are things going at Watson's? How are Karen and Andrew?"

"Oh, they're great!" said Kristy. (She loves to talk about her little stepsister and stepbrother. I knew I could get her off the subject of babysitting. I just knew it.) "And I'll tell you something," she went on. "I hardly think of the house as 'Watson's' any more. It's just 'ours'. All of ours. Mum's, Watson's, Charlie's, Sam's, David Michael's, Andrew's, Karen's, mine, and even Shannon's and Boo-Boo's" (Shannon is David Michael's puppy, and Boo-Boo is Watson's cat. Shannon is named after Shannon Kilbourne, the associate club member. It's a long story.)

"That's great," I said. "So you feel as though you're fitting in? I mean, in the neighbourhood?"

"I'm getting there," Kristy replied.

"How about you, Dawn?" I wanted to know.

"How about me?" Dawn repeated vaguely. She had painted her fingernails and was now putting a tiny dot of silver polish in the centre of each toe-nail. She looked up. "Oh, you mean fitting in in Stoneybrook?"

I nodded.

"I hardly even think about it any more," she replied. "Getting used to the Jeff thing is much harder."

"The Jeff thing?"

Silence. Four heads turned towards me.

"Don't you know?" asked Claudia, aghast. "I was sure I told you."

"Know what? I don't remember you

391

telling me anything. Tell me now!"

My friends glanced at Dawn, who had finished dotting her toe-nails.

Dawn handed the bottle of polish to Mary Anne, and looked quite uncomfortable. At last she said. "My brother moved back to my dad."

"He moved to California?" I cried. Then I clapped my hand over my mouth, realizing how loudly I'd spoken. "I knew there were problems," I went on quietly. "I think I even knew your mum was considering letting him go back, but I didn't know it had actually happened. Oh, Dawn, I'm really sorry."

I don't know how close Dawn and her younger brother are, but being an only child I sometimes fantasize about having a brother or sister. It seems like the most wonderful thing in the world. So losing a brother or sister seemed like the most horrible thing in the world.

Dawn's eyes filled with tears. She blinked them away. Then she said, "Well, it's no wonder you didn't know. Remember what was going on at the same time Jeff was getting ready to leave?"

Claudia, Mary Anne and Kristy burst out laughing.

"The Little Miss Stoneybrook Contest!" Claudia cried. "What a mess!"

"Tell me more about it," I said eagerly, wishing I'd still been in Stoneybrook then.

"I only heard bits and pieces."

"It started with me," said Dawn, who seemed to have recovered. "It was a contest for five- to eight-year-old girls, and Claire and Margo Pike were dying to be in it, so their mother gave me the job of preparing them to enter. Each girl had to have a talent. You know what Margo's was? Peeling a banana with her feet and reciting *The House That Jack Built*."

Every single one of us became hysterical. We grabbed pillows and stuffed them over our faces to muffle our laughter.

But Dawn wouldn't stop. "And you know what Claire's talent was?" she went on. "She sang, *I'm Popeye the sailor man. I live in a garbage can. I eat all the wor-orms and spit out the ger-erms. I'm Popeye the sailor man.*"

We could barely contain ourselves.

Then Dawn said in a whisper, "You guys, I have just had the *best* idea. Let's make a joke phone-call to Jeff in California. It's only eight-thirty out there."

"Okay," I agreed, "but just one call. It's expensive. What should we say?"

"Let's see if he falls for the oldest joke call in telephone history," suggested Mary Anne. "Oh, please Dawn, can I call him?"

"Of course," replied Dawn. She gave Mary Anne her father's phone number.

Mary Anne dialled it. "It's ringing," she told us. Pause. Then she cupped her hand over the receiver. "*Jeff* answered!" she whispered loudly. She removed her hand. "Hello?" she said. "Is your refrigerator running?"

"Yeah, I think so," Jeff replied.

"Then you had better go and catch it!" cried Mary Anne gleefully, and hung up.

Further hysteria. I laughed until I rolled off the bed. Then an awful thought occurred to me. "Dawn!" I said. "What if Jeff thought that was you and he rings your house? *Now*? He'll wake up your mum."

After a moment of horrified silence we started laughing again. We just couldn't help it.

"I bet," said Mary Anne, "that if he phoned *my* house now, he'd get an engaged tone. You know why?"

"Because your father has a girlfriend and spends hours talking on the phone to her?" I teased.

"*No*. Because Tigger knows how to take the phone off the hook and he does it all the time."

"You're kidding!" I cried. "Tigger's only a kitten."

"It's true!" said Dawn. "I've seen him do it. It's the phone on Mr Spier's desk. He knocks the receiver until it falls off."

At this point, I was afraid my parents were going to come in and tell us to stop being so noisy (it was impossible to calm down), so I told my friends we had to move into the living room.

"Good," said Claudia as we tiptoed down the hall. "I'm hungry and the living room is closer to the kitchen. Got any junk food?"

"Party leftovers," I told her.

We raided the refrigerator. Then we sat around the living room eating French bread and potato crisps and pretzels. (Well, not me. I just had a diet lemonade. I have to be extremely careful about my food intake because of my diabetes. And Dawn had only pretzels and the tomatoes from one of the French bread sandwiches, since she won't touch meat.)

"Boy," said Kristy after she swallowed a mouthful of potato crisps. "I wish we'd had as much fun at the party last night as we're having now."

"I expect you guys were too nervous," I said. "Maybe a party your first day here wasn't such a good idea."

"I don't know why I was so nervous," spoke up Claudia. "Maybe I was trying too hard to fit in. I'm sorry about Coby, Kristy."

"That's okay," Kristy replied. "I over-reacted. Anyway, Coby has my phone number and address and I have his. I bet we'll be in touch soon." Kristy blushed, but I knew she was pleased with the idea of writing or talking to . . . a boy!

"As long as we're apologizing," said Mary Anne, "I'm sorry I've been such a pain. I mean about New York. It's just that it's such a glamorous place."

"Well, *I'm* sorry I've been such a scaredy-cat," said Dawn. "New York always seemed like such a frightening place."

"I'm sorry I haven't been very understanding," I added.

And Kristy said, "And I'm sorry I have such a big mouth."

With that, we started giggling again. We talked and giggled until Mum really did have to get up and tell us to be quiet. Then we went to bed.

15th CHAPTER

Dear Jessi,
Writing this postcard is
ridiculous, because we're on the
train coming home now. It's a
New York postcard and I'll be
sending it in Stoneybrook! Oh,
well. Today was great, but it was
also sad. It was great because
the five of us were just being
ourselves so we were having a
great time. It was sad because
we had to say good-bye to Stacey.
Anyway, this is
    Guess what just happened?
Kristy is asleep next to me and
her head keeps falling on my
arm! I better end this here.
Claudia wants to go to the buffet
car for M&M's and   Love, Dawn

It was our last day together and guess how we spent half the morning? Sleeping! We were exhausted. We hadn't fallen asleep until about one o'clock the night before. I hated to waste time sleeping, but it felt so nice to keep stretching my legs out in bed and rolling over for "just five more minutes." (Each five minutes lasted at least fifteen minutes, and I must have done that eight times.)

Anyway, when my clock read 10:08, I finally yawned and stretched and struggled to sit up. Then I wandered into the living room to see what was going on. I found a note from my parents saying they'd gone to church and then planned to take a walk. I felt a bit sorry for them. With the club members asleep in the living room and study, there was nowhere my parents could go except the kitchen or their bedroom— or outside.

I hated to wake everyone up, but it had to be done. My friends' train was leaving at two-thirty that afternoon, and we didn't want to sleep away our last few hours. I began making kitchen noises. I put on the kettle for tea, got out plates and knives, and then opened the refrigerator, hoping to find what I usually find there on Sunday morning—smoked salmon and cream cheese. In a paper bag in the bread drawer were fresh bagels. Goody!

"Oh, you guys!" I called. "Breakfast time!"

I heard rumblings and muffled, sleepy sounds from the other rooms, but nothing else.

I put the bagels on a platter, the smoked salmon on a plate and the cream cheese on another plate. A breakfast assembly line was now ready—if anyone would get up.

"Yoo-hoo!" I called.

"*Yoo*hoo?" replied Kristy. "You sound like my grandmother."

"Come *on*. Get *up*. I've got a great breakfast for you. Even you will like it, Dawn." We had whole-wheat bagels as well as white ones, so Dawn wouldn't have to poison her body with white bread.

I heard thumps and rustlings, and soon my bleary-eyed friends had found their way into the kitchen.

Kristy's eyes popped out at the plate of bright orange smoked salmon. "*What* is *that*?" she asked, pointing.

"Salmon," I replied.

"I'm hoping," said Kristy, "that it isn't what it looks like, which is raw fish."

"Smoked."

"Is it like sushi?" asked Mary Anne warily.

"No, it's cooked," I said. "It just looks raw."

"I'll try it," said Dawn. She paused. "How do you eat it?"

"Like this," I answered. "I'll make you a breakfast you won't forget."

"I bet," muttered Kristy.

I sliced a bagel in half, toasted the halves in the toaster, covered them with cream cheese, placed some smoked salmon on top, arranged the bagel halves on a plate, and presented the plate to Dawn.

She took a bite. "This," she said, closing her eyes, "is heaven. Food heaven."

"I now pronounce you a true New Yorker," I said.

"You mean I won't be a true New Yorker until I eat smoked orange fish?" asked Mary Anne.

"That's right."

"Oh, lord," said Claudia.

Well, in the end, all my friends wanted to be true New Yorkers, so they ate the smoked salmon and bagels. Even Kristy. Then we got dressed (we wore our Hard Rock Cafe T-shirts), and we sat around and read *The New York Times*, which Mum and Dad brought home with them when they finally returned.

"A New York City Sunday morning tradition," I said.

"Really?" asked Mary Anne. She looked quite pleased with herself. Then she glanced at her watch and her expression changed to utter sadness.

"What's wrong?" asked Dawn.

"It's noon."

"Oh, wow. In less than two hours we'll have to leave for the train station," I said.

At that moment the doorbell rang.

Good. A diversion. I ran for it.

"Who's there?" I called.

"It's Mrs Walker."

I opened the door. There stood Mrs Walker with Henry and Grace.

"Hi!" I said.

"Hi," answered Mrs Walker.

Henry and Grace scooted behind their mother and peeped around at me, but they were smiling.

"Come on in," I told them.

They did. Henry and Grace each held out a piece of drawing paper.

"These are for you ... and your friends," said Henry.

"Hey, you guys, come here!" I called.

Kristy, Dawn, Mary Anne and Claudia joined us in the hallway.

"This was the kids' idea," said Mrs Walker. "They were up early, drawing pictures, and they said they wanted you to have these. They had a great time yesterday."

"Thanks!" said my friends and I.

Henry's picture was identifiable as a dinosaur. (A stegosaurus, he informed us.) Grace's was a blue circle with some squiggly pink and green lines around it. She said it was Central Park.

After the Walkers left, my friends decided that they wanted to say goodbye to the other kids we had sat for, so we did just that, only this time we started with the apartment on the lowest floor and worked our way up. Dawn rode in the lift as if she'd been doing it all her life. Mary Anne didn't quote one fact about New York, Kristy didn't make a single snide remark and Claudia mentioned that she was going to write a letter to Laine when she got home.

So my friends said their goodbyes to Dennis and Sean, to Carlos, Blair and Cissy, and to Natalie and Peggie. As we left the Upchurches' apartment and headed for the lift, Kristy stopped in her tracks.

"Do you know something," she said. "I don't *want* to go and say goodbye to Leslie Reames. We'll probably get stuck in that penthouse listening to a lecture on wheat allergies . . . or what would happen to Leslie if she ate goat cheese."

We laughed.

"Well, we have to go," I said. "You can't say goodbye to all the kids except Leslie."

Reluctantly, we went to the penthouse. But Martha was the only one there. Hooray! Unfortunately, now my friends had to pack their things. It was time for them to get ready to leave.

The packing was done silently. We weren't angry, just sad.

We lugged Claudia's goods wagon into the living room.

My friends said goodbye to Mum and Dad.

Then my father gave me some money for a taxi, and we left the flat.

"Thanks for everything!" said my friends.

"Come back soon," my father replied.

"We loved having you," added Mum.

Claudia looked at me mischievously and whispered, "Have fun and be careful."

"Have fun and be careful!" Mum called, just as the lift arrived.

We zoomed to the ground floor.

"Have a good day!" said Isaac as we trooped by.

I hailed a taxi. The driver put Claudia's goods wagon in the boot. My friends and I squeezed their duffelbags and rucksacks and souvenirs into the taxi.

The trip to Grand Central was pretty quiet. We weren't sure what to say to each other. But as soon as we entered the train station we all began talking at once.

"What a weekend!" exclaimed Mary Anne.

"Oh, my lord, it's been awesome!" said Claud.

"I'm glad we got to meet Laine," said Dawn.

"This building is the hottest place I've ever been in," complained Kristy.

"Worse than Bloomingdale's?" I asked her.

"Hmm. That's a close one to call."

Unfortunately, my friends' train was

announced then. In a split second, every one of us burst into tears, even Kristy.

We hugged and cried and said how much we would miss each other and made all sorts of promises about writing and phoning and visiting.

Then I walked the members of the Stoneybrook branch of the Babysitters Club to their platform.

"Goodbye," said my friends together.

"Goodbye," I replied. "Have fun and be careful!"

The Babysitters Club

Need a babysitter? Then call the Babysitters Club. Kristy Thomas and her friends are all experienced sitters. They can tackle any job from rampaging toddlers to a pandemonium of pets. To find out all about them, read on!